F   B733   Lg. Print

Brand, Max

Danger Trail

DANGER TRAIL

**Center Point
Large Print**

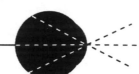

**This Large Print Book carries the
Seal of Approval of N.A.V.H.**

ॐ श्री गणेशाय नमः

DANGER TRAIL

MAX BRAND

CENTER POINT PUBLISHING
THORNDIKE, MAINE

This Center Point Large Print edition
is published in the year 2001 by arrangement with
Golden West Literary Agency.

The text of this Large Print edition is unabridged.
In other aspects, this book may vary from the original
edition. Printed in Thailand. Set in 16-point Plantin type by
Bill Coskrey.

ISBN 1-58547-092-9

Library of Congress Cataloging-in-Publication Data

Brand, Max, 1892-1944.
    Danger trail / Max Brand.
      p. cm.
    ISBN 1-58547-092-9 (lib. bdg. : alk. paper)
    1. Large type books. I. Title.

PS3511.A87 D35 2001
813'.54--dc21

                                                    00-065735

~1~
A Happy Man

TAG Enderby rode whistling down the trail. He only stopped whistling to begin a song. His pockets were empty, but his heart was light. His horse was a ragged cartoon, but his seat was sure. He had fasted a day, but still he sang, because he knew that he was a scant mile from a new horse, full pockets, and as much food as he could wish.

He turned from the trail and broke into the thick of the pines. They were so lofty and crowded that they made a gloomy green sky above his head. The sun could not beat down to him, but neither could the wind reach him. It merely washed currents of stifling heat among the tree trunks. And still he sang.

Presently a man stepped out from behind a tree, his rifle held at the ready.

"Hello!" he called sharply. "That you, Tag?"

Tag Enderby did not answer. His song simply swelled louder. He gave no greeting, but rode past, heedless of the scowl that followed him.

He cared not for scowls. For he was of a happy nature. He loved his friends and enjoyed his enemies. He found the world so entirely good that he would not have changed it. It was as perfect as if he had himself composed it in a daydream.

The trees broke from their solid ranks and opened to show him a clearing with a shack in the center of it. Over the green, naked acres horses were straying—fine thin-legged horses, with square quarters, and reaching necks that promised striding length.

At the door of the shack he dropped to the ground, six feet of him, lean and tough, light in the saddle and hard in the hand. He peeled off the saddle, stripped off the bridle, and turned to face a man in the door.

"Where you been?" asked the man in the door.

"Oh, around," said Tag.

"Whatcha do with your horse?" asked the other.

"Faro," said Tag.

"And your swell clothes?"

"Faro," said Tag.

"And your coin—where's that gone?"

"Faro," said Tag.

"Yeah, faro," said the man in the door. "You'll be faro, one of these days. Hungry, I guess?"

"Yeah," said Tag. "I can eat. Throw on a couple of venison steaks. I don't care how thick you cut 'em. I'll have some fried trout while the steaks are cooking, or a couple of chickens to take the edge off. Gimme about three gallons of coffee. That'll be a start. I'll think of something that I really want to eat, while I put that stuff away."

He entered the shack, threw down his saddle and bridle, and strode to the stove. A great iron pot of beans was simmering upon it. They had been flavored red with peppers and tomatoes. There was no other food in sight, but a huge, two-gallon coffeepot steamed at the back of the stove.

"I was dreamin'," said Tag. "Beans was what I wanted."

He poured out a pint cup of coffee, drained it dry, dumped a couple of quarts of beans into a granite basin, pulled a vast chunk of stale corn pone out of a storage barrel, and sat down to eat. Even with his mouth filled, he still managed to hum, from time to time.

The other had turned from the door and sat down in a corner. He put his hands upon his knees, fingers turned in, and stared at Tag. He was the wreck of what had once been a magnificent physique. Now his face had fallen into loosely flowing lines. His stomach flowed loosely against the belt which was too big for the band of his trousers. The two top buttons were undone to give him breathing room. Even his greasy black mustaches drooped from the corners of his mouth. They were so glossy a black that he continually looked as though he had just drunk and failed to dry his mouth satisfactorily. His eyebrows jutted forward. They were black, also, but his hair was the snowiest white. There was no good humor about his expression. His mouth was sour, and his glance was fixed, half in criticism, and half in thought.

"Busted," he said at last.

Tag shifted his mouthful a little.

"Yeah," he managed to say. His eyes were blank and blissful, as he continued to chew.

"Always busted, ain't you?" said the other.

Tag shifted again.

"Mostly," he said.

"Now you want a new hoss, a new layout of coin, and everything, don't you?"

"Yeah," said Tag.

"You're going to go to hell, one of these days," said the other.

"Sure, Dan," said Tag.

He filled his mouth again, with beans, and then with bread. His cheeks bulged. Dan Malley regarded him with a sort of fascination, like a little boy watching a snake swallowing.

"I'd like to turn you off, if you wasn't Tag Enderby," said Malley.

Without a word, Tag Enderby drank coffee noisily.

"By thunder," said Malley, "don't that boilin' stuff take the skin off your throat, and your stomach, too?"

Tag drank again, and said nothing. He was refilling his mouth with beans and with pone.

"Who took you to the cleaner's?" asked Malley.

"Faro," said Tag, with difficulty.

"Yeah. You've said that about a thousand times. But what layout, I mean?"

"Si Dumphy's."

"You been there? You're a fool! Didn't you know that Dumphy was a crook?"

"Yeah," said the youth.

His eyes remained blank, mild with content, like the eyes of a cow as it chews its cud.

"But you went there anyways, did you?"

"Yeah," said Tag Enderby.

"You're a fool!" said Malley.

Tag washed down his last mouthful with coffee. He cleared his throat.

"You were saying—" he said politely.

"I'm older than you. I gotta right to tell you something," said Malley hastily.

"Sure you have," said Tag.

The gleam passed from his eyes. He replenished his basin. The first supply of beans had vanished.

"Whatcha do? Drink them beans?" asked Malley.

"Kind of," said Tag.

He refilled his pint cup with bubbling, steaming coffee.

"You beat me," said Malley.

Tag said nothing. He was causing food to flow steadily down his throat again. The swallowing act was with him, at a mealtime almost continuous.

Malley laid a hand upon his own stomach. His expression was sad.

"There is onions in them beans," he suggested grimly.

"Yeah," said Tag. "That's why I like 'em." He filled his mouth again.

"Don't they never give you no indigestion?"

"Huh?" said Tag quickly.

"Indigestion—pains in the stomach—wake you up at night—double you up, pretty near."

"Uh-huh!" grunted Tag.

"You never had no indigestion?" asked Malley, leaning forward with almost savage challenge in his voice.

"Uh-huh," said Tag.

Malley leaned back hopelessly.

"Yeah. You're young," he declared, with disgust.

"Uh-huh," said Tag.

"I was young, too, once," said Malley.

"Uh-huh," said Tag.

"I could eat rawhide, when I was your age," boasted Malley.

"Uh-huh," said Tag.

"Stop grunting like an Injun!" shouted Malley. "Ain't you got a tongue?"

"Uh-huh," said Tag.

He finished his second basin of beans, looked critically

at the great iron pot, decided in the negative, refilled his coffee tin, made a cigarette, and leaned back on his stool until his shoulders rested against the wall of the house. He closed his eyes, the better to enjoy the sweet flavor of that smoke.

"You had twenty-five hundred dollars, when you left here," said Malley.

"Uh-huh," said Tag.

"Whatcha been and done since you left here—outside of that faro that you been talkin' so much about?" asked Malley bitterly.

"Had a party with Jess Culver and his friends in Tuckerville. That lasted two days. I still had a hundred left."

"Yeah. You're gettin' economical," said Malley. "Only spendin' a thousand a day! What did you do for drinks? Let the boys treat you?"

"Then I spent a coupla days playing poker, and came out with five grand and—"

"What?"

"Reached Wilson City, and it seemed kind of slow, and after it got speeded up, and greased up, my funds had sunk again, to a coupla five hundred, so I looked at some dice and they talked to papa, and I got another breath, and kept Wilson City running a coupla three days more, and then hopped along to James Crossing, and got wrecked on Si Dumphy's plant. So I'm back again, holding out my hand."

"You only got nine, ten thousand left," said Malley. "Whatcha want to be a fool for? Whatcha wanta throw everything away?"

"I don't throw anything away," said Tag. "I'm going to sleep."

"When'd you sleep last?"

"I disremember," said Tag.

He went over to a bunk, pulled a blanket off it, swept it in an expert curl around his body, lay down on the hard boards of the floor, closed his eyes and was instantly asleep.

Malley went to him, stirred him in the ribs with the toe of his boot, and said, "Listen!"

The body moved loosely. The eyes did not open. So Malley went back to the door and sat down there, shaking his head while he made a cigarette.

~2~
A Job for Tag

ANOTHER rider came into the clearing on a fine horse, covered with the salt of much sweating. He, like Tag, pulled the saddle and bridle off his horse and went to the door of the shack.

"Hullo, Dan," said he.

" 'Lo," said Malley.

He moved over a little so that the other could go inside.

"What's the news, Joe?" he asked.

The newcomer was a big man, with a deep chest, and a back rigidly straight, a horseman's back. His voice came from his toes.

"There ain't no news," he said, "except that son of a gun of a low-down watchman has gone and lost his job. They got them a new night watchman at the bank."

"Couldn't you get to him?"

"He didn't like the cut of my face," said Joe.

"Didn't he like the cut of your money," asked Malley.

"He's Irish," said Joe, explaining. "If an Irishman don't like your face, he can't see your money, never! You better send down a slicker. Send down Tag, or somebody. I hear Tag's come in?"

"Yeah. He's in there."

"Is he been raisin' hell?"

"When did he raise nothin' else?" asked Malley sourly.

"Is he all together?"

"Yeah. When was he ever apart?"

"Yeah. I know. But I been expecting, all the time—"

"When they take 'him' apart," said Malley, "it'll be in the papers. It'll be front page, with pictures of how the town looked after the explosion."

"He's a mean kid, all right," said Joe.

But he was thoughtful, and plucked at his short mustache.

"You don't know him," advised Malley. "You oughta study him some, Joe."

"It takes a pretty fast eye to study that kid," said Joe.

"Yeah, it takes that," said Malley.

"Any coffee on the stove?"

"Sure. All the time."

Joe went inside and dropped his saddle and bridle.

"Hold on," he said, "I didn't know that the kid was in here."

"Why?"

"I wouldn't 'a' wanted to wake him up."

"You can't wake him up."

"Can't?"

"No."

"Yow!" screeched Joe.

The sleeper turned a little on his side, sighed, and continued his slumber.

"It beats me," said Joe. "He ain't batted an eye when I yowled."

"He knows your voice," said Malley, grinning in spite of himself.

"He ain't waked up to know it," said Joe.

"No, but he knows it in his sleep. That's the way that he is."

"He beats me," said Joe.

"You ain't the first," said Malley.

"Somebody'll step in his face, one of these days, sleepin' like that," declared Joe.

"Not if it's a stranger," said Malley. "Watch this."

Joe came out carrying a cup of coffee.

"Hey, Mack!" called Malley.

A broad young man with a red, freckled face came sauntering from the shed at the side of the house. He had in his hand a bridle which he was repairing.

"They's some fresh coffee brewin' in there," said Malley.

"Yeah?" said Mack. "I'll take a shot. Hullo, Joe."

"Yeah, that's my name," said Joe. "How are you, Mack?"

Mack stepped through the door; Malley looked up expectantly.

"Well?" said the sharp, wide-awake voice of Tag Enderby.

"Hullo?" said Mack. "I'm Mack. Who are you?"

"Your grandpa," said Tag Enderby. "Why don't you take the hobnails out of your feet?"

"Say," shouted Mack, "if you're lookin' for—"

"Shut up, Mack," said Malley. "That's Tag Enderby. Shut up, Tag. Mack is a new man. Lay down and go to sleep again."

"All right," said Tag. "Why'd you keep changing the deck so often, in a little friendly game like this?"

They heard him yawn, as Mack came tiptoeing through the door, the coffee sloshing recklessly in the tin cup he was carrying.

"You might 'a' tipped me off!" he whispered. "I didn't know who he was. I thought he was just a kid. I didn't know he was—"

"Yeah, he's just a kid, too," said Malley. "What did I tell you?"

"It's a funny thing," said Joe. "You wouldn't believe it. It's like he had somebody standing by to watch over him."

"Yeah," said Malley.

Mack went back to the shed.

"I'd like to ride with Tag sometime," said Joe.

"So would I," said Malley.

"Whatcha mean by that?"

"I mean he works alone. He only spends in company."

"Yeah. I've heard that he spends."

"You've heard an earful," said Malley. "When he spends, he spends!" He waved toward the broken-down mustang on which Tag Enderby had returned to the camp.

"I give him a thousand-dollar thoroughbred. He brings me back a ten-dollar nag. Yeah, he spends!"

"Well, he works, too," said Joe.

"He works, all right," said Malley grimly.

"If he loves to work by himself so much," said Joe, "Why don't he cut loose from you and do his own stuff all the way through?"

"Because he's lazy," said Malley. "He don't mind usin' his hands, but he hates to use his head. That's why he loves a gun. It stops so much argument."

"Yeah, he's got his list," said Joe.

"You don't know half of it," said Malley. "Neither do I. But I know more than Tag does. He's forgotten most of their names. He hates to use his head. So I rig up the plants, and give him the jobs. He works 'em alone, all the time."

"You don't hardly need nobody but him, if he's so good," said Joe critically.

"He ain't only here one day in ten," said Malley regretfully. "The rest of the time he's working, or spending. One day here, one day to work, eight days to spend. That's about the way with him."

"I'd like to work with him sometime," said Joe. "Only he's touchy. He always wants to fight."

"He never wants no fighting," said Malley, "if folks leave him alone. He just takes some understanding. That's all. I understand him. That's why I get along with him so good."

"It takes a pretty good head to understand him," repeated Joe, as he moved off around the corner of the shack.

Malley sat patiently in the heat of the sun. One hour, two, and three passed. The sun hung halfway down from the zenith, raging with strength. Then a shadow slipped across Malley's face. It was Tag Enderby, stepping catlike, silently, from the open doorway.

He stood in the sun, facing it, his head thrown back a little. He stretched, rising on one foot, and then on the other, his arms straining at their sockets. Then he yawned, shook his head, and started across the meadow on the run.

Malley watched him go without a word.

He saw him go through the trees, shedding clothes as he went, and saw the bronze flash of his body as the youth leaped from the bank and disappeared into the silver streak of the pool. A few minutes later he came back, the clothes flung over one arm, while he whipped the wet from his skin with the edge of one palm.

He stood before Malley, letting sun and wind finish the drying. For the hundredth time he reminded Malley of a whipstock, quiveringly supple and subtly made, remarkably strong.

"What's in the air?" asked Tag.

"Trouble," said Malley.

"Yeah. There's always trouble." Tag Enderby yawned. "How do you spell this kind?"

"Champion's out of the can."

"Champion of what?"

"Ray Champion."

"Don't remember him."

"You remember that red-haired fellow that you slung a gun on down in Tucson?"

"No, I don't remember?"

"Wait a minute. It was in Perry's Bar. You shot him through the hip. The fellow that was cussing you because—"

"I don't remember," said Tag. "I never liked redheads, though. What about Champion?"

Malley looked at him more sourly than ever.

"You don't remember nothin'. You're goin' to lose yourself, and forget that you're lost, one of these days," he declared. "Anyway, Ray Champion was a bunkie of that redhead. Champion used to be one of my boys. He quit. He was goin' to split to the law, I think. So I had him salted away."

"Whatcha mean by that?"

"Got him pinched, and let some evidence leak through. They sent him up for five years. Out at the end of three on good behavior. Paroled, or something."

"What about it?"

"All he wants is my hide."

"It's a good tough skin, at that," said Tag critically, almost eagerly.

"I need all my hide for myself," said Malley.

"There isn't much charity in you," said Tag. "Go on. What about Champion?"

"He's a mean fellow, Tag, and I want him salted again."

"Well, go get him salted, then."

"That's the job for you, Tag. That's what I want you to do."

"Not me," said Tag. "You have the trouble with Champion. I never even saw him. Salt him yourself. I have nothing to do with the law. You salt him yourself. I don't work the double cross."

"I tell you, he's so mean that he makes your head ache," said Malley. "He's hired men to get my throat cut. That's what he's done."

"That's dirty. That's low," said Tag Enderby. "You better go and take it out of him."

"Besides, he's a redhead himself," said Malley.

"Is he?" murmured Tag. "Then maybe I'd better go down and have a look at him."

At Grove City

I N Malley there were several virtues. One was that he paid his employees, with a scrupulous exactness, just that part of the spoils which had been agreed upon. They could always count upon him. An even greater virtue was that he cast up, as it were, a smoke screen between the public and the deeds of his men. Nearly everyone knew that there was a Malley. Nearly every one knew the look of him. His face appeared upon posters, offering liberal rewards for information leading to his apprehension. His death was desired. The law said that it was desired. There was a price upon him, dead or alive. But beyond Malley, little was known. As for his gang, its existence was well-proved.

That was why Tag Enderby could ride into Grove City boldly, in the middle of the day, looking to the right and to the left, heedless of what eyes fell upon him.

He had been in Grove City before. In fact, he knew every nook and corner of it, and Grove City knew him, as a wild young man through whose hands money flowed freely. There was nobody in the town who took Tag Enderby to be a tenderfoot, or a greenhorn in any way. And yet there was no one willing to connect his name with that of Malley, the pernicious.

If Enderby had been of a philosophical turn of mind, he would have been surprised to find himself in that town. For he had come down to find out what he could about Mr. Ray Champion. And his secret motive was a desire to put Ray Champion securely behind the bars once more. Yet he had no personal grudge against the man, and he would not be lining his pocket by jailing him.

Logically, there was only one thing to drive Tag forward to his goal, and that was a will to please his chief. But he had not such a will. Malley was to him a plain rascal, and rather a low one. He knew all about Malley. He had forgotten more of Malley's rascality than he could remember at the time, because he was a forgetful young man. But there was no reason why he should stick to Malley, except that if it were not Malley, it would be some other man.

What Malley did was to point the way to certain places out of which money could be taken. And money was necessary to a pleasant life. If Tag Enderby knew one thing from life, it was the great importance that attaches to hard cash. Therefore, he was glad to have a magic arrow, like Malley, which told him just when and where he would be able to find certain sums, large sums. For only large sums would do for him. Small change, such as five or ten thousand dollars at a time, sifted instantly through the liberal interstices between his fingers.

As a matter of fact, if he had stopped to reason—which he did not—the only cause that brought him there to Grove City was that he had heard that Ray Champion was a red-headed man. And, as he had said to Malley, he hated redheads.

He had no good cause for his hatred. In fact, he never searched for the causes that underlay his emotions. If the emotions were there, that was enough for him. He might have traced the feeling back to his early school days, when a certain red-headed youth had regularly thrashed him, four or five times a year, until he grew to a sufficient stature to thrash the redhead. But he had forgotten that particular boy, and all he knew of the matter was that he loathed the auburn-headed tribe, and all the clans thereof.

Grove City was not very large, but he thought that it might prove large enough when he saw the extensive fronts of some of the saloons. They looked as though gambling halls were to the rear of them.

And he had nine thousand dollars in his pocket to spend!

He went to the store, first of all. There he fitted himself out in a blue serge suit, and a white shirt, and stiff, boiled collars. He only retained his riding boots, with the spurs thrusting out behind until they caught his attention. Then he unbuckled them, and wrapped them in a silken handkerchief. Thereafter, they remained in an inner pocket, close to his heart. They were his first spurs. He would love them until his death day.

Then he crowned himself with a gray Stetson with a soft, wide, furling brim. The paleness of the hat made his face seem very dark.

He bought a handkerchief with some thin blue threads running through the hem of it. He allowed a corner of the handkerchief to project from his breast pocket, and the sight of it in a mirror made him wish for a flower to balance it in the opposite lapel.

Ready-made as it was, the suit fitted him to a T. The shirt and the collar troubled him for a few moments, but after all, it was not his first excursion into the realm of town neatness.

He pivoted before a mirror.

"How do I look?" he asked the grinning clerk.

"Like a tenderfoot, stranger," said the clerk.

"I'm goin' to be a tenderfoot," said Tag Enderby. "I'm

goin' to be as soft as a three-minute egg."

As he spoke, he took from his discarded clothes two long, ponderous Colts. They were extra size, and it made them a fraction of an eye wink harder and slower to draw and to handle than the ordinary gun. But they shot almost like rifles, and they were the standard .45 caliber.

The sight of these weapons caused the clerk to gape. He gaped still more when he observed that they disappeared into the clothes of the stranger without leaving visible exterior signs.

Tag Enderby pivoted again.

"See anything?" he asked.

"Not a wrinkle," said the clerk.

"That's good," said Tag Enderby. "It keeps folks from thinking too much. There ain't a thing in the world, I'd say, that's more nuisance than a lot of folks thinking about what might be in your hip pocket. Is it a handkerchief, a flask, or a gun? They begin by thinking and then they wind up asking. And there you are, all started for trouble. Me, I'm a fellow that loves peace."

"Yeah, I can see that," said the clerk. "With a couple of rods like that to lean on, you must love peace. I wouldn't suspect you of loving nothing else."

Tag Enderby paid his bill.

"You haven't seen me in here, I guess?" said he.

The clerk looked into his eyes.

"Why, no," said he, "I don't guess that I ever seen you at all, Mr.—"

He stopped.

"Then I'll be running along," said Tag.

"Wait a minute. There's more'n twenty dollars change

coming to you," said the clerk.

"If I haven't been in here, how's there anything coming to me?" asked Tag Enderby.

He went out. The clerk, staring after him, began to grin, and then to lick his lips. But he was a discreet young man, and it was not the first suit of clothes that he had sold. He started to pick up the rumpled castoffs of the last customer. He hummed a little to himself. He felt that spring was in the air.

Tag Enderby went down the street to the first saloon. He looked for a moment at the gilded sign that ran down the front. Then he pushed the swinging doors ajar and looked first at the sawdust on the floor, then at the dusky forms lined up along the bar in the half light, then at the row of bottles in front of the mirror, and at their reflections in the glass.

"Hey, you long-eared son, you wool-bearing fool!" bellowed a voice. "Shut that door, and keep the draft out, will you?"

Tag Enderby stepped inside.

"Gentlemen," said he, "when I hear talk like that, it makes me feel right at home. Change hands, friends, because the drinks are on me!"

A big Negro with a black and shining face frowned upon the newcomer. He was dressed in regular cowpoke attire, with a blue handkerchief of shimmering silk around his bull neck.

"How old is you, son?" he asked. "They don't liquor kids in this here bar."

"I was born on Friday," said Tag. "That's why I have all the luck. Back up, and give me room."

He stepped to the bar, walking straight at the big black, who drew up as if to defend himself from expected attack. But Enderby simply dropped his elbow on the bar, in the space thus made, and turned his back upon the Negro.

"Now, boys," he said, "name your pleasure."

They named it, but they looked past Enderby at the Negro, expecting action. The action did not come. It may have been the erect bearing of Tag's head. At any rate, the Negro began to think the thing over, and he never came to any decision.

The first drink went down, and with it was washed home the conclusion in every mind that Tag Enderby was quite a man.

"Feathers, they show how the wind blows," said one of those present, later on, "and that was a whole eagle's wing. That Negro, Cressey, has done some mighty hard hitting and straight shooting in his time. He's a white Negro, he is, a regular fellow, if you know how to handle him. The kid, he knew the trick without anybody teachin' him."

Tag was talking of other things.

"Is there around this town," he said, "a red-headed boy by the name of Ray Champion?"

"Champion's back now," said a man at the far end of the bar.

"Are you a friend of his?" asked Tag.

"Yeah. I'm glad to say that I'm a friend of Ray's," said the other. "You know him?"

"I only know that he's got red hair," said Tag Enderby. "The next time you see Champion, you tell him that I got a natural peevishness for rusty tops, will you? I never knew a redhead that was any good, and I guess that Ray Champion's no exception to the rule. You tell him, will you, and I won't have to write a letter."

He went out of the saloon, and stood for a moment in the sunlight, letting the drink percolate to the farthest corners of his being. The sun was bright and hot. Heat waves shimmered upward from the roofs of the houses across the street. It seemed, just then, a good town to be alive in, and Tag Enderby felt quite alive.

He drifted down the street to see the inside of the next saloon. For now he felt that he had set the ball rolling, and that he could afford to wait for things to happen.

At the next corner, he passed the imposing front of a bank, decorated with lofty cement pilasters, with a broad expanse of plate glass. He peered at the sign above the door, which announced that Telford and Mays were bankers. He peered through the windows at the glimmering steel and gilding of the cages inside. For he had a strange affection for banks. He had seen many of them from the inside!

Then he stepped through the next pair of swinging doors, and found his footstep gently muffled in a fresh layer of sawdust. The pungency of whisky and beer was in the air. Peace settled upon his spirits. For he knew that he had started mischief on the wing, and that was the bird he loved best.

~4~

Ray Champion

THE spirits of Tag Enderby being high, the stakes he played for were high, also. Roulette he favored at the present moment, and lost seven thousand dollars in exactly seven minutes.

A thrill passed into the very air of Grove City. The flush and fairness of the earlier mining days seemed to be returning. Luck then faltered. In the next fifteen minutes Tag Enderby lost only fifteen hundred. When he reached into his pocket and found that there remained to him only three hundred, he decided that it was folly for him to weigh himself down with such a trifling sum. All or nothing!

He put the whole sum on the single number nine. At the same time his shoulder was touched, and he turned to look into the withered face of an elderly man, sickly in appearance, but all fiber and bone. Spent as he seemed, perhaps he would still outride and outlast a hundred sturdy youths. The flap of his coat hung open and plainly showed the steel shield of a sheriff on his blouse.

"I'm Sheriff Bud Hay," said he. "I wanta talk to you."

Glances were exchanged around the roulette table. When men spent as freely as this, a sheriff generally had more than a distant interest in the source from which the money flowed.

"I'll be with you in a minute, sheriff," said Tag Enderby. "This wheel is just about through talking to me—"

It paused, stopped with a light click. The nine paid! Ten thousand five hundred dollars passed into the hands of Tag Enderby, and he scooped it up without emotion, merely saying:

"A lot of play for a short winning. Sorry I have to stop for a minute, boys!"

He waved to the croupier and turned away with the sheriff. A buzz arose behind him, deeper and more significant than that of bees, and with a greater sting in it. Grove

City was past its flourishing prime, but still it knew enough to recognize a man when it saw one. And the qualities of Tag Enderby were not obscure.

Sheriff Bud Hay was speaking with the newcomer in a corner of the room.

"You want Ray Champion?" he said. "What for?"

"I wanta see him," said Tag Enderby.

"You're gunning for him," said the sheriff.

"No, I'm not gunning for him."

"Then you come along with me. I'll take you to Champion."

"I don't need an escort," said Tag.

"You're going to have one, though."

Tag Enderby shrugged his shoulders and went out onto the street with his guide. The sheriff explained somewhat as they passed along toward the hotel.

"Champion's a friend of mine," he said. "I'll tell you why. I think that he was framed when he was sent up three years back. Now he's out, and just wants an even break to make good. He's got enough money left to make a start. And I'm going to see that he gets his chance. If you wanta talk to Champion, you can talk with me umpiring. He's been laid up for three years. He's pretty nigh forgotten how to jerk a gun, I reckon!"

"The good ones never forget," said Tag Enderby. "It's like milking. Once you learn the knack, it never gets out of your fingers again. And they tell me that Champion was good one day."

"He was too good," said the sheriff rather sadly. "When a boy learns more about guns than he knows about books and people, folks get scary about him. That's why it was easy to frame Ray—if he 'was' framed. Here we are."

He led the way into the hotel. Two minutes later they were being admitted into a small, dingy room by Ray Champion. He was one of those men who have heavy-weight shoulders, neck, and head fitted upon a lightweight body. Such a build makes a pugilist. It also makes a horseman. And the slightly bowed legs of Champion were in themselves almost a sufficient proof that he had grown up in the saddle.

His hair was a brilliant red; his eyebrows were red, also, and thick; they were the brilliant, pinkish color of brick dust. They even seemed to impart some of their glow to a pair of pale and thoughtful eyes below them.

His facial expression was depressed, gloomy; there was compensation in the extreme depth and gentleness of his voice.

Said the sheriff: "This is Tag Enderby. He's been looking around the town for you, Champion. I thought that maybe he was a friend of yours. Anyway, here he is. Now, whatcha wanta see Champion about, Enderby?"

"Why, just to look," said Tag Enderby, failing to see the extended hand which Champion was proffering by way of acknowledgment of the introduction. "I heard that this fellow had the reddest hair in the world, and I just wanted to see for myself."

Champion, drawing a little back, eyed the young stranger narrowly but quietly. He uttered not a word of criticism.

"Trouble," said the sheriff, "is what you're aiming at in this here town, Enderby, it looks like to me. Whatcha got agin Champion, will you tell me that?"

"Look here," said Tag Enderby. "Why should I have anything against him? I never saw him before. I wanted to see his red wig. I've seen it. That makes a good day for me, doesn't it? And there's that roulette wheel waiting for me up the street. So long, Champion. So long, sheriff. Hope to see a lot of you both."

He went out of the room and left the sheriff in close consultation with Champion. The fists of the latter were balled into hard knots.

"I hate to take it," he said rather hoarsely. "I'd rather be horsewhipped than to have to stand up and take the tongue of a young fool like that!"

"Sit down," said the sheriff. "You and me may be able to work something up out of this. You never seen him before?"

"Upon my word, I never laid an eye on him."

"He wants your scalp," said the sheriff. "I never heard a lingo as fresh as that talk about your red hair."

"I wanted to bash him on the jaw," said Champion through his teeth.

"Mind yourself!" said the sheriff.

"I know," said Champion. "The first lick I make, I've broke parole. I know that."

"It ain't fists, likely," said the sheriff. "That's an expert gun toter, that boy is. He packs around with him a pair of specials. How he can flip around a pair of long cannons beats me, but they say that he makes 'em come and go like card tricks."

"If it comes to gun play," said Champion, "I'm not afraid. I'll stand up with most of them, Bud. You know that."

"I know you were a fast trick in the old days. But three

years is a long time to rust."

"I rusted for six months," said Champion, "and since then I've been polished and scoured every day."

"How come?" asked Sheriff Hay.

"The warden was a white man, the whitest that ever was seen. He let me be for six months, and then he took an interest in me. He used to have me into his office and talk to me. Finally I told him how I'd been framed, and he seemed to believe it. He tried to get me pardoned. That wouldn't work. So he gave me work as a trusty, and my job was teaching the guards every day in the shooting gallery and out on the open range. That warden keeps his guards up to snuff. And I used to coach the boys with the rifles, but most of all in quick draws and snap-shooting."

He conjured forth a pair of Colts.

"That's about the sixth pair of guns that I've had in the last two years and a half," he went on. "I've burned out the other ten Colts blazing away at the prison. I used to keep it up for hours every day, giving demonstrations to the boys, showing them how to throw a gun fast. I was pretty quick before. I'm half a second faster now, and ten times as accurate. No, Bud, if it comes to a pinch, I'm not afraid of any man in the world. But I don't dare pull a gun, unless it's life or death. I wouldn't have a chance. They'd railroad me straight back to jail."

The sheriff nodded reluctantly.

"This Enderby," he said, "has something on his mind. He's a wild young hawk, but there's something right about him. His eye is straight enough."

"So's a wild cat's eye," said Champion gruffly.

"I'm behind you all of the time," said Sheriff Bud Hay.

"Don't you forget that for a minute. If they frame you, it'll have to be on top of my testimony. But still, you're right to be careful, and mighty patient. How's things?"

"I've been to Telford & Mays. I saw old Mays. He's hard and he's mean. But Telford is a friend to me. He may give me a place in the bank."

"That's a good break, son."

"It may be a start," said Ray Champion. He opened his hands and extended them a little. "If I ever get a fair grip, I'm going to show this town how I can work up!"

"You'll work up," said the sheriff with a sort of confidential kindness. "I know you, Ray. How does Molly take things?"

"She takes things well. She always takes things well," said Champion. "She's patient, too. You know the way that she is. Nothing upsets her. She's the only person in the world that it doesn't matter to—my being in jail. Her old man is a worse deadbeat than ever. She and her mother are going to take in boarders if they can get 'em. She and I figure that if I can work for six months steadily at the bank, I'll be enough ahead to marry."

"She's a good girl," said the sheriff with a devout enthusiasm. "There used to be more like her, but the breed has sort of played out thin. There ain't a finer girl in the world," he added, "than Molly Benton!"

Champion nodded. His eyes were abstracted, his brow troubled.

"You know how it is?" he said slowly. "It's too good to be true, that I should have her for a wife. I don't believe it. I can't believe it. God bless her," he added quietly.

The sheriff stood up.

"This wagon is going to drive right through and deliver the goods at the door," he said. "I got my money on you, Ray. And I've got some spare cash to help you out the minute that you say the word. Now I gotta drift along and keep an eye heaved chiefly in the direction of that Tag Enderby, as he calls himself. I'd like to know the record of that boy. If he ain't wanted by a coupla dozen sheriffs one place or another, I'm a fool! I'll see if I can't find a boarder to go to the Benton place, Ray. So long."

~5~
Gathering Information

THERE was no need of the good offices of the sheriff to secure the wanted boarder at the Benton house. The place was already filled, and the filling came about in the following manner.

When young Tag Enderby went down the street from the hotel, he passed a back lot in which a fourteen-year-old lad was seriously laboring with a forty-foot rope, striving to make it perform in the air.

Tag Enderby paused and made a cigarette and watched.

"It's the wrist, son," said he.

"Lemme see you do better before you talk," said the sweating boy.

Tag Enderby was pleased, for he liked to see spirit in the young. He could himself remember when he had been fourteen, and he considered that age the prime of life. For a boy was then able to ride, shoot, and do nearly all that a man can do. Yet he was still not required to take a man's responsibilities upon his shoulders.

Responsibilities were the bane of Tag's life. He had spent his years in running away from them, and hitherto they never had caught up with him. But he always felt that they were hot upon his trail.

So he took no offense at the curtness of the lad, but accepted the challenge. He opened the eyes of the youngster. He made that rope stand in the air, coiled like a spiral spring. He made it fall like water into the cup of his hands and spring upward again in three high-darting sprays. He appeared in the center of a whirling, inextricable mass of coils, which presently dissolved, reformed in the air, became three magic nooses that whirled around above the head of Tag and straightway dropped over the lad. He found his legs bound at the ankles and again at the knees, and his arms lashed tightly to his sides.

He was stunned. He stood gaping, while the stranger set him free.

"You must be Three-handed Stringer!" he cried when he got his breath back.

"No. I'm only Tag Enderby. You must have better ropers than I am in a big town like this."

"They wouldn't be here if they was better than you," said the boy. "They'd be out with a circus getting about a hundred dollars a week, I guess."

"That's a lot of money," said Tag.

"Yeah. But that's what 'you'd' get if you wanted it," said the boy.

He stared bewildered at the natty blue suit which clothed the slender, supple body of Tag. Such clothes he could not fit into one picture with such dexterity.

"You've got Ray Champion here in town, and he's a

great rope dauber, they tell me," said Tag.

"Him? Aw, maybe he's daubed a rope on a few cows, same as any other puncher. But I ain't heard about him being anything extra special. He ain't even going back on the range, they say!"

"Oh, he'll go back on the range, all right," said Tag Enderby.

"Will he? Then why's he tryin' for a job in the bank, you tell me?"

"He wouldn't want a job in the bank," persisted Tag Enderby. "Not Ray Champion!"

"Wouldn't he?" demanded the boy sharply. "Then maybe my old man didn't tell me that Ray was already hired, and maybe my old man ain't the president of the bank!"

"The deuce he is!" said Tag Enderby.

"The deuce he ain't!"

"It's a good job, being president of almost anything," said Tag Enderby.

"I dunno," said the boy. "I been president of our club for three whole weeks, and I'm going to resign."

"Why?"

"You know. Everybody gets jealous. Every time you say anything, everybody says 'No.' It ain't any kind of a life, being president of a club. I'm going to resign."

"You resign, then," said Tag Enderby, "but not till you've licked the boys that have all said 'No.' "

"Yeah," said the lad, "but that ain't my job. The sergeant at arms, he does the head punching. I wanta be sergeant at arms now. Everybody in the club wants to be sergeant at arms, though, specially after he's been president."

"I can't see why Ray Champion would want to work in a bank," said Tag Enderby.

"He's gotta save a lot of money before he can marry Molly Benton," said the boy.

"Yeah, that's true. He's gotta have money to marry her," said Tag Enderby, learning little by little.

"You gotta have a lot of money to marry," said the boy wisely. "Molly and her ma, they're going to take in boarders now. That'll help to get money for the marriage, I guess."

"You bet it will," said Tag Enderby. "They ought to get a lot of boarders."

"Oh, I dunno," said the boy. "There ain't many people that want regular steady board here in Grove City. The boys come in for a time, and they go away again after a coupla days. I hope the Bentons have luck, though. Molly's so swell!"

"Yeah. She's mighty good-looking," said Tag Enderby.

"Ain't she, though?" said the boy. "She's about the best-looking that ever I seen! Say, how did you get those three nooses working for you?"

"I'll show you that trick one of these days," said Tag. "What did you say your name was?"

"I didn't say, but it's Tommy Telford. I'm Telford's son—him at the bank, I mean to say."

He yawned. The bank did not seem to be important on the horizon of his life.

So Tag Enderby said good-by and sauntered on down the street. He was learning a good deal about Ray Champion, bit by bit. He might need all of that information before he was through. And, with every moment, he was gladder and gladder that he had consented to come to Grove City for the purpose of spiking the guns of Ray Champion. It might be considered dirty work by some. But he looked upon it in a different light. Never in his life had he seen hair more burningly red than that of Champion. Besides, there was something about the outthrusting head and the solid shoulders of the man that promised a hard battle before the end.

And Tag lived for fighting. Money was a mere sad necessity. One had it or one did not. That was all. It came and went, but a good fight now and then was the spice of existence.

At the next corner he found a cow-puncher sauntering down a cross street. Of him he asked the way to the Benton house. First of all he had to endure a slightly sneering survey of his neat clothes. Then he received the required information.

Everybody knew where the Benton place was, or everybody ought to, it appeared from the tone of the cow-puncher. It was right down the street a way, and you came to a couple of oak trees in a front yard. And mostly there was a brindled cow staked out there on the grass. And there was a fig tree around at the side of the house, and a windmill on the left as you faced it, and there was a tank house with latticework down the front of it, and honeysuckle growing up the slats, and there was a grindstone under the fig tree, and the corral fence was next—and you couldn't miss the place, anyway.

So Tag Enderby went on. It was true that he could not miss the place after this elaborate description. It was a low-fronted little house, with three windows looking out upon a veranda that ran from corner to corner. Before it was a great bower of shade produced by the spreading of the oak limbs. It seemed small and poor, to be sure, but it seemed cool, also, and very comfortable.

He opened the front gate and checked the in-swing of it as the iron weights dragged down against the pulley. For he hated noises—sudden noises, most of all.

Then, with his light step, he went up the path, keeping to the edge of it. For in the center there was rough gravel that would grate underfoot, and perhaps hurt him through the thin soles of his boots. He was a sensitive plant, was Tag Enderby.

Light and noiseless as a shadow, he went up the steps to the front door. Only the screen was closed. He could look through the rusted mist of this and stare down a straight hall that cleaved the house in twain from front to back. A similar door at the rear opened apparently upon a similar veranda. It was a double ender, this Benton house.

"Hey, Molly!" bawled the voice of a man.

"Molly's in the front room doin' the churning," screeched a woman from the back of the house.

"Why's she always churnin', or washin' clothes, or something?" complained the man. "I'd as good as have no daughter at all around the house, I guess."

Tag Enderby smiled.

He tapped upon the screen door, and at once the figure of a girl appeared upon the farther side of it. He knew it was Molly. For even through the screen he could see that she was lovely. He could remember still the ecstatic voice of Tommy Telford.

"This is the Benton house, isn't it?" said Tag. "And I hear that you want boarders here?"

"Yes," she said.

"I'm Tag Enderby," said he. "I'm in town for a while. Will you let me see the rooms?"

She pushed the door open, and instantly he received a shock. His peculiar prejudice caused him, always, to look first at the color of the hair, and he saw that hers was red!

It was not flaming fire, like that of Ray Champion. It was a darker color, and at the edges, where the light could get through the smoothly drawn strands, it was almost golden and shining.

Still, it was indubitably red hair. And the heart of Tag Enderby hardened within him.

She pushed the door open and waited for him to enter. He passed in, and was shown into a front room. It was quite large. There was a capacious double bed, with four tall posts and the iron frame for a canopy over it. The rug on the floor was good, though the pattern was badly frayed by the scrubbing of many feet through many years. On the walls hung several family portraits, enlarged photographs.

Those walls were a plain white, unpapered, but the room was so drenched with shadow that the white would never be glaring. There were two windows, one to the front, and one looking upon the fig tree at the side, and the grindstone under it. Under the first window stretched a comfortable-looking couch. He could veritably feel his bones resting on that couch, while he watched cigarette smoke curling toward the ceiling.

"I'll take this room," said he.

A Quiet Game

THE moment he had spoken, he felt as though he had always lived in that room, as though he had been raised in it. He was almost tempted to fumble in his memory to find the names of the stiff-faced ancestors who were ranged along the walls. He saw the writing table. He saw a hanging shelf filled with books. Like all lazy men, he liked to read. And like most of the excessively indolent, he read with intelligent discretion. For the truly idle don't wish to waste their strength and their eyes upon what is dull or cheap. Your successful business man, the vigorous and active machine, will devour trash to fill up vacant hours or to rest his mind. Your dilettante lives his only life while drifting among the words which others have written well.

Tag Enderby stifled a yawn. He felt that he could live here for a month, as inactive as a dormant bear in winter.

"Yeah, I'll take the room," said he.

" 'And' meals?" she asked him.

There was little inflection in her voice. He looked across at her and met very odd eyes. They were as blue as any he ever had seen, but it was a flat blue—not the sparkle of lapis lazuli, but mere daubs of dull color. He wondered if the sunshine could light them, or if any emotion ever rose to them. She had one of those white skins which burns but will not darken from exposure. There was no color in it. It was like milk. Not a hint of pink was in her cheeks. Yet she looked perfectly healthy.

"And meals," he agreed.

"We want to ask a dollar a day—thirty a month," said

she. "Is that all right?"

In those days a cow-puncher would work for a salary no larger. It was quite a competent price to ask, considering. But he said: "That's all right. Three meals?"

"Yes. Of course."

"I'll pay forty," said he, "if I can have second helpings."

"You can have second helpings," she answered.

He watched for a smile. There was none.

"We'll call it forty," he said, "and plenty of chuck."

"You'll have plenty of food," she said. "Mother's a good cook Thirty dollars is the price we are asking."

Suddenly he saw that he could offer no more. He was almost abashed, which was a strange feeling in Tag Enderby.

"It's closed, then," said he. "I'll go get my stuff. Have you got stable accommodations for an extra horse?"

"Yes."

"What sort of hay?"

"Volunteer oats. It's good hay. Father knows when to cut it, before the grain has shaken out of the heads. It never sweats or molds in the barn, either. It always has a sweet smell."

"You know something about horses," he said, nodding as he listened.

"Yes, I know something about horses," she said.

She was so plain and simple in her manner of speech that he found no corners, as it were, to take hold of. Conversation fell to the ground.

He said that he would go at once for his things, and she went with him and opened for him, again, the screen door. He looked down at her hand. It was as white as a white glove, and the nails were startlingly pink. They looked as though they had been stained.

He was rather thoughtful when he went back to the hotel to get his horse. If he was to make trouble for Ray Champion, perhaps he might begin with the girl. But he felt that the task would be a hard one. He had, in fact, no definite plans. He simply wanted to understand the field in which he was to work. The goal of his work would be the ruin of that red-headed fellow with the solemn face—Ray Champion. Guns, probably would be the final solution to the problem.

He went back to the Benton place, opened the gate to the corral, and rode up to the barn. The sliding door was open on one side, so he rode straight in. There was a box stall filling one end of the aisle, and obviously it was not being used. So he put his horse in that place. It was a beautiful gray, darkly dappled about the body, with stockings and muzzle of the most glossy black. It had points, and it had heart. It was the best horse that Malley could give him for a mount, and Malley knew horses.

The mow was half filled with hay. When he forked some into the manger of the box stall, pigeons flew out from above, their wings squeaking in the air. The hay itself, as the girl had said, had a sweet smell. It was clean, moreover. No dust flew with the forkfuls that he shoveled into the manger. And he knew that clean hay is apt to mean clean wind to a hardworking horse.

When he had hung up saddle and bridle on the wooden pins which thrust out from the wall of the barn, he unlashed his pack from behind the saddle and carried it into the house. He went in the front door without knocking this time, for he felt that he might as well make himself at home at once.

Already the room had been prepared for him. One ray of sunshine managed to slide through the foliage of the oaks. It glided through the open window and struck into a glow a bunch of little single roses which had been placed on the writing table in a vase of blue-and-white china.

He leaned over the roses and breathed of them. Their sweetness filled the mind of Tag Enderby, and filled the room, also, he felt. Then he undid his pack and laid away his things carefully. His Winchester he leaned in a corner of the room behind the table, so that it would not be too conspicuous. His extra clothes, and his chaps, he put into the closet. Then he went to the back of the house to become acquainted with the rest of the family.

He found Mrs. Benton in the kitchen. She had a short leg, supported on a shoe whose sole was a good four inches thick. Her back was humped with time and labor. But she was cheerful; her eyes sparkled. She came to him and gave him a wrinkled, work-reddened hand that had a good grip in it.

"I'm going to make you a happy home here with us, Mr. Enderby," said she.

"You know," said he, "everybody calls me Tag. It's shorter."

"Sure, it's shorter, and it's handier, too," said she. "Where's pa? Have you seen pa yet? Hey, pa!"

"Hello," said the man's voice which Tag Enderby had heard before.

He turned about and saw a man of sixty, straight as a tree, big, wide-shouldered. At the first glance he seemed to have the face of a conqueror. At the second glance he seemed rather one who has tried to conquer and has failed. Failed to conquer himself, at least. His hair was snow-white; so were his eyebrows. But under them were eyes exactly like the eyes of the girl—big eyes, and of the same flat blue. These, perhaps, were a little misted over.

Henry Benton introduced himself, shook hands, and took his guest onto the back porch.

That was apparently the stronghold of Mr. Benton. He had a padded rocking chair on the porch, and by it stood a bamboo table with a wicker top. The low section, where the legs crossed, was jammed full of all kinds of newspapers and battered magazines.

"Sit down and rest yourself, son," said Henry Benton. "What might you be doing in Grove City?"

"Just resting," said Tag. "And looking around for something to do."

"And what's your line? Not punching cows?"

He looked at the lean hands of Tag Enderby. They were not scarred and broadened and thickened, as are the hands of most toilers on the range.

"No," said Tag, who believed in total frankness up to a point, "my line is blackjack, or poker, mostly. I've played a little euchre, too, but that's rather slow. I don't mind a game of craps now and then. And the way I lose my honest money is faro."

Mr. Benton, saying nothing, looking out from those flat, blue eyes, allowed this information to soak in upon him. Gradually he responded to the news with a very broad smile.

"Bucking faro was where my money went, too," said he.

"But I never regretted it none. I had my fun. I'll never say that I didn't have it. You finding any pickings here around Grove City?"

"I haven't looked very far. I just had a shot at roulette to get the circulation going."

"We got a sheriff here," said Benton, "that looks pretty hard at the boys that make their living out of cards."

"I shoot them square," said Tag Enderby truthfully. "I shoot them honest with the honest fellows. And crooked with the crooks. The sheriff can't object to that."

"Yeah, I guess you do that," said Benton. "But you know the way that things are now. The world has got so a man can't spread his elbows at the table any more. Not without havin' the whole town shakin' its head when you walk down the street. Son, you're goin' to be a powerful relief to me. You're goin' to be a rest. That euchre game that you was speaking about—I play that a little myself."

So Tag Enderby sat down to a quiet game of euchre. It did not take him long to see that Mr. Benton had a few parlor tricks with the cards. They were very simple little manipulations. Tag himself had known them and forgotten them years ago, at the beginning of his career. But he did not mind watching them. He allowed himself to fall into trap after trap. He was amused, and the rising light in the eyes of Henry Benton pleased him. For, above all, it proved to him that eyes of a flat blue, blue of the deep, deep sea, can have a sparkle rising through them from the bottom of the soul.

He wondered if he might some day see that same light appearing in the eyes of the girl.

Euchre continued until the light began to wane, and the fragrance of cookery pervaded the air. Supper was announced at last, and Mr. Benton rose, the winner of twenty-two dollars in hard cash.

"Hello, Molly," he said. "You mean to say that supper is ready now? Is it as late as that? And here I've been and forgotten all about Jake Winton, that I said I'd go and see him this afternoon. I'll just run down the street and ask him what he wants. And you folks sit down. Don't wait for me. I'll be right back."

He started through the door, exclaiming: "All you need to do to your game is to take a little more care of them bowers. The bower play is the thing that makes euchre a good game!"

He disappeared, and as young Tag Enderby rose from his chair beside the wicker-topped table, he found that the girl was standing before him.

"How much did he win?" she asked.

"Oh, nothing. Twenty dollars, I suppose," said Tag.

"He'll be back again before morning, then, I suppose," said she. "Please don't do it again, Mr. Enderby."

"The cards ran his way—" he began.

But he found the blue, dull eyes fixed upon him, and he knew suddenly that they were looking straight through him, as if through a window into his mind.

~7~
A Caller

SUPPER might have been a dull affair, for Molly Benton spoke not a word during the entire course of it. She was neither sullen nor gloomy, but simply removed, and grave. But her mother made up for that silence.

Mrs. Benton rattled on cheerfully, picking up one topic before it had been more than touched upon, and moving lightly to another. She talked about the cows, and the pity that summer pasture made the butter so pale a yellow. She had to put in coloring matter. No, it didn't hurt the butter at all. It was an extract from carrots, she said. And if you didn't put the coloring in, you couldn't get any price. People were silly that way, she said. As if color made any real difference! But in the spring, when the grass was young and rich and green—that was the time when the milk pails came in steaming full, and the butter was as dark as gold! Spring, after all, was the glorious time of the year!

"Isn't it true, Molly?" she would say at the end of nearly every remark.

But Molly never answered, except for that grave, silent lifting of the eyes. That seemed response enough to please her mother.

They arrived at coffee at the end of the meal when Ray Champion came in. He was introduced, and shook hands.

"I've met Enderby before," was all he said.

He pulled up a chair, and took a piece of the mince pie and a cup of the excellent black coffee.

"You oughta use this cream, Ray," complained Mrs. Benton. "Here's a whole half pitcher of it goin' to waste. You had oughta try it. You used to take cream always. Coffee ain't coffee without some good rich cream to it, I always say."

"I got used to black coffee in the penitentiary," said Champion.

He spoke without emotion. Tag Enderby noticed two things about his voice—that it was low, like that of the girl, and that it was nearly always grave and unemphatic, like hers. There was something to this man, he felt—if only that hair had not been such a flaming red. It irritated him— through his eyes—to the very soul.

On the good side, he could not help admiring the ease and the untroubled calm with which Champion met his eye as he sat at the table. He had showed no surprise at seeing him there. And yet he must have felt that there was trouble in the air.

No doubt Champion would talk when they were alone, he and the family. And then, perhaps, Tag Enderby would be invited to leave. He hardly cared, except that there was something about that girl that intrigued him, like the solving of the problem of a combination lock. He was annoyed to think how little progress he had made since his arrival in Grove City.

Immediately after supper he went to his room and lay down on the sofa. He did not even take a book or light a lamp, for there was still a warm glow from the sunset streaming rosy through the window, and a gentle breeze puffed upon him and stirred the blond curls across his forehead.

He smoked, and let the smoke drift idly in pools and swirls above his head.

From the back of the house he could hear from time to time the clatter of dishes in the kitchen. They would be washing and drying them in there, and no doubt Ray Champion was leaning in the doorway, quietly telling the tale of his first interview with Tag Enderby.

Yes, something was astir. He had made Grove City realize that he was in town. It would realize that fact a little more vividly on the morrow, if luck came his way.

He closed his eyes. The sweet, sharp odor of the harvested fields blew in to him. Dew would fall this evening. He could feel the cool moisture of it in the air. The end of his nose and his lips were growing cold. And peace covered the soul of Tag Enderby.

A knock came at the door. The quick, light step of the girl passed down the hall, and Tag heard a man asking if a Mr. Enderby were stopping there.

He got up, and, nodding to Molly went out to meet the stranger. The light was dim, but he felt that there had been no change in the manner of the girl. It was as though Ray Champion had said nothing to her, and yet that seemed hardly possible.

He stepped on to the porch with the caller. It was a biggish man, who stood with his legs spread, braced. Deep-chested and long-armed, he looked like a heavyweight pugilist. He had one of those craggy faces in which the prominence of the cheek bones sets off the hollows of the sunken cheeks.

It was vaguely familiar to Tag Enderby, this face. He reached into his memory, but he could not strike upon the proper connecting links. The face was lost in his past, and yet he was almost sure that he was not looking at it for the first time.

The stranger said simply: "You're Enderby?"

"Yes."

"I've come up with a message from Sheriff Hay. There's some trouble in town, and he wants to have you with him. He wants to talk to you, Enderby."

"What sort of trouble?" asked Tag Enderby.

"I dunno what. He just wants you. He sent me down here in a hurry."

"Shall I saddle a horse?"

"Well, I dunno. No, I'd come straight along if I was you. He's in a mighty hurry, Enderby."

"All right," said Tag Enderby. "I'll go along, then."

He started as he was, not even pausing for a hat.

"The sheriff'll be mighty glad to see you," said the stranger.

"You know me," said Tag Enderby. "Do I know you?"

"No, I reckon that you don't know me. You never seen me really, I suppose."

"Dead sure?"

"Yeah, dead sure."

They had passed down the walk beyond the embowering foliage of the oak trees. The mustang on which the stranger had come began to lift its head at the hitch rack in front of the swinging gate.

"You're a double-crossing liar," said Enderby suddenly.

"I'm a what?" said the other. "I'm a—"

He didn't finish his speech. His wits consumed the idea with which Tag Enderby had jolted him, and the stranger reached for Tag's head with a beautiful long left lead, and at the same time snatched for a gun.

His punch missed Tag Enderby as the stroke of the hand usually misses a dead leaf, swaying in the air, repelled by the very wind of the stroke. And Tag, stepping in lightly, smote with the edge of his palm upon the base of the other's neck.

Try it for yourself—even a tap. It sends a shooting pain into the brain; it drives a tingle down the shoulder and the center arm. That is the result of a mere tap, but the edge of Tag's hand, from practice, was as hard as a stone. It is said of the Japanese that they can break a bar of marble an inch thick, using the iron-hard edge of the hand in this manner. And the stroke which Tag gave to the other paralyzed his gun arm and hand, benumbed his brain. He did not fall. He stood wavering back and forth, like a scarecrow that rocks in the wind.

Tag slipped his hand down and took from the senseless fingers of the big man the gun which was already sliding out of them. He waited for a moment, the gun's muzzle resting gently against the chest of the other.

Then he said: "What's your name?"

"I'm Doc Tyson," muttered the stranger.

"Where did I see you before?"

"When you came out of the First National at Blodgett, carrying the canvas sack. I was on the corner. I saw you go by. I took a shot at you as you jumped your horse. I missed, and then my gun clogged."

Tag Enderby heard the recital without anger.

"You saw me to-day, before?"

"Yes. I seen you talking to Tommy Telford."

"And then you saw the sheriff?"

"Yes."

"What did you tell the sheriff?"

"Nothing."

"Listen to me, Tyson. I've got a gun in my hand. It's 'your' gun. If you have an accident with your own gun, and happen to shoot yourself through the heart, is it my fault?"

The other waited a moment, evidently thinking the matter out.

"No, you got me sewed up," said he.

"Then tell me what you said to the sheriff."

"I said that I'd seen you somewhere," confessed Tyson. "I said that I wasn't quite sure, but that I wanted to get in another good look. He said to come down here, and if I remembered anything worth talking about, I was to bring you back to him. Well, the minute I laid eyes on you standing at the door yonder, I remembered how you'd run past me on the street there in Blodgett."

"D'you live in Grove City?" asked Tag Enderby.

"No. I'm just looking around for a job on the range near here."

"You'd better go home," said Tag Enderby.

"You've got the drop on me," said the other.

"How much money have you got?"

"I've got ten, twenty dollars. Plenty."

"Here's a hundred to give you a long start," said Tag Enderby.

The other shook his head.

"I don't want your coin," he said sourly.

"Listen, Doc Tyson."

"Yeah, I'm listening."

"If I should see you here in Grove City, you wouldn't expect me to stop and waste any time explaining, would you?"

"No, I guess not."

"Doc, you climb on board of that horse and tell the conductor to let you off a hundred miles from here, will you?"

"You got the drop on me," repeated the other sullenly.

"Then start along."

Tyson, without a word, turned slowly, strode to the gate,

mounted his horse, and then paused, as though he were fighting a battle in his mind. But eventually he turned the head of the mustang up the road and let it go off at a slow walk.

"A slow start makes a long finish," said the voice of Molly Benton just behind Tag Enderby.

He whirled around on her. She was very close. Her face and hands seemed almost luminously white in the darkness.

"Maybe that's true," said Tag Enderby.

"What did you do to him?" asked the girl.

"I stung him in the nerve center," said Tag Enderby truthfully. "That's all that there was to it."

"Well," said she, "he's gone, and that's one trouble out of your way. But will you tell me now just why you've come here? Why do you want to do harm in this house?"

~8~
An Observing Girl

H E was not entirely surprised by this direct attack. He had sensed hostility and suspicion in her from the first. "What harm is there in resting?" said he.

"You've started dad on one of his silly little sprees," she answered, "and you've run another man out of Grove City. Are those the usual results when you—rest?"

He waited a moment, turning his thought of her over in his mind.

"Why start a war?" he asked at length.

"I'm not starting a war," she answered. "I'm afraid of you. That's why I'm asking questions. I know that you don't have to answer them."

"Do you want me to move out?"

"No," she said. "We need the money you pay for rent and board. Besides, if you have some scheme up your sleeve, it's better to have you here. It may give you a better chance of working, but it also gives us a better chance of keeping you under our eye."

Tag Enderby laughed.

"You're all right, Molly," he said. "You hit out from the shoulder. I'll tell you. There's nobody in your family that I'll hurt."

"It's Ray Champion, then," she said instantly.

"Tut, tut," said he. "I never saw Ray Champion before today. What makes him think I'm out for him?"

"He doesn't think so. At least, he hasn't said anything."

"What makes 'you' think so?"

"You're not here for your health," said she. "You're not here for our money, because we haven't any. You're not here to harm us, because you've told us so. Then you're here to harm Ray Champion."

He was amazed.

"You're logical," he said, "but you really can't run a fellow down like that. Am I the first man you've ever known who drifts around and follows his nose? Am I the only man in the world who doesn't live on a schedule?"

"Humph," said she.

"Come up there on the veranda," said he, "so that I can watch your face. You're a strange one, Molly."

"Yes," said she. "Let's sit there, where we'll have more light."

They sat on chairs within the glow of the lamplight that streamed out of the windows of her room. She placed herself so that he could look straight into her face, but he saw that her glance did not waver. She was studying him with fully as much intensity as he was bestowing upon her.

"Now, Molly," said he, "you tell me why we shouldn't be friends?"

"Because I expect to marry Ray Champion," said she. "I want him alive and happy, not dead or ruined."

The directness of her thrusts and the hits which she was making well nigh staggered Tag Enderby. He had to shake his head a little to tell himself that he was not dreaming.

"You have that fellow Champion still on your mind," he said.

He wondered if it were true that Champion really had not said a word about him. If so, Champion stepped a long distance upward in his mind.

"Of course, I have him on my mind," said she. "If it's not Champion that you want, then it's buried treasure, or some such stuff!" She laughed faintly at the thought of such a thing as buried treasure in her house. And he bent his head a trifle, to listen more keenly to the musical flowing of the sound.

"Laugh some more, Molly," said he. "I wouldn't know you when you laugh like that. I still don't see what makes you think I'm after Champion."

She remained silent for a moment, always studying him.

"Listen to me, Tag," said she.

"I'm listening like a church," said he.

"Suppose that you see a hound running with his head close to the ground and his tail out straight. What do you think?"

"That he's on a trail, of course."

"And suppose you see a wild cat creeping with its belly to the ground, and its tail curling around its sides now and then, and its head stretched straight forward?"

"Trying to catch a bird in a bush, I suppose."

"Now then, Tag, what am I to think about you?"

"Why? In what way? Have I been creeping around with my nose to the ground?"

She said, and tallied off the items on the slender tip of a forefinger:

"When you look at people, you weigh their hearts in your eyes."

"Come, come!" said he.

"You do," she answered. "Also, when you step, you make no sound."

"I wear soft soles, and very thin ones," said he.

"You walk close to the wall, even when you're going down the hall, and you slow up a little every time you pass an open door."

"You're imagining that."

"While you were eating supper, you looked toward the open door over your shoulder at least a dozen times."

"I don't remember doing it once," said he.

"It wasn't a full turn of the head. Just a glint out of the corner of your eye. Perhaps you didn't know that you were doing it."

"I can't argue about things I don't remember," said he.

"Inside your hand," she said, "there isn't a single sign of a callus. When I met you, I found your hand as soft as mine."

"I wear gloves," said he.

"I know," she answered, "the sort of thick, spongy calluses that grow under gloves."

"What do you draw from that?" he asked her.

She shook her head.

"You carry a gun with you, Tag."

"I do?" said he. "What makes you think that?"

"Because of the way you walk, talk, and look about you. I'd be less surprised to find a cat without teeth than you without a gun. And yet you know so well how to dispose of it that I can't see a wrinkle or a bulge as a sign of it."

"If I wear a gun, why should I advertise it?" said he.

"You shouldn't," she replied. "I merely say it's another thing that proves you're an expert."

"An expert what?" he asked her abruptly.

"Man-killer," said she.

This time he started. She had struck him in many places, but the weight of this last blow really stunned him.

"Listen, Molly," he said. "That's a little steep, even to take from a nice girl like you."

She shook her head.

"I'm not really asking you to answer. I don't expect you to confess. I don't actually hope, like a fool, that you'll tell me how you were cornered by the three Mexicans and dropped them all—"

He jumped to his feet. In one stride he had reached her. He bent over her. His face was as hard as stone, and his eyes shining. Yet she did not wince.

"Who the devil has been telling you about me?" he asked her in a fierce whisper.

She tilted back her head, and a faint smile stirred on her lips.

"Not a soul has told me a word about you," said she.

"You lie, too—do you?" said Tag Enderby.

"I'm not lying. Nobody has told me one word about you."

He sneered.

"The three greasers—you just happened to see that with second sight, I suppose?"

She shook her head. Her smile even deepened.

"It was a hit in the dark, but I'm glad that it hit home," said she. "I know that I haven't been making a fool of myself, talking like this and thinking as I do about you."

"A hit in the dark?" said he, angry now. "How could that be a hit in the dark? Do you think I'm a half-wit, Molly, and that you can pull the wool over my eyes?"

"I know that you've been in Mexico by the way you roll a cigarette," said she. "And by the rest of you, I guessed that you've fought in Mexico—that you've fought every-where you've been. As for the numbers, that was sheer guess."

"By—" he began.

Then he stopped himself and returned to his chair.

"You're wonderful," he said. "Truth teller or liar, you're wonderful."

He stared at the coppery gleam of her hair. That was the one fault he could find in her.

"Go away, Tag," said she. "I don't want you to hurt Ray. And I don't want him to hurt you. And it's to make trouble for him that you've come here. I believe you when you say it's not to bother my family. But go away. You can't gain very much out of it. Go back to the man who sent you, and tell him that you don't want the job. Ray was railroaded before. Why should you do the job a second time?"

He stood up once more. He wanted to be alone. She baffled and bewildered him, and he felt that he had to get away from the steady probing of those big blue eyes. For all her thought, there was not a trace of a wrinkle in her forehead. It was low and broad and smooth as the brow of an Indian girl. The hair was bound sleekly about her head like a copper helmet.

If only it had been black, or brown, or golden, or even the color of straw.

But it was red!

"There's no use saying yes or no to you," he said. "You've written me down as a man handler."

"I saw you working, Tag," she said. "Don't forget that. I've seen you—sting a nerve center, as you put it so aptly. You broke the spirit of that big man. He's ready to take water from a Chinaman after this evening."

"I can't change your thinking," said he. "I'd better turn in, anyway, if you'll excuse me."

"I have to go in, too," said she, and went before him to the door. She rattled the knob, twisting it from side to side.

"Bother!" said she. "Mother's been absent-minded and locked the door already. I'll have to rout her out."

"Let me see it. Maybe it's only stuck," said he. "You can call Champion, though."

"He's already gone. He took the short cut to the hotel across the fields."

He was leaning above the lock only for a moment.

"Just as I thought," said he. "The door was only stuck. There you are."

He pulled it open for her.

"Thank you," said Molly Benton, and went in before

him. As she passed, she gave him a smile so suddenly brilliant, so lighted with understanding, as it were, that it left him somewhat staggered, and groping for the reason as he went into his own room.

An Old Acquaintance

H E undressed very slowly, pausing for thought after every move of his hands. Several times he shook his head, and when he had slid in between the coolness of the sheets, he murmured: "Except for the red hair—"

He shook his head again and fell fast asleep.

When he awakened in the morning it was the gray of dawn, just coloring with the morning rose. He got up, washed, shaved, dressed, and went out to the barn to see his horse, Doctor. He found that Molly already had the beauty at the watering trough.

"Turn him loose and let him run," said Tag Enderby.

She slipped the halter off obediently.

The tall gray, having finished his drinking, shot suddenly away. He went around the corral like a stone swung in a sling. He was leaning in at a sharp angle all the way to maintain his pace without losing his balance.

"He's as wild as a cat," said the girl. "You'll have a job catching him!"

"No. Not after he's loosened himself up," said Tag Enderby.

Wreaths of dust, flung up by the hoofs of the horse, hung in thin silver streaks in the air. His speed seemed to increase. He ran all straight, stretching like a thing made of rubber. Then, coming to a canter, a trot, and a stop, he hung his head over the fence and looked across the wider pastures beyond.

"That hawk wants the whole blue to fly in!" said the girl.

She smiled and nodded—not toward the horse, strangely, but at Tag Enderby himself.

"Now, why do you look at me when you say that?" he asked her.

"Oh, I won't make any more remarks. I was too personal last night," she admitted. "But I was frightened. I had to talk. This morning I've stopped drawing deductions."

"Thanks," said Tag.

"I'll go down on the right side and try to drive him toward the barn," she suggested.

"There's no need of that."

He whistled sharply. The big gray wheeled about and came straight up to him at a trot.

He put on the halter once more.

"You've spent a long time teaching him that trick," said she.

"I've trained a lot of horses," he answered rather vaguely, for his mind was back in the green meadows of the clearing before Malley's cabin. There, to be sure, he spent far more time with the horses than with the men. He had worked on them until the whole herd would come in answer to his whistle. They would obey him in other ways. And when new horses were added to the old herd, they quickly learned from the ways of the others. It was almost the only innocent pleasure—aside from food and drink—in which he employed himself.

Now he took the gray back to the barn, gave him a liberal feed, and looked up to find that the girl was there, still watching.

"You ask Doctor here," he said, pointing to the horse. "He'll tell you a lot about me."

"He could tell me some nice things," said she. "But I know some nice things already."

"You do?"

"Of course I do. But we're not talking personalities this morning. I suppose that breakfast will be ready by the time we get back."

They walked in together, and she sang all the way beneath her breath. She was as fresh as the morning, and as gay. He opened the swing gate that gave on the board path to the back of the house, but he stopped her with a gesture as she was about to step through.

"You've done a lot of mind reading since I've been at the house," said he. "Let me do a little mind reading of my own."

"Why, yes," said she. "I'd like to have you try. Read my mind for me, Tag. What am I thinking about now?"

"Hawks—and blue skies," said he.

"Yes," said she. " 'A' hawk, though."

She looked straight at him as she spoke.

"But I'm going to find something more important than this in your mind," he assured her.

"You go on and tell me, then, Tag," she urged him.

"It's about Champion."

"Is it? Tell me what I think about him, then. But you know already!"

"I know something new," said he. "You like Champion a

lot. You think he's the salt, all right. But you don't love him a rap."

He saw her draw a breath for a quick denial. But suddenly she was thoughtful.

"There shouldn't be this sort of talk in the morning," said she. "Come on. I can smell coffee and bacon, and I know there are sour-milk biscuits, too."

Henry Benton was at the breakfast table, looking very seedy, and with a muttered account of a "sick friend" with whom he had had to sit up most of the night. The family paid no attention to him. Mrs. Benton could speak of one thing only: It was the first day of Champion's work in the Telford & Mays bank!

After breakfast, Tag Enderby lounged in his room, smoking one cigarette from the butt of another, and finding that his thought dissolved in the air to nothing, even like the smoke that rose above his head and formed like a dying shadow upon the ceiling. He could not fix his mind upon any process or current of thought, but only the face of the girl kept forming and dimming and growing again between him and his ideas.

It was nearly noon when he got up, put on hat and coat, arranged the handkerchief in his breast pocket, left word that he would not be in for lunch, and sauntered down the street to the center of town, moving with a snaillike slowness in the shadow, but with a brisk swing in the sun.

He went into the first saloon that he reached, so abstracted that he forgot it was the very same in which roulette had first stolen his money, and then returned more than all to him. The bartender favored him with a sour smile, which he answered with a nod, and went into the back room. For he wanted a dark corner. In darkness he felt that he could think best.

In the very darkest corner, therefore, he settled down and tried to group his thoughts effectively, and still the image of the girl stepped between him and his ideas with a sunshine clarity that made all other things dim.

"She's getting on my mind," said he to himself. "What's the matter with me?"

A voice in a husky whisper sounded near by.

"Don't turn, Tag. It's me; Charlie Magnum!"

He did not turn. He was glad of any interruption just then, but he had to fumble far back in his bad memory before he could recall the man. Charlie Magnum, he then remembered, was the yegg who had worked with such success through the small towns of Colorado some years ago.

"Where you been, Charlie?" he asked, just turning his head enough so that his whisper could come to the other. And he kept his cigarette near his mouth, so that the movement of his lips might not be observed by the four men at the other end of the room, shaking dice on a blanket.

"I've been up for a stretch," said Charlie. "I'm out now, and I'm full of ideas. I got an idea right here for you and me."

"You know me, Charlie," said Tag. "I work alone."

"Usually. Mostly you do. But not right now. It's such a cinch," said Charlie.

"Then pull it yourself if it's a cinch."

"All I need is an outside man. I can crack this mug. I can read its mind."

With the skill learned from a long prison life, Charlie Magnum laughed, and made a sound no more vibrant than his whisper had been before. It was rather a ghostly thing to hear.

"I'm not an outside or an inside man, except when I'm alone," said Tag Enderby. "You can't talk to me. Don't blow your hand."

"You're restin', son," persisted the whisper. "But I tell you what: You oughta step in and take some of the easy cash."

"Why not keep it all for yourself?"

"I wanta make the job that extra safe, is all," said Charlie. "Bein' alone and inside the joint—it's hell. I've got more nerves than I used to have."

"You find another bunkie," said Tag Enderby. "I'm resting just now."

"Is that the end of the story?"

"Yes, that's the end for you."

A few sibilant curses, directed vaguely at all of life and fate, answered him. Then a shadow rose behind him, and he saw the hunched back and the hawklike profile of Charlie Magnum pass from the place.

Tag was disgusted. He was disgusted with the profession which he had made his life. He was disgusted with the knowledge that even such poisonous rats as Charlie Magnum could call him by name.

To wash his mind free from such distractions, he joined the dice game, bet high, lost a cool thousand, and wandered out onto the street again. He felt better, able to stand straighter, and yet none of the amusements of the town were exactly to his taste just now.

The coming of Charlie Magnum had thrown a shadow over everything. Tag went to the hotel, ate a very bad lunch, and returned, at a snail's pace again, to the Benton place.

Life was pleasanter to the taste, in his estimation, when he was stretched lazily once more upon his couch under the window, and again, like a dormant animal in its winter sleep, he lay there only semi-conscious, hour after hour, not even smoking, but with his hands clasped behind his head, and his dull eyes fixed upon the ceiling.

"Something's happened to me!" he assured himself several times.

But that assurance gave him no nearer approach to the solution of the mystery.

At supper he sat like a stone, and after supper he went to bed almost immediately, and fell into a troubled sleep.

He was up in the first of the morning light again, and, as he dressed, he heard hoofbeats approach, stop before the gate, and then running footfalls rounded to the back. A screen door slammed. Voices murmured rapidly from the direction of the kitchen. Then a woman's voice screamed high and long and loud.

It sent the chills running up his back.

A moment later, as he was about to open his door and go back with inquiries, he heard a loud rapping, and, as he turned the knob, he found the girl in front of him, with two bright-red spots in her cheeks.

"Mr. Man-killer Enderby," she said, "you've done the thing perfectly this time. You've jailed Ray Champion; I hope that you suffer for it!"

On the Trail

H E was so angry at the confidence of the accusation that he exclaimed at once: "Champion's in jail? What of it? I hope he stays there. But who says that I put him in?"

She controlled herself, smiling in the coldness of her fury.

"You didn't put him in," she said. "You merely cracked the safe; you took the loot; you sneaked from the bank to the hotel; you kept the seventy-five thousand cash and planted the unnegotiable bonds in Ray's room; you left the trail marked so that people would be sure to follow to that place. Now—deny it—lie to me. I wasn't to see what face you put on it!"

She was not snarling at him. Anger made her voice lower. It did not tremble, either, but a heat went through him, like a flame.

What he saw most clearly was not the girl at all. It was the sneaking form of Charlie Magnum.

"I was in my room all night," Tag said.

She smiled, and said nothing in reply.

"I was in my room all night," he repeated, his voice harsh and flat.

"The other thing—just happened, I suppose," said she.

She stepped a little closer.

"Why do you do it, Tag?" said she. "Why don't you let the truth come out to me? I can't send you to jail for it. You've done what you wanted to do—you or the devil inside of you!—you've ruined Ray Champion's life for good, now. He'll never be able to lift his head again. It'll make him a crook. He's already—"

She stopped herself on the unspoken word.

"I'll tell you what I'll do," said Tag Enderby. "I'll make a bargain with you."

"Bargain? What will you bargain with?"

"I know the man who stole the stuff from the bank. I didn't know that he intended to plant it on Champion to cover his own trail. But, suppose that I should find him, and bring him in, and make him give up the money—"

He waited for her to speak.

"You're a complicated man, Tag," said she. "What am I to say to that? You want to smash Ray. You've done it. Now you say that you'll undo it?"

"I haven't smashed him. He's broken, though. Suppose that I patch him together again?"

"Well?"

"What will be in your mind then? That it was all a complicated plot of mine from the first?"

"I don't know what I'll think," said she. "I only know that just now my brain is whirling like a top."

"Good-by, Molly," said he. "I'm riding out now. You'll be wishing me luck. If I get the stuff, I'll be back soon. If I don't get it soon, I'll stay on the trail till I get the man, at least. Only—tell me one thing. What made you think that I'm a cracksman?"

"The front door, before last night," said she. "I suspected those clever hands of yours. So I simply locked the door while I was pretending to open it. The key was on the outside, you know."

"You wanted to see what I'd do with it, eh?"

"Yes. And you found that the door had simply—stuck!"
She did not smile.

"Then, this morning, you were sure?"

"Honest men don't learn the minds of locks as quickly as all that," she said.

He left her, closed the door, made up his pack swiftly, and carried it out to the barn, where he saddled the gray and was quickly on the street again.

Now minutes, he knew, might count enormously.

He rode the gray downtown and went straight to the railroad yard. There he dismounted, tethered the gray to the fence of the yard, and hurried inside.

The agent sat upon a box on the platform, his back bent, a toothpick thrusting out from his mouth.

"Looking for a cousin of mine," said Tag Enderby. "And he came down here yesterday. Rather small, back sort of bent, and a big beak of a nose."

"Yeah, I remember him. He told me a couple of funny stories. He was just down here to see the train come in. You know that one about the Scotchman that lost the penny and—"

Tag already had turned away.

For he had learned all that he would be able to get from this fellow. If it were true that Charlie Magnum had come down to the station yard the day before, it was simply because astute Charlie wanted to know about the movements of the trains during the night and the early morning.

He stood in front of the big blackboard on which the movements of trains for the last twenty-four hours were chalked up. Between midnight and this hour, no passengers had been through. But two freights had stopped. Each was going east, and therefore, he had no doubt, Charlie Magnum was now east of Grove City.

At the far end of the yard a freight was even now preparing to pull out. He ran to catch it.

A burly brakeman confronted him as he approached. He held an unlighted lantern in his hand, one of those iron-framed and barred lanterns which are used along all American railroads. They give a strong light. Also, they make an effective club.

"You're headed the wrong way, kid," said the brakeman. "The next train is the one you want."

"Hello, friend," said Tag Enderby. "Why, if it isn't Uncle Joe! Hello, Uncle Joe. You don't mean to say that you've forgotten me?"

He put two silver dollars into the hand of the brakeman. The latter rang the coins together before he answered.

"Sure I remember you, Willie," said he. "Where have you been keepin' yourself all this time?"

"I've been to college," said Tag Enderby. "I've got to hurry now to graduate and get my diploma, and all of that."

"Yeah, I'll bet you gotta hurry," said the brakeman. "Maybe they's somebody back there in Grove City that wants to hand you a diploma with a nightstick inside of it. Is that the way?"

"Uncle Joe," said Enderby, "you got fine eyes. You could see through plate glass, pretty near."

"Hop on, kid," said the brakeman, swinging his signal hand to the engineer. "You can ride my division."

There were no useless formalities. Tag Enderby walked into the caboose and sat down at a window. The brakeman joined him a moment later as the long train began to groan and shudder, and pick up speed.

"Been on this run long?" asked Tag Enderby.

"Three months. That's enough. There's only about one jack rabbit to the mile. Where do you come from, boy?"

"I come from over there," said Tag Enderby, including half the points of the compass in his gesture.

"I thought that was your home town," replied the brakeman, with a grin. "They got a new fire department, ain't they?"

"Yeah. They've got a red one. What about jungles along this line?"

"Is that the sort of hotel that you want?"

"I don't mind," said Tag Enderby. "I like to have elbow-room."

"You'll look sweet, in about half a day, if you live in a dirty tramp jungle," said the brakeman. "Why don't you brace into a big town and put up at a big hotel? That's the best way to lose yourself—the very best!"

"You know, brother," said Tag. "But I've got something on my mind besides hair. Not so many jungles along this line, are there?"

"Not so many. I keep a lookout for the hobos about ten miles from here, where we hit the first long grade. They try to hook on there, now and then. It's a little jungle, right under the trestle. Sometimes you can look down, at night, and see the wink of their fire. It's only a little jungle."

"Where's the next one?

"That's an hour from here, the way we run it. Yeah, nearer to an hour and a quarter. Outside of Bear River."

"What's Bear River?"

"You oughta learn your country before you campaign it,"

said the brakeman, in stern reproval. "Bear River is where the W. & O. line crosses this one. It's a pretty good-sized town. Smoky, though, because there's always so many engines firing up in the yards."

A railroad junction was, very likely, the place where Magnum would change from the first train. The more angular he could make his course across the country, the more it was apt to please him.

"Do you slow near the Bear River junction?" he asked.

"Yeah. There's a heavy grade there."

"I'll leave you when you hit that spot," said Tag Enderby. "Lean back and rest yourself. It's a hard life that a shack has in this world. I'm sorry for you fellows. Up by day, up by night, work as many as five or six hours a day, except when you're sitting in the caboose, eating the apples that you've pried out of some shipment, or working open a case to slide out a little bottle of hooch. It's a mean life, and a hard life, and a life that's hard on the eyes."

The brakeman grinned. He was big enough to be magnanimous. Besides, he seemed to possess a sense of humor. In addition, he had two heavy silver dollars, which made a great difference.

"You're right, son," said he. "It's a hard life."

"And hardly any exercise," said Tag Enderby, "except bending a lantern frame over the head of a hobo, now and then?"

"That's about all. We get real soft," said the brakeman, flexing and relaxing his huge, hammer head of a fist. "What's your line?"

"I'm an entertainer," said Tag.

"Yeah. Midnight entertainer, ain't you?"

"Yeah. I've performed at midnight, too."

They talked with mutual pleasure, so that the hour slid rapidly by. And as the train slowed for the grade, the engine laboring mightily, Tag Enderby stepped to the rear platform, waved farewell to the brakeman, and climbed down the steps.

He saw on both sides of the train a sweep of low trees and a tangle of brush. A mile away, arose the red and brown roofs of a town. And now he saw a narrow gully, with the silver blink of water running through its midst.

That was the place for a comfortable tramp jungle. He gripped the guard railings with both hands, swung out, dropped lightly to the ground, sprinted to keep from falling, and then turned off into the brush. He felt that Magnum might be no more than two jumps ahead of him!

~11~
A Formidable Pair

THE smell of wood smoke first gave Enderby promise that he would find someone in the jungle. He went on rapidly but soundlessly through the shrubbery until he came to a clearing on the verge of the stream. By the number of tin cans of all sizes which were heaped in a pile at one side of the place, it was certain that this was a tramp "jungle" of long standing. It was strewn with pebbles and big stones. And through the center the stream made a quick turn around a bend.

Here were water and fuel to the heart's content, a town less than a mile away, and a railroad at hand. What more could the heart of the tramp desire?

The fire which he had smelled from the distance was blazing cheerfully in the middle of a number of blackened rocks, a natural outdoor hearth. Supported above the flames by the rocks was stretched a small washboiler that might hold as much as five gallons, all told. The cover was on it, and from the crevices around the fire exuded a fragrant steam of the cookery.

Two obvious vagrants were there. One stood by the washboiler, scanning it with a proprietary frown, and sometimes moving the coffee pot a little when it was beginning to seethe at the verge of the fire. The other sat at a little distance away, busily putting a patch on his coat, his sewing kit spread out on the pebbles beside him.

They were a formidable pair in size and looks. Their lined faces were shadowed with beards of several days' growth. It was plain that they were old companions. Each was over six feet in height. They were well-matched in ugliness and in power, being solidly made men with the look of those who can take and give hard knocks.

"Brisk up the fire, Bill," said he who was seated, as Tag Enderby came to the verge of the brush.

"Brisk it up yourself, Indiana," said Bill gruffly.

"Go on and brisk up the fire. I'm gettin' hungry," said the other.

"Get hungry, and see if I care," said Bill.

"Listen, Carney, don't get proud," said Indiana.

"I ain't proud," said Bill Carney. "I'm tired of the way that you set around."

"Who got the chicken?" said Indiana.

"Who dug the spuds, and brought the coffee along?" demanded Bill Carney.

"Who swiped the canned tomatoes?" asked Indiana.

The latter remark seemed to settle the dispute. Bill Carney grinned.

"That was pretty slick," said he. "You got a pair of hands. I never said no to that!"

"I got a pair of hands, and I always split the profits," declared Indiana.

"Yeah. You do that," admitted Carney. "You gotta pair of hands, and you use 'em for two. Only, you're a lazy galoot, Indiana. You ain't ever going to come to no good end."

"You jailbird," said Indiana cheerfully.

"Yeah, and what about yourself?"

"I never done a stretch in my life," said Indiana proudly.

"You'll get your neck stretched, to make up," remarked Bill Carney. "This mulligan smells pretty good."

"You always make it good," said Indiana, willing to admire. "I never seen anybody like you, Bill. You could make a good mulligan out of hot water and wood chips. I dunno how you manage it."

"It's a kind of a gift. It's the way you put things together. I dunno just how I do it. I've tried to explain to blokes. But they never catch on, mostly."

"Yeah, you've tried to teach me," said Indiana. "But somehow or another I never could get the hang of it."

"Because you're too dog-gone lazy," said Carney.

"Listen," complained Indiana. "Do we have to start and argue that all over again?"

"Aw, let it go," said Carney. "Nothin' will ever change you except the hangman."

Tag Enderby stepped into the clearing.

"Hullo, boys," said he.

They looked at him without enthusiasm—his neat clothes, his cheerful face.

"Dog-gone me if we ain't picked up an undertaker," said Carney sourly.

"Whatcha got with you, buddy?" asked Indiana.

"I pay," said Tag.

"He knows his way around," said Carney, looking at his partner.

"Yeah, he knows his way around," admitted Indiana. "Rustle some more wood for the fire, will you, stranger?"

"I pay," Tag repeated. "I don't work."

"He saves his hands," said Indiana.

"Where's his gloves then?" asked Carney.

"I left home in a hurry," explained Tag Enderby. "I had to leave the gloves behind me. What have you boys got in that pot?"

He approached.

"Keep your hands off that lid," said Carney. "It ain't ready for the unveiling yet."

Nevertheless, Tag Enderby raised the cover and peeked inside, and sniffed the steam.

"He's fresh, too," said Carney to his partner.

"Yeah, he's pretty fresh," said Indiana. "He's got the manners of a counter jumper. He ain't been raised right."

"Chicken," pronounced Enderby. "Tomatoes, potatoes, onions, and a bottle of ketchup."

"You missed something," said Carney, with an obvious interest.

"Garlic," said Tag Enderby, studying the fragrance of the steam that escaped.

"He's got a nose in his head, too," said Carney.

"Yeah, he's got a nose," admitted Indiana. "What's your little line, brother?"

Tag replaced the cover upon the boiler.

"Green goods, or a little kiting," he said. "I've got lots of talents. I'm not lost at cards, and I've rolled dice, in my day. Got a set, you boys?"

"He's a penman," said Carney to his companion.

"Yeah. He's got the hands," said Indiana.

He regarded Tag Enderby with some interest.

"You don't go heeled, buddy," said he, surveying Tag's closely fitted suit carefully.

"Why should I go heeled like a cop?" said Tag Enderby. "Fast feet are better than a gun in the hand, any day."

"What do you pay, stranger?" asked Carney.

"Fifty cents."

"There's chicken in here," said Carney.

"Fifty is a lot of cents," explained Tag.

"Yeah, fifty is a lot of cents," said Indiana. "Let's see it stacked up in one pile, will you?"

"It's up my sleeve," said Tag.

He shook his arm, and turned his hand. A fifty-cent piece appeared on the back of his hand. He tossed it into the air, let it drop on a stone, and while the ring of the piece was still in the air, he caught the coin on the rebound, and made it disappear, as though a rubber string were hitched to it.

"He's been around," said Indiana.

"He knows his piece good enough for Sunday school," admitted Carney. "This chuck is about ready."

He took off the cover from the stew and peered into the rising mist.

"You boys been here long?" Tag asked.

"Just long enough to get settled in," said Indiana. "Why?"

"I was looking for a friend. I thought you might have seen him around this place."

"What's his moniker?"

Tag Enderby avoided the question.

"He's not very big," said he. "Got a hump on his back and a nose and a half on his face. That mean anything to you?"

The two tramps looked at one another.

"Never saw him," said Indiana.

"Nope, never," said Bill Carney.

Tag smiled faintly. He knew instantly, from the readiness and unanimity of their responses, that they were lying. And his heart gave one triumphant throb. It was plain that they had seen Magnum, and perhaps that gentleman was not far away at this moment.

"Makes no difference," said Tag. "He was just a friend of mine; that's all."

"Friends make the world turn around," said Indiana absently. But his eyes were steadily fixed upon his partner.

"Yeah, they make the world turn around," said Carney.

He dropped the cover of the boiler to the pebbles. It made a loudly ringing clatter.

"Quit that!" cried Indiana.

"Yeah? Why should I quit it?" said Carney.

"You give me the jumps," said Indiana. "You got no nerves in your ears. You must 'a' been raised with a brass band. I never seen a guy that liked noise so much."

"I'm musical; that's why," said Bill Carney. "Where's the tins you found? This stuff is ready to dish out."

Several tin plates were produced. They still were marred and marked with rust, which had been only partially scrubbed away with water and sand.

"Wait a minute," said Tag Enderby.

He stepped into the shrubbery, and came back in a few minutes carrying a natural dish of bark, which he had cut from the side of a tree. By crumpling up one end of it, he produced the effect of a good-sized scoop. In this he received the portion which Carney ladled out to him, serving with such care that some of all the ingredients of that noble mulligan came to the share of Tag Enderby.

There were two loaves of fresh baker's bread. And he got a chunk from one of these, and a fairly clean tomato can more than half filled with coffee.

Then he sat down cross-legged, and began to taste the mulligan from the end of the scoop. He had had no breakfast, and his appetite was very sharp.

He flipped the fifty-cent piece to Carney.

The latter threw it back.

"We don't want the cash," said he gruffly.

"It's about time," said Indiana.

"Yeah, it's about time," said Carney.

And suddenly Enderby was covered by two man-sized Colt revolvers!

~12~
The Loot

HE had a chunk of bread in one hand and the scoop of the bark in the other, which made him reasonably helpless. He continued to eat.

"What do you want, boys?" he asked. "The insides of the goose, or just the golden eggs?"

"Stick up your hands, son," said Indiana.

"Wait till they're empty," said Tag.

"That's fair," remarked Carney. "You oughta let him eat something. He's hungry. I been hungry myself."

"He's a slicker," said Indiana. "You, stranger, stick up your hands. You hear?"

"Oh, take it easy," said Tag Enderby. "If you want my cash, you can have it—after I've finished breakfast."

"He's cool," said Carney, sighting down the barrel of his revolver at Tag.

"Yeah, he's cool," said Indiana. "But he's going to be more than cool in a coupla seconds, if he don't hoist his mitts. He's going to be cold, what I mean!"

"You're going to be cold, if you don't stick 'em up," said Carney.

"D'you mean that, boys?" asked Tag, aggrieved.

"Yeah, we mean that," said Carney.

"Go ahead and drill me then," said Tag Enderby. "I'm hungry, and I mean to feed."

"Why, you fool!" exclaimed Indiana. "D'you think that you can back-chat with us, when we've got the drop on you? I'll count to three, and then we both drill him, Carney!"

He began to count, slowly, making a longer pause between two and three than between one and two.

But when he had pronounced "Three," Tag Enderby was still eating cheerfully.

And the guns had not exploded.

"That's all right, boys," said Tag. "It was a good bluff,

but I know you're too white to bump a fellow off like that. You're too far West to be that tough."

"He's got a head on his shoulders," said Carney.

"Yeah, and he nearly lost it, that time," said Indiana. "You was only a hundredth of an inch away from the dark, that time, brother. I give the trigger a squeeze, but I didn't squeeze quite hard enough."

"You'll get the silver lining out of this cloud," said Tag, "if that's what's worrying you. You'll get the money. What makes you want the hide, too?"

"I dunno," answered Carney. " 'I' don't want the hide. This guy is all right, Indiana."

"Yeah, he seems all right," said Indiana thoughtfully.

There was a faint rustling sound at the edge of the brush. Tag turned his head a trifle and saw a most unwelcome sight—Charlie Magnum stepping into the clearing.

The latter gave him one glint from beady eyes, and then turned fiercely upon the two hobos.

"Bright, ain't you?" said Magnum. "Going to let him kid you along, ain't you? I just stayed there and watched, for a while. I wanted to see what he'd do, in a tight pinch, like this. Why, you fat-headed fools, he blarneyed you almost to death. He'd 'a' had your scalps in another thirty seconds. You jackasses, this here is Tag Enderby! Steady—watch him—keep your guns on him! He's liable to start it, any minute!"

He himself was looking down the barrel of a gun toward Enderby.

"All right," said Tag cheerfully. "What upsets you so much, Charlie? What makes you so excited?"

As he spoke, he put down bread and bark scoop and

slowly, carefully elevated his hands until they were level with his head.

"Enderby?" queried Carney.

"Enderby, you sap," said Indiana, snapping out the words. "He's the boy safe cracker, the handy gun fighter, and card sharp. You don't know Tag Enderby?"

"Tag Enderby?" cried Carney. "Now you speak of him again, seems like I remember something."

"Give him a half second," said Magnum, "and he'll make you forget everything that you know—forever. Enderby! You boys don't know him, but I do."

"What's the matter, Charlie?" repeated Tag. "What's biting on you? What have I done to upset you so?"

Now that the hands of Tag Enderby were in the air, Magnum approached closer. But his face was working, and he kept his revolver leveled.

"Too good to do a job with me, weren't you?" he said.

"I wasn't too good," explained Tag. "But I always work alone. That's the main reason I wouldn't throw in with you."

"I told you that it was a cinch," said Magnum. "But you were too good. You wouldn't work with me. I was too common to suit you."

Tag shrugged his shoulders.

"I'll tell you the straight of it, Charlie," said he. "I didn't know that you were such a smart worker. But when I saw how you cleaned up there in Grove City, I made up my mind that you and I could work together and make a lot of money out of it. Am I wrong?"

"You're wrong, and you're dead wrong," said Magnum. "I see through you, you double-crossing sneak, you!"

"How have I double-crossed you?" asked Tag.

"That Champion, he was a friend of yours," declared Magnum, vicious suspicion twisting his face. "You know that he was. You can't lie out of it. And you came on my trail, because of him!"

"Listen, Charlie," said Tag Enderby. "I'll tell you something. I came to Grove City to get Champion. Does that mean anything to you?"

"Not a thing," said the other.

"Then pull the stuffing out of your brain and try to think all over again, will you?"

"You're bright," said Magnum. "I always said that you was one of the brightest. But you've stepped too far, this time. You've stepped right off the edge of the cliff. Don't trust him, boys," he added to the other pair. "He's crookeder than a snake's path. The thing for us to do is to sock him on the head, and let him lay!"

"You've told the boys about your haul, have you?" said Tag Enderby. "Are you splitting with them?"

"Shut yer face!" commanded Magnum. "Or I'll—"

"He blew the Grove City bank last night," said Tag. "That's why he's all excited to-day. Did he promise you boys a couple of hundred if you'd take anybody off his trail?"

"You dirty—" began Magnum.

His face was white with passion.

"Steady, Charlie," said Indiana, waving his gun toward the safe cracker. "Seems to me that we're hearing something like reason. Don't pull that trigger, Charlie. You hear me talk? He cracked the bank in Grove City, did he?"

"Yeah. He cleaned out about seventy-five thousand in

hard cash," said Tag. "How was he going to split with you boys?"

"The sneaking crook was only going to give us twenty apiece, if we took anybody off his trail!" exclaimed Bill Carney, red with almost honest indignation.

"Never heard anything like it," observed Tag. "But some fellows are like that, you know. No sense of humor in them, even. Twenty apiece, eh? Well, he's got about seventy-five thousand on him. That's all!"

"Do you hear that music in the air?" said Carney to Indiana.

"I hear it," said Indiana.

"Seventy-five thousand," said Carney. "That's pretty sweet, for one small man to be packing around with him."

"It's sweet, all right," commented Indiana.

"Listen, boys," said Tag. "For my share, I don't want a penny. Not a bean. All I want is young Mr. Charlie Magnum. He's tried to fix me with a plant. Now, I want to plant him. You boys are welcome to the stuff. I just want the man!"

Magnum made a step closer. He stood just over Tag Enderby, with his face twisting to one side, in a hard knot, as though an electric current were flexing the muscles. It was a ghastly picture of rage and fear that he showed as he glared down at Tag.

"I'd like to cook you, a slice at a time!" declared Magnum.

"You ain't going to cook nobody, brother," observed Indiana. "It looks like you're going to be cooked, instead."

Magnum flashed a desperate glance at the two hobos.

Then, with a groan, he saw that he had extended his hand

too far, and allowed himself to be drawn into a trap.

There was only one way out that presented itself to his mind. It cost him almost more than blood to conceive of such a thing, but he was cornered.

"Boys," he said, "I'll tell you the straight of it. There was no call for me to talk about what I had. If I could get you at a reasonable price, I was to get you. Otherwise, I would have been a fool. This bird has spilled the beans for me. Well, then—I put it to you straight. We've got him cold. I hired you to get him. And I'll make a fair split with you. I'll tumble everything out of that satchel, yonder. It's more than seventy-five thousand, all told. There's nearly thirty thousand apiece for us, in there. Ain't that enough? I hired you. You started for me. Once we make the split, I forget about it. But you leave this hawk loose on your trail, and he'll have the coin, and pick your bones, besides. That's his style. He's Enderby. He's a devil! Everybody knows that Enderby has no heart in him!"

He spoke with the enthusiasm of an utter conviction.

"Maybe there's something in that," declared Indiana.

"I dunno," said Bill Carney. "You know, boys, there's something about Enderby that I like."

"Because he knew that there was garlic in the stew—that's about all!" exclaimed Magnum.

"He's a cool one—he's pretty cool," argued Bill Carney.

"He's so cool that he'll make a pair of chopping blocks out of you," declared Magnum.

"Listen, Bill," said Indiana. "This here Charlie Magnum, if that's his name, is right. We could handle him"—he winked with evil meaning at his companion—"but I dunno about this Enderby. He's slick."

"Yeah, he's pretty slick," agreed Bill Carney.

"I throw in with Magnum, for one," said Indiana.

"Where you go, I guess that I go, too," said Carney. "We've always played things that way!"

"D'you hear, Enderby?" snarled Magnum. "D'you hear what they say? Now say your prayers, you slick—"

As he spoke, he made a half step nearer, drawn by his hate. That last movement brought him an inch or so inside the danger line. And the next instant he was aware of it.

~13~
Menacing Guns

As for Tag Enderby, he had been watching the movements of the yegg with the greatest attention, measuring distances for the last few moments. If he jerked down his hands, he would draw the fire of three revolvers. But the readiest of the three to fire was, undoubtedly, Magnum. The other two were still in the process of the argument.

"You think, boys," said Tag, "that he's given you the argument that can't be answered, do you?"

"It can't be answered, Enderby," said Indiana, with a sober conviction. "Don't you waste words trying to argue yourself out of the hole. You're stuck, Enderby. Magnum, whatcha want done with him?"

"I want him—cold!" said Magnum.

As he spoke, he allowed the fierceness of his hate to master him for a fraction of a second, so that his squinting eyes were almost shut, and the gun wavered in his hand with the very intensity of murder in his grip.

That was the small opening for which Tag Enderby had waited. Now he did several things at the same instant. He jerked down his hands out of the air, flung himself on his right side, and at the same time his supple legs uncrossed and swung out with the speed of a striking whiplash.

Charlie Magnum fired, point-blank, but the nervous contraction which had tensed his muscles sent that bullet a full foot wide of the mark. Almost at the same instant, the driving feet of Tag Enderby knocked the legs from under the yegg, and he pitched forward on his face. He flung his hands out to save himself, instinctively, from the shock of the fall, and the revolver flew far ahead of him, clanging on the rocks, and exploding a second time.

Straight down upon Tag fell Magnum, to be received with a jolting short-arm punch that flicked across his chin and turned him limp.

The two hobos, in the meantime, had been ready to shoot, but the move of Tag Enderby came so suddenly, and took them so by surprise—helpless in their hands as he had seemed—that before they could fire, their associate, Charlie Magnum, was sprawling upon the prostrate body of their target.

"He's got no gun!" yelled Indiana to Carney. "Get around on the far side of him. Enderby, your goose is cooked! Sit up and stick up your hands or else—"

The answer was a bullet that clipped through the two thighs of Indiana, cutting through the big muscles between knee and hip, behind the bones of the leg.

He fired in the air as he fell, cursing in a groaning voice. Bill Carney, as he heard the shot, leaped into the air as though the bullet had been intended for him, and he hoped to jump out of the path of it.

He landed in time to receive a .45-caliber slug through the tip of his right shoulder. It being his right shoulder, the revolver dropped instantly from his nerveless hand.

And he stood like a bewildered child, clutching at the wound, and staring at Tag Enderby.

The latter disentangled himself from the loose body of Magnum, which had served him as a shield.

Indiana was obviously the more formidable of the two hobos. Also, he still had control of both hands, for the moment, at least. So Tag went to him.

"That was a slow play of yours, Indiana," he said. "You might have shot me to pieces right under the body of your little partner, there—Mr. Magnum. But you didn't. You were humane, Indiana. And that's a foolish thing to be!"

As he spoke, he was behind the fallen form of Indiana, and facing toward the other tramp. But Carney did not move, still standing bewildered by the suddenness and the completeness of the tragedy which had fallen upon him.

As he talked, Tag Enderby dexterously relieved Indiana of a knife, and a second revolver.

Having made him quite helpless, he went to Carney and fanned him in the same manner, but aside from the gun which he had let fall, poor Carney had no semblance of a weapon on him.

Tag picked up the gun. He collected that which had been flung away by Magnum as he toppled forward.

"Hullo, Charlie," he said to Magnum, as the latter sat up with a groan. "When you went to sleep, I was only a loafer, like yourself. But now I'm ready to set up a hardware store. Stand up, Charlie. That's the man! Now hold out your hands behind your back. You won't have to carry the suit-case. I'll manage that for you."

He lashed the narrow wrists of the yegg behind his back.

"Oh, I'm going to get you for it!" snarled Magnum, with a sob of rage and grief and incredulity in his voice. "I'm going to get you when the getting's good. What happened? Indiana—Bill—why don't you do nothing?"

"You yella dog!" said Indiana, sitting up, regardless of the blood which was spouting from his wound.

"You yella dog, it was you that balled up the game, and gummed the deal. I'd like to have the cracking of your head for you. You let us down. You flopped like a—"

He sank back on the ground, weak, but still cursing. Tag Enderby went to him in haste. It was he who cut away the cloth and rapidly made two secure bandages for Indiana and it was Tag, also, who wound up and stopped the rapid bleeding from Carney's wound.

"Now what's the play?" Indiana askcd Tag. "You've turned over and got yourself to be a stool pigeon and a cop, have you? You're going to turn us in?"

"I'm not going to turn you in," explained Tag.

He counted out two hundred dollars and placed the money in Indiana's hand.

"Here!" he said, and gave him, in addition, the long-bladed knife which he had just taken from him.

"What's the main idea?" asked Indiana, puzzled but now hopeful.

"This is the idea," said Tag. "You boys are all right. You just saw more of the long green than you could digest, and it gave you a brain storm. I don't want to see you in too much trouble. Now, you look here! You have the money,

Indiana. And you have a knife to keep Carney from taking the coin away from you. He has a pair of legs left to him, good and sound, and he can walk into town and get a wagon out here to take you to a doctor. You have the money to pay the doctor's bill. And it will keep you going till you're on your feet again. You understand?"

"Hold on," said Indiana. "You talk like a white man!"

"I'm white in spots," said Tag. "Any one who wins can afford to be white. Carney, you've heard my talk?"

"Think of it, Indiana," said Carney. "We listened to that hatchet-faced, long beaked son of trouble, instead of to this gent!"

"My fault," said Indiana. "I made a fool of myself. And I know it. Don't you rub it in!"

He braced himself on one elbow. He extended his hand.

"Enderby, shake!" said he. "The blood you've let out of me is the bad blood. I'm your friend, from now on!"

Tag Enderby took the hand.

"You know, Indiana," he said, "it was in the cards, or it wouldn't have happened. Carney, so long. I have to start back with my friend Magnum."

"Take him and give him free lodgings," said Carney. "If I ever meet up with him again, I'll sock him so's he'll remember it. One thing more, Enderby. You only grazed me and Indiana. Was that on purpose?"

Tag Enderby looked him in the eye.

"You make up your own minds about that," he said. "So long, boys. Work it out the way I tell you. If you get into more trouble, send word to me. I may still be in Grove City."

Then he left them, and walked up the steep of the gully

bank, with Magnum driven before him.

When they got to the top, the yegg turned and faced him. His complexion was a gray-green.

"Now what, Tag?" he asked.

Tag Enderby raised a forefinger at him.

"Your hands are tied behind your back, Charlie," he said. "But if you speak to me again before I get you where I'm taking you, I'll knock you flat. You meant murder—don't speak, I tell you—and I saw the killing in your eyes. I hope to die like a rat if I don't want to throttle you this moment!"

Charlie Magnum seemed about to speak in spite of the double warning, but at the last moment he changed his mind, blinked, moistened his white lips, and went on in front of his captor.

They came to the line of the railroad tracks, which stretched out in shining length east and west. Already, in the east, there was the black smudge of an approaching engine, and a dim vibration sounded from the rails.

~14~

Tag's Day

I T was the noon hour at Grove City, and the sheriff like an honest working man took his full hour off for lunch; when he was on the trail, a bit of hard-tack eaten in the saddle, and a mouthful of lukewarm water were too often the substitute for a solid meal. Therefore he made a special point of taking his time over the table when he was in town.

So he locked his office, walked home, bought a newspaper on the way, slammed the front gate to let his wife know that he was punctual, and went into the front room.

He was the only one who ever sat in it. His wife entered it only to clean it thoroughly, on Saturday, and to sweep and dust and tidy it every morning of the week. When the sheriff was not there, she then darkened the windows and locked the door upon the sanctum. It was the one bright place in the house, for her. It had a red-flowered carpet, and lace curtains, and an old upright piano which sounded like tin pans when it was struck. It had a leather-upholstered armchair, and a footstool, and a funeral wreath in wax under glass on the wall, and several family photographs, and a cabinet filled with varnished sea shells and other knickknacks.

But when the sheriff was in town, he always spent his spare time in the front room.

The first thing he did was to take off his boots and slip his aching feet—vanity condemned him to boots a size too small—into a pair of huge, thick carpet slippers. Then he laid his heels on the footstool, extended his legs, lay back in the rocker, and groaned with comfort. Only one window was uncurtained. Through it, he could see the white blaze of the street under the full noon sun. He could see it, and feel the blessing of cool shadow in the room.

Then he moistened his right thumb and began to thumb the pages of the newspaper.

He could hear the hissing of steak in the pan in the kitchen, when a knock came at his front door.

He waited. The knock repeated.

Then he realized that his wife had lost the fine edge of her hearing.

"Hey?" he called at last.

"Wanta see you, sheriff," called the voice.

"About what?"

"Business."

"See me in my office. One sharp," said the sheriff.

"Wanta see you," repeated the voice cheerfully.

"But I don't want to see you!" yelled the sheriff, in a sudden fury.

He was easily enraged; he was easily pacified.

"Oh, yes, you do," said the voice of the persistent caller. "You want to see me pretty badly."

~15~
The Hero

THE sheriff leaned forward in his rocker. He was about to stride to the front door and deliver his opinion to the face of the other. Then he remembered in the nick of time, that he was a salaried public servant. He gritted his teeth at the thought! However, votes were votes.

"I don't keep office hours twenty-four hours a day," he called. "See you at one!"

"You keep 'em twenty-four hours a day for me," said the other.

"Are you the governor?" shouted the sheriff, infuriated more than ever.

"No, I'm only Tag Enderby."

The sheriff suddenly found himself at the front door, gaping through the screen at two men who stood on the porch. He had paused only long enough to make sure that his revolver was loose and ready in its clip holster beneath the pit of his right arm, the handle pointing well forward.

That gun made a decided protuberance. But the sheriff did not care. He did not wear his Colt there for secrecy, but for a quick draw.

Tag Enderby's handsome face he knew well enough. The other was a rather humpbacked man, with a great, crooked nose.

The sheriff thrust the door open.

"Come in, gents," he said. "Come right in. I'm glad to see you, Tag. How are you?"

"Better than you think," said Tag Enderby.

He shook hands.

"Excuse Mr. Magnum if he doesn't shake," said Tag. "The fact is that his hands had to be tied."

The sheriff had observed the fact before. It was one of the reasons for his pronounced hospitality.

He ushered the pair into his sanctum, just as his wife shrilled down the hall to announce that lunch was ready. He bellowed back that lunch could wait.

"Now, gentlemen," said the sheriff, putting his hands on his knees, and smiling a little grimly upon the pair, "what can I do for you?"

"Soak him in jail!" cried Magnum, gasping out the words, half throttled by the excess of his emotion. "He's a crook. He's the biggest crook in the West. He's—he's Tag Enderby!"

"I know he's Tag Enderby," said the sheriff. "What have you got on him?"

"I've got the dope," said Magnum. "I know he's a yegg—same as me. That's how I know—because I'm in the same line as him!"

"It's a good trade," said the sheriff, his upper lip curling like the lip of a dog about to bite. "It keeps a lot of the boys pretty flush, I guess."

"It keeps 'him' flush!" shouted Magnum, his gray-green color beginning to turn purple. "He's the worst thug in the West. You hear me talk? I'm Charlie Magnum, and I ought to know!"

"He wants facts, Charlie," advised Tag Enderby gently. "It isn't just wind and words that he wants. He can find all the words that he needs in the newspaper for instance. What have you on me, Charlie, to come to the point?"

"I could dig up enough to soak him in the pen for life. I could hang him for you!" shouted Charlie Magnum. "I know where to go and get the dope on him!"

"You'd need to be free, to find that dope, wouldn't you?" asked his companion.

"Yah!" snarled Magnum, turning toward Tag Enderby. "I hate the dirty heart of you!"

"What have you got on Enderby?" asked the sheriff eagerly.

"I tell you," said Magnum, "inside of two days, I can be back here with—"

"But you'll be in jail, Charlie," said Tag. "And that's a pity. He really wants to help you about me, sheriff," he added sympathetically, to the sheriff.

The latter growled wordlessly.

"All right," he said, "if you can't give me anything that's real, Magnum—suppose I get to know why your hands are tied behind your back?"

"I'll tell you," said Magnum. "It's all a fake and a joke, and this dirty crook, that robbed the bank last night, wanted to get a goat and hang it on him—and I was the—"

The sheriff looked earnestly at Magnum.

"I'd like to believe you, Magnum," he said. "But I can't. Enderby never did that job!'

"Why not? Why not?" cried Magnum.

"Because," said the sheriff, "Enderby's neat. I've seen some of the jobs that was laid to his door. And they was all neat. There was that Culver Creek job. That First National job at Culver Creek. You remember that job you did there, Enderby?"

"Has Culver Creek got a bank in it?" asked Tag Enderby innocently.

"It did have!" said the sheriff.

Then he sighed.

"Oh, Enderby," he said, "how I'd like to get the goods on you. How I'd love that!"

" 'I'll' get the goods on him for you," said Magnum. He shrilled out the words, desperate with eagerness. "I swear that I'll come back, afterward, and put the whole case in front of you. I'd go to jail for fifty years, if I could put him in for a week. And I know that I could do more than that. I could soak him. I could plaster him. I could 'hang' him, for you, sheriff. I could make you famous because of him and—"

The sheriff lifted his hand.

"I've heard enough out of you," he said.

Then he turned.

"Now, Enderby," said he. "What is it?"

"It's only a little thing," said Tag Enderby. "It begins with Ray Champion, your friend."

"He 'was' a friend of mine," said the sheriff, thinking how many votes he was losing because of his outright advocacy of Champion after the latter's release from the penitentiary. "The kid was straight, I think. But they must 'a' got to him in the pen. He must 'a' learned bad habits there."

"He learned 'mighty' bad habits there," said Tag Enderby. "He learned to crack a bank and then spill signs all over the street and lead the man hunt straight into his hotel room, where he's tucked away all the unnegotiable securities in a bag, for the sheriff to find. He 'must' be a friend of yours, to make it so easy for you, man. Or else, he's the biggest fool in the world!"

"I thought of all of that, too," said the sheriff. "But what's a man to do? There was the stuff cold on him!"

"Think some more," said Tag Enderby. "And there's something to start your train of thought."

He pointed to a satchel which he had brought in with him and placed on the floor.

"He done the job himself— he framed me!" cried out Magnum. "And now the rotten sneak wants to—"

The sheriff had opened the satchel. He took out a thick sheaf of bills, held together with a wrapping of brown paper around the middle.

In response to Magnum's words, he merely lifted his head, and in silence glanced at the yegg. Magnum grew silent. He settled far back in his chair, gloomily.

"I'm not going to say a word," he declared. "It's a frame. It's a plant. That's what it is. It's a dirty, crooked plant to grab me. You ain't got a thing in the world on me. Enderby ties me up. He brings this loot to you—"

The sheriff glanced inquisitively at Tag Enderby.

"Is that all you can tell me, Tag?" he asked.

"I've got two witnesses who'll tell you that Magnum had this satchel, that I caught up with him, that he tried to murder me with their help, that I had the luck, and that's why he's here."

"A pair of worthless hobos!" screeched Magnum.

The sheriff stood up.

"I've got a place for you in the jail, son," he said to the yegg. "I've got the best cell ready for you. Ray Champion has just been warmin' it up a little. That's all. Come along, Magnum. You'll fit it a lot better than he did!"

Charlie Magnum rose slowly to his feet. He favored Tag Enderby with one long look, green-tinted with hatred.

Then he walked toward the door.

The sheriff lingered behind. He gripped Tag's arm with fervor.

"I thought you were out to get him—I mean to get poor Ray Champion. Tag, I love that kid for what he's been through. I'm going to prove to you what this day of yours means to me and—"

"Cut it out," urged Tag Enderby. "The rest will keep for Sunday."

Tag Enderby wanted relaxation. It was not that he had been giving his attention so solidly to business. It was rather because his mind was baffled by the circumstances in which he found himself.

In the first place, he had been sent to Grove City to "get" Ray Champion. In the second place, Champion, through no effort of his, had been lodged in jail, due for a long term—a term equivalent, no doubt, to the lifetime of Malley. In the third place he, Tag Enderby, had exerted himself to free Champion from danger.

That was the point at which he ceased to understand himself.

Champion was nothing to him, personally. He only appeared in his mind as the enemy of Malley. Therefore he was to be removed. Chance had removed him, but he, Enderby, had brought him back upon the scene at the cost of much effort and great risk.

It was a thing not to be believed. And, above all, it was incredible that he should have done so merely to settle the doubts which were in the mind of a girl—a redhead, at that!

He was so baffled, so irritated, that he sought consolation in whisky, but the first rising of the stifling fumes of the redeye changed his mind. He turned from bars to gaming tables. He wanted excitement. He worked feverishly all the rest of the day to get that excitement.

But he failed.

What he lost at dice, he made at poker. When he was deeply in the hole at blackjack, he turned to lose still more at roulette, and only succeeded in filling his pockets. Poker, in a brief round, trimmed him down to his last thousand. He decided that he would clear the air by going broke, so he found a faro outfit, which was opening up full blast with the usual crew of spotters.

It was a crooked layout. He could sense that at once. But he stepped up and played it, nevertheless. And suddenly he was winning.

The pale, bitter face of the man behind the bank told him why. The man was afraid to cheat him! And luck was running his way.

He turned the single thousand into twelve.

The faro banker folded up his tents and fled.

"Damn this town," said Tag Enderby. "There's no excitement in it!"

He turned, and found at either shoulder a sober-faced citizen, obviously each loaded down with weapons.

They looked Tag Enderby in the face and one of them said:

"You may damn Grove City, Mr. Enderby, but Grove City will never damn you!"

Tag Enderby scowled at them.

"Now what d'ye mean by that?" he asked.

Thereat, they smiled at him.

The second of the pair said: "We know you, Enderby. You're young. You're wild. But we know what you did for Ray Champion. I'm Telford, of the bank. I'm Tommy Telford's father. That may help to spot me, for you. He told me about the great rope expert! Well, Enderby, I and Mays, here, would have been ruined. So would a lot of innocent depositors in our little bank. We don't forget what you've done. Neither does the rest of Grove City. You can work at the end of a long tether, Enderby. Nothing will ever happen to you in this town!"

The speech should have pleased Tag Enderby. It would have pleased most other men, but it merely irritated him.

Friendship was, to be sure, a sacred thing. But he had had little use for it. His work had been lonely work. His hand had been working against all other hands, more or less, except those actually within the gang of Dan Malley. And even inside that gang, he had no intimates. Like a bee in a garden, like a hawk in the air, he roved where fancy and prey led him.

And now the entire town of Grove City had determined

to wrap him in cotton batting, and take care of him!

Disgusted, he left the game room of that saloon. He went to the bar, to wash away the unpleasant taste of the last conversation. The bartender instantly stopped serving the other guests and stood before him, both fat, white hands spread out up on the bar. He beamed upon the youth.

"The house has been waitin' quite a spell to set up the drinks for you, Mr. Enderby," he said. "Just name your brand of poison, sir."

"Mr." Enderby and "sir," both in a sentence.

He glanced up and down the bar. Broad smiles and approving nods greeted the remark of the bartender.

"I've changed my mind. I've had enough to drink," said Tag Enderby.

He walked hastily into the street. It was sunset time. The west burned with golden and crimson fires, and the unpainted roofs were stained with it, and the western windows blared out like trumpets of light.

"Gosh," sighed Tag Enderby, "they're going to take and make a hero out of me!"

He was late for supper at the Bentons', but he decided that he would return to the place. The sea of unusual friendliness in which he found himself lost disturbed him mightily.

But even as he walked jauntily up the street, a pair of cowpokes passed him, dusty, hard fellows with thorn-ripped chaps. They looked aside at him; they waved their hands to him.

"That's him. That's Tag Enderby," he heard one of them saying loudly as he went by.

"Damn this town!" muttered Tag again.

And just then, a burly citizen came out from a grocery store, settling his hat on his head. He saw Tag, and grunting with haste and with pleasure, fell into stride beside him. What could be done to shake him off?

Nothing!

Grimly staring ahead, Tag Enderby had to submit to a flow of honeyed talk, from which it appeared that the grocery store proprietor knew all about the history of that day, and the heroism of Mr. Enderby. He was, himself, a large depositor in the bank. If the money had been lost, he would have had to close his shop. He would have had to move out from this cheerful and growing town to the country. He would have had to settle down, with his wife and children, upon a barren patch of range land. And it was late in his life to make such a change.

"Serving the public behind my counters, that's what I'm fit for," said he. "I'm a kind of public servant, in a quiet way, Mr. Enderby. But I'll never live to do for the town what you've done in one stroke!"

He turned in at the gate of a big, decently painted house. Tag went on, more rapidly, buried in gloom.

A woman cried out upon a porch. Only from the corner of his eye did he dare to mark her, and he saw her standing up—a gaunt, gray-headed, bent creature, with a wisp of a tow-headed lad at her side, agape.

She was calling out a blessing upon the head of Tag Enderby.

He hurried on, embittered, puzzled.

"I've gone and ruined myself," said Tag Enderby darkly, to his own wretched heart. "Here's a thousand people that know my face by heart, and information like that always spreads and crops up where you don't want it. I'd better hop onto a ship for Australia. That's where I'd better go. Champion, I wish you'd rotted in jail, before I ever lifted a hand to help you out!"

Two young girls came hurriedly around a corner, skipping hand in hand. When they saw him, they jumped to a halt, as though at a signal. They stood still, pressing back against the fence. With broad smiles, with adoring eyes they followed him as he strode past them.

"Terrible!" said Tag Enderby to himself.

But soon he came to the edge of town, and now he was turning in at the Benton place.

He could be thankful that he was well past the supper hour. That would give him a chance to have a solitary lunch by himself. Then he could go to bed and try to think himself out of the wretched tangle.

Grove City!

It was synonymous, to him, with misery.

So he entered the front door of the place, shied his hat into his room, and went with his light step through the hall toward the dining room. He remembered what the girl had said, and forced himself to walk down the middle of the hall.

She saw everything, it appeared. That was the trouble with her; she saw too much. That was the trouble with all redheads, he swore. They were always seeing too much. They were too sharp, like red foxes, their natural kin!

So he came out into the dining room and there halted abruptly. He would have turned back, but he was already committed. For there were grouped the three Bentons—and Ray Champion! Yes, the last man in the world that he wished to face was there, present.

"Here he is!" said Mr. Benton. "We thought that you'd be along pretty pronto, Mr. Enderby. Not that we wouldn't 'a' waited longer. I guess you don't have to keep sharp hours in 'this' house!"

She came to him and put a hand on his arm. She looked up to him with trembling lips, with tears in her eyes.

Cold dismay poured through the soul of the outlaw. He wanted desperately to turn and flee. Sweat beaded his forehead. He would rather have faced guns than the melting love and admiration in the eyes of that woman!

"It's all right," said Tag Enderby. "I'm sorry that I'm late. I should 'a' stopped at the hotel, only—"

"Stop at the hotel? Well, of all things!" said Mrs. Benton. "Molly, let's get the food onto the table. Of all things in the world! And I've got Parker House rolls, special made for you, Mr. Enderby. They won't be as good as your mother makes for you, I guess. There's something wrong with that oven. I declare, Henry, I'm going to be in despair if you don't get that worthless oven fixed up for me."

She passed into the kitchen as her husband comforted her by saying:

"It's a poor workman that complains of his tools, ma! You been complaining about that stove for thirty year, about, and that stove ain't never said a word back to you. I reckon you might be a little ashamed, kind of!"

"Hear him talk!" said Mrs. Benton, from the kitchen. "Mind that pan, Molly. It's boilin' hot. Take the dishrag to it. There! They 'look' pretty good, anyway. But looks ain't the only thing in this world, the more's the pity! Hurry with the coffee, Molly. I reckon he likes his coffee right at the beginning and straight through to the end. What stomachs these young people have!"

Tag Enderby was glad of the noise. He was glad of another thing—that neither old Benton nor Ray Champion were pouring out words. But the grave, steady eyes of the latter were upon him. He had to meet that glance. Champion made no attempt to thank him, not even to shake hands. But curiosity, gratitude, respect were in his eyes.

It finished the wretchedness of the day for Tag Enderby. It completed the twenty-four hours like a tombstone at the end of a grave!

~16~
A Voice in the Dark

SUPPER was a triumph for Mrs. Benton, a torment for poor Tag Enderby. He thought that the meal would never end. Henry Benton was a savior. Tag's exploits on this day—it seemed as though the sheriff had proclaimed them from every housetop, and the confession of Magnum had established the tale, with marginal embroiderings—reminded the father of the family of stories of the old days, when, as he said, men were men. He drew deeply upon his memory. His imagination also worked somewhat overtime. But he was amusing, and he took attention from the grim face of Tag.

The ordeal ended. Mr. Benton produced cigars, the last relic of his recent euchre winnings, but Tag escaped from the smoking and went outside to walk and cool down. Two things had chiefly impressed him, the reserved manliness of Ray Champion, and the peculiar thoughtfulness in the eyes of Molly.

He went into the corral and walked up and down there, close to the garden fence. He was not surprised when he heard the light step of Molly coming out the board walk. The gate creaked behind her. She joined him at once, and fell into step beside him. They strolled up and down for several minutes, and in spite of himself some of the irritation began to depart from Tag. He was amused by this silent walk together. He began to smile in the dark.

"It's been a hard day for you, Tag, I suppose," said she, at last.

"Kind of crowded," said he.

She chuckled. She had a chuckle like a man's—deep, and hearty.

"I know," said she. "You've been the bad boy so long you don't know what to do with a new sort of reputation. Isn't that it, Tag?"

"Humph!" said he. "I know you're laughing at me, Molly."

"No, I'm thanking you," said she. "Nobody else could have done such a thing. You're giving Ray another week or so."

"Hold on," said he. "You talk as if he were condemned to death."

"And he is," said she steadily.

He stopped in his pacing.

"What do you mean by that, Molly?"

"I think you know," said she. "They're after him. People a lot stronger than that Magnum, the thief."

"Who are they?" asked he, feigning ignorance.

"Malley. Dan Malley is the man behind the gun,

according to Ray. And Ray ought to know. Malley's the one who had him framed and sent up. Malley's the man who'll be after him now."

"I've heard of Malley," confessed Tag Enderby. "I hear that he's a bad egg."

"He's poison," said she. "He uses brains—and long arms. Other people are his arms. And his men are all hand-picked."

What she said went home in him. He felt as guilty as a child, caught red-handed stealing from the pantry. He was silent, after this, and off in the distance they heard the bawling of a cow, frantic for the calf which had been newly taken from it for the butcher.

"Champion can keep out of Malley's way, I guess," said he finally.

"Ha!" cried the girl. "You don't see the rest of the story, do you? Champion will never try to stay away."

"Then Champion's a fool, if what you say about Malley and his picked men is true."

"Ray's a fool, of course, to want to fight the thing out, one man against such numbers. But there's no use arguing with a bulldog."

Tag Enderby recalled, then, the heavy shoulders, the thick neck, the projecting, resolved jaw of the man. It was true that he looked like one who would hold on to a project. He had the calm of the fighter who will be cut to pieces before he surrenders, just as the bulldog keeps his grip strong even while he is dying.

"That's bad," said Tag. "That may lead him into a lot of trouble, of course."

"It may," said she. "And it will. Sooner or later, he's

bound to come across some sort of a trail, and then he'll follow it till he has been drawn into a trap. I know it. I've known it from the very first."

"Why doesn't he go hunting for the trail now, then?" asked Tag Enderby, suddenly irritated. "Why does he go through all the form of settling down to a bank job? Why doesn't he clear off the fighting end of things first, and then get to work in the bank—if that's what he's going to do!"

"Why," said the girl, "he thinks that he's given up the whole Malley affair. He thinks that he has buried the grudge and that all he's got ahead of him is simply to work away and be a prosperous business man. But maybe you've noticed his red hair, Tag?"

Tag Enderby turned sharply on her.

"I've noticed it, all right," said he.

"He never can tell when he'll break into a flame as red as his hair. And if ever he comes across the Malley trail, he'll be off on it faster than an old fire horse to a fire signal."

"No," argued Tag. "He wants to marry you. That's the chief thing in his mind."

"It's the chief thing that he knows about," she answered. "But he doesn't care for me as much as he hates the three years he spent in prison. The more honest the man, the more he hates to suffer when he hasn't been in the wrong. Ray always was honest. Almost stupidly honest. And the three years burned him up. It's a fine school for hate, a penitentiary."

Tag Enderby reflected and nodded.

"You know a good deal," he said.

"I know Ray Champion," she corrected.

"Why do you tell me?" he asked.

"Because you're curious, aren't you?"

"I don't give a hang about Champion. Only it made me mad—the way you talked about me this morning. That's why I went on the trail."

"It was a wonderful piece of work," she said.

"No, it wasn't. This fool town is shouting about nothing. I'd seen Magnum before. I knew what he had in his mind. I knew that he was the one who had tried to work the plant on Ray."

"Malley wasn't behind it?"

"Malley knew nothing about it—I suppose."

He was afraid that he had been a little too emphatic in speaking to this effect.

Then he said: "This fellow Champion—you're fond of him. You like him pretty well—but you'll never marry him."

"He'll be dead inside of a month," she answered calmly. "There'll be no wedding. You're right there."

"You don't like him well enough to marry him," said Tag Enderby.

"You think not?"

"It's more than thinking. I know! I've watched you looking at him. Your eyes are as flat as when you look at me."

"I'm not emotional, as some people are," said she.

"Oh, you could catch fire, too," said he. "You're a red-head yourself, you know."

Through the starlight he could see the flash of her hand as she raised it instinctively toward her hair.

"No, Tag," she said, with her chuckle. "Auburn is the word. Be polite!"

"Auburn, coppery, rusty, red—it's all a lot of names for one thing," he told her. "You tell me, Molly—what you're trying to pull out of me, to-night, talking about Ray Champion?"

"Nothing," said she.

"Humph!" muttered Tag Enderby. "You want me to mount guard over him and shoo the flies away when he takes a siesta every day?"

"My," said she, "what a bad boy you want to be."

"Stop it, will you?" he protested.

She was chuckling still.

"I'm going in," she said.

"No, you stay here and explain what's up your sleeve."

"I'm going in," she repeated. "Good night, Tag. This is a day that Grove City will never forget, even if you want it to!"

And he heard her still laughing to herself as she went in. He stood stock-still, glaring after her, hating her. Then he went in turn, and took the front way toward his room.

From beneath the fig tree a shadow stirred. He fell flat upon the ground, a gun in each hand, the hammers raised, bullets ready to fly.

"Steady, Tag!" He heard a husky voice, lowered cautiously.

"Step out," said Tag.

A man walked forward, hands raised. And Tag Enderby gathered himself from the ground.

He distinguished more clearly now the outlines of the other.

"You're getting careless, Malley," he said.

"Hush," murmured Malley, and drew him back into the

shade. "What's this I've been hearing about Champion in the can, and you getting him loose again?"

"It's right. That was a dirty play of Magnum's. I couldn't let that yegg put the thing over. He planted the deal on Champion."

"What the devil do you care who he planted it on?" said Malley. "I sent you down here to get Champion. And he was got by somebody else. That was your signal to forget about him and come home."

"I didn't like the deal," said Tag Enderby. "That's all."

"I've taken a lot from you, Tag," said the other, panting with anger. "I'm not going to take this. Listen to me. This Champion is a bulldog."

It was the second time Champion had been called by this name in the course of a very few minutes, and Tag Enderby was vaguely impressed.

"I framed Champion," said Malley. "It was that or a lot of trouble for me and the boys. I framed him. He knows I did. He's going to get on my trail one day and never leave it till he's got his teeth in my throat. I sent you to get him— and instead, you pry him out of the can. What sort of work is that, I ask you?"

"It's the way I saw the thing," answered Tag. "I have to do a few things my own way. You oughta know that!"

"You've pulled some good jobs for me," said Malley slowly. "Now you're undoing them. You can do me more harm here than you ever did good before."

"You and your good and bad can go to the devil, for all of me," said Tag Enderby.

A long silence followed.

"You mean it, eh?" said Malley. "You wanta bust away

from me and the boys?"

"I'm tired of the lot of you," said Tag. "You send me down here on a dirty job. I don't like it. I'm tired of you. You and the rest of 'em can go to the devil!"

"Can we? You'll light the way for us, though," said Malley.

He turned on his heel, and in three steps he was lost in the darkness under the trees.

~17~
A Talk with Molly

FOR two days, Tag Enderby rested. He had broken with Malley, and that was a dangerous thing to do, as he well understood. It was not usual. Men joined Malley and stayed with him till their deaths. If they left him, their deaths followed as a rule with an odd suddenness. The suddenness was in fact so very odd that most people were able to draw deductions of their own.

He had broken with Malley while he knew the face and the record of every man employed by the arch crook. Would the men stand for it? Would Malley ask them to stand for it? The quickness with which Malley had accepted Tag's resignation seemed to show that the chief was himself sufficiently excited and enraged. It might very well be that he would want no urging to put his men upon the trail not only of Ray Champion but of Tag Enderby as well.

Malley had plenty of hands available to undertake both of these tasks at the same time. He had but to whisper, in order to fill a house with armed men, every one hand-picked, as Molly had designated them. He had brains, money, and an ample supply of tools. He could make himself formidable to twenty brave men all in an instant.

Then why had Tag Enderby chosen to break with him?

For the sake of red-headed Ray Champion?

Never!

For the sake of the red-headed girl?

Absurd!

Why, then?

Was it that some taste of the pleasures to be derived from public service had stirred him? Had the applause of Grove City moved him so much?

That was the most ridiculous idea of all. He had detested public clamor and loathed public attention from the first.

Most of the second day, after his break with Malley, he spent in his room lounging. In the late afternoon, at that time when the sun is westering fast and begins to take on a golden face, Molly came and stood at his window.

"Hullo, Molly," he said. "What's the news?"

"Nothing much. Only Ray," she said.

"Got promoted?" Tag asked.

"No. Gone," she said.

"Gone?"

He sat up and looked through the window at her. She was perfectly composed. There was nothing about her face to indicate that she was in the least excited.

"The way you said he'd be gone?" he asked her. "On Malley's trail, you mean?"

She shrugged her shoulders.

"I don't know. He's gone. He's left no word. I suppose it's on the Malley trail."

"What makes you think so?" he asked.

"Well, in the middle of the afternoon, he just looked through the window, chucked down his pen, and started through the door. That's the last that was seen of him, except at the livery stable, where he hired a horse. He said that he'd pay the hire when he got back with it."

She turned a little and looked toward the road.

"Look at the dust blowing," she said. "They're going to lay down some gravel next month, though. It'll be better, then."

"Yeah. It'll be better then."

The window had a low sill. He ducked his head and stepped through the opening onto the veranda.

"Listen!" he said.

"Well?" she answered.

She did not look at him. She was looking idly across the white shining of the road, where the dust blew in parallel drifts of white. The gold of the sun was distinctly in them.

"You're all heated up," he said. "Why do you pretend it doesn't matter to you?"

"I don't know that it matters so much," said she. "You tell me why you've been lying around like a snail in a shell for the last couple of days."

"I've been waiting for trouble to pop," said he.

"So have I," said she.

"I don't mean for Ray Champion," he qualified.

"Neither do I," said she.

"Then what 'do' you mean?"

"Go on," said she. "Give me a lead. What's in your mind?"

"I'll tell you. I'm a yegg. I've split with my boss."

"Malley?"

"What makes you think Malley?" he demanded.

"You came after Champion. Who'd want him, except Malley?"

"You're a bright kid," said he.

She looked at him and deliberately chose her words.

"All redheads are bright," said she.

His color changed a little.

"You're fresh, too," said he.

"All redheads are extremely fresh," said she.

"Listen," said he. "What's the main idea of all of this?"

"Oh, nothing. There's trouble in the air. That's all that I know."

"You know enough. You guess a lot more," he told her.

"Yeah, I guess plenty already," said she.

"You don't have to talk down to me. You don't have to use slang," said he, sneering with pride and disdain.

"I want to use slang," she said. "It makes me feel better. I'm sort of sick. That's why I want to talk low, too!"

He grew a little afraid of her, as of some incomprehensible thing. She seemed to include everything of which he had experience, men and women.

"I'll talk," said he.

"Go on then," said the girl.

"You look at me first."

"I'm looking at the road," said she.

"You're looking at the mountains beyond the road," he corrected.

"Maybe," said she.

"You know I'm Tag Enderby. But you don't know me."

"You tell me then," said she. "Tell me how many men you've killed, and all of that stuff."

He straightened, his nostrils flaring.

"It doesn't get you anywhere to be so hard-boiled," said he.

"I don't try to get anywhere," said she.

"What are you driving at?"

"You want to tell me about yourself," said Molly. "But I don't want to hear your stories. You make me sort of tired, just now."

"Do I?" asked he, in a dangerous tone.

"Yes, you want to prove how romantic and dangerous you are, don't you?"

He got hold of one of her wrists and pulled her around. But he could not make her turn her head.

"I've been Malley's right bower," he said. "He sent me down here to get Champion, just the way you think."

"Yeah, I know that," said the girl.

"Shut up!" he commanded. "I don't need to have you say how much you know."

"Well, I'll say it, anyway," said she. "I'm tired of mysterious men."

"I'd like to wring your neck," said he.

"Go on and try it," said she.

"You talk like a baby. You talk like a fool," said he. "I'm trying to make sense with you."

"Well, try again," she said. "You're missing pretty far, it seems to me."

He dragged in a great breath.

"Look, Molly—" he began.

"Go on," said she. "You're so mad at me that you'll begin to make love pretty soon."

"What a mean devil you are!" said he.

"Yeah, I'm mean. I'm not even halter broke," said she.

"I'll tell you something," he declared.

"I'd like to hear it, too."

"Suppose that I went out and got your boy, your Ray Champion for you."

She was silent, still staring out across the dust films that blew down the road, one after another.

"Well, suppose I should?" he insisted.

"I'm trying to suppose," said she.

"Suppose that I broke Malley and his rotten lot. Suppose that I brought back your beautiful boy, with his skin still hanging together. What then?"

"I don't know what you're driving at."

"Yeah, you know what I'm driving at," he said fiercely. "You turn your head and tell me what I mean."

"I don't know what's in your mind," said she.

But he saw a cord in her neck suddenly stiffen and thrust out a little, breaking the bronze curve. He knew that she had firmly locked her jaws.

"Don't fight," said he. "Play fair. I'm not fighting. I'm letting everything slip, redhead. I'm coming clean. You come clean, too. Tell me what's in my mind!"

"You want to go out and jump your horse over the moon, and ask me what I'll think of you when you hit the ground. I'll tell you. I'll think that you're a pile of blood and broken bones. That's all. Ray Champion's gone. He's a dead man."

"I'll bring him back to life then," said he. "And after that—what?"

"Nothing," said she.

"Look at me," said he.

Little by little she turned her head. All at once he knew

by his grip upon her wrist that she was trembling violently.

And so her eyes met his.

They were flat, dull, steady blue, as they always had been.

"Now you tell me what I want," said he.

"You want me," said the girl.

"How much do I want you?"

She drew a breath; he heard it drawn. Yet she did not answer directly.

She said: "Do a job like that, bring Champion back—and then I'll let him go hang. I've been looking all my life to find a man. Do a job like that, and you could whistle me off a throne. I'd marry you and follow you around the world. I'd take in washing, so you could blow the money on faro. I know you. I know you're no good. I know you're spoiled. But do that—and I'm yours to the end of time!"

~18~
The Strange Rider

H E made his pack, took it out to the barn, saddled the gray, and went back to the house. The gray waited at the corral gate, hanging his head over the top bar, impatient for the roving road. Tag went back to the house and saw the girl. She was waiting under one of the oak trees, plucking off the leaves, crumpling them, and letting them fall to the ground.

"You say good-by to your father and mother for me," he said. "Here's my month's rent."

Her lip curled a little.

"We don't need that," she said.

"You don't. The old people do. You take it," he commanded.

She held out her hand in silence and took the money.

"That's making a beggar out of me from the start," she said.

"You were a beggar before to-day," he answered. "You've been bleeding me—you and your pride and your sneers. You've been riding me all the time. Oh, I saw through it. Only, you made me so mad that I wanted to show you."

"You're still showing me," said she.

"Yeah, I'm not through, but I despise myself for wasting time. Listen—don't make any mistake about me."

She nodded, watching him all the time with careful thought.

"I know what you mean," she said. "You're not in love. I'm not the fool to think that. And I won't cry my eyes out while you're gone. I'm only curious. That's all."

"That's a good way to start me out—full of enthusiasm," said he.

"That's my way of starting 'you'," said she. "Good-by, Tag."

"Good-by, Red," said he.

He went back to the corral, mounted the dappled gray, and galloped down the road toward town. As he passed the front gate of the yard, he saw that she had not moved from beneath the tree, and he had half a mind to draw rein, and pause to speak to her again. Instead, he waved his hand to her, and went on.

He had changed to a cow-puncher's clothes, the only dress for such rough riding as he was likely to have before him, and he relaxed and rejoiced in the easy, sloppy fit of everything that was on his body. Yet he was not happy.

He had played too many games of chance, and therefore he knew that the odds against him were very great indeed.

First there was the bank.

Telford himself came hurrying to meet him.

"I don't know what to make of it," he said. "I've been waiting here for the sheriff. I know that something is wrong. He hasn't been seen out at the Benton place?"

"The sheriff?"

"No, of course not. Ray Champion."

"No, he hasn't been back there. Just when did he leave?"

"At four thirty-three. It seemed strange. I looked at the clock. A business man has to note minutes like that."

"What had happened before he left?"

"I was talking to him myself. I was joking about his day off in the jail. And he laughed a little, though laughter comes hard with that young man. However, he was laughing a bit, and just then some one rode past the window in the front of the bank. I didn't see the rider very clearly. But apparently there was something about him that fastened Ray's eye. He jumped up without a word to me, and snatched a revolver out of the drawer of his desk."

"A revolver?"

"Yes. And he ran out through the front door, bending low, sprinting hard. I think—from the look of him—that he had seen somebody he intended to open fire on."

Tag Enderby nodded.

"He didn't come back. I sent out after him. Found that he'd gone to the livery stables and hired a horse to—"

"What was the color of the livery-stable horse?"

"Yes, I asked for that information, too," said Telford, pleased with his own intelligence. "I asked, and they told me that it was a pinto."

"A paint horse, eh?"

"Yes."

"That rider who went by—you didn't have a chance to see the color of his horse?"

"No."

"But it wasn't a pinto, or a white, or a black, or a gray?"

"It might have been a black—covered up with a good deal of dust. It wasn't white or gray or pinto. I would have seen colors like that."

"Bay or chestnut or brown, likely," said Tag Enderby. He added: "Was he riding fast, or at a slow lope?"

"A slow lope, but quickening."

"If he just flashed past the window, how could you tell that he was quickening?"

Telford smiled again, as a man does when he is pleased with his own intelligence.

"He was leaning forward, pretty sharply, the way a man does when he's about to urge a horse ahead."

"You have an eye," said Tag.

"You take a banker," said Telford, "and he has to have an eye. A flicker of an expression, a twist of the mouth, a turn of the head—that makes all the difference between a loan put out to chance, and money kept safe in the vaults!"

"Safe?" said Tag, grinning.

"I'm putting in a safe that nobody will ever be able to force!" said Telford sourly. "That Magnum—that contemptible crook—"

Tag had heard all that he guessed could be of importance.

He left the bank and went back to his horse. He knew that some one had ridden slowly past the window of the bank, and that that slowness had been in the hope of attracting the eye of Champion. The man had put his horse to a high speed, probably, immediately after going by. And that was why Champion had found the other out of pistol range when he came onto the street, rapidly as he had started for the door.

But it was very important to learn a description of the rider.

He mounted, rode down the main street until he came to the blacksmith's shop, and there saw the blacksmith himself working at the ticklish job of setting new spokes into an old wheel.

Tag drew rein.

"You're putting new wine in an old bottle, partner," said he.

"And who the devil needs to tell me that?" shouted the blacksmith angrily. "Is it my fault if I got cheap customers?"

He turned around to follow up his counterattack. Then he saw Tag, and smiled, embarrassed.

"Didn't recognize your voice, Mr. Enderby," said he.

"That's all right," said the latter. "Look here, partner. About four-thirty, a fellow went down this street lickety-split."

"That was Tom Sanders," said the blacksmith. He paused to grin. "He'd been in town since early morning—buying groceries and things, I guess. And a long about that time, I guess he seen that he was already four hours and a half late to get things back to the place for lunch. So he went down this here street with the hosses hopping as lively as fleas in front of his buckboard."

"The man I'm talking about wasn't driving. He was riding," said Tag Enderby. "A bay, or a brown, I think."

"Most hosses are bays or browns," said the blacksmith. "I wasn't out here just then, though. I just glimpsed Sanders through the door. Anything important?"

"Well, I'd like to know."

"Hey, Danny!" called the smith.

A sooty boy came to the door.

"You was out here about four-thirty," said the blacksmith, "planing off these spokes. Who rode down the street lickety-split, about then?"

"Four-thirty?" said the boy vaguely.

Tag Enderby pointed at an angle of forty-five degrees toward the western sky.

"The sun was right there," said he.

"Oh," said the boy. "I dunno who he was. He was sure hitting it up. He went by mostly dust, and not much hoss or man."

"What color horse?" asked Tag.

"Bayish, or brownish, or chestnut, or something," said the boy.

"Yes. Something I guess," said the smith, disgusted. "Ain't you got eyes in your head? A fine blacksmith you'll make, some day."

The boy stood in sullen silence.

"That's all right," said Tag Enderby gently. "It's not important—very."

"You dunno that this is Mr. Enderby, maybe?" asked the smith of his apprentice.

"You think that I dunno 'nothing'!" exclaimed the boy.

"I'll bet," said Tag, "that you could tell me how many white stockings that horse had."

"White stockings? How many? Why, there was only one. His near foreleg. That had a white stocking right up to the knee. That was the only white on him, except a star on the forehead."

"Biggish horse?" asked Tag.

"Fairish. Kind of fifteen handish, and maybe an inch or two."

"Mustang?"

"You bet. Neck like a ewe."

"Biggish man?"

"Fairish size," said the boy, growing more confident. "Kind of fairish. He had on an old felt hat, and the brim was so plumb soft that it didn't look like no brim at all in the front. It furled right back agin' the crown."

"Heavy man, would you say?"

"Nope. Pretty lean. He could ride, that buckaroo. He set right into the saddle, and that gallop wasn't no bed of feathers, neither. But he set it, all right! He'd been in a saddle a coupla times before, maybe. I watched him slide down the street. He rode kind of slanting."

"In?" said Tag Enderby.

"No. Out. Like that—out."

"Oldish man?" said Tag.

"Yeah. Pretty old. About thirty something, I guess."

"You talk like a fool," said the smith. "A kid of thirty—and you call that old!"

"Well, he had an oldish look," persisted the boy.

Tag thanked them both. Then he turned the gray into the

street and started off, adding up his facts.

He wanted a man riding ·a mustang with an ewe neck, and one white stocking, and a blaze on the forehead. He wanted a man who rode like a real horse breaker, with a limp in the left leg, and an old felt hat on his head.

It was not a great deal, but it was a lot better than nothing.

He began to wonder how he himself had so often been able to avoid the strong hands of the law.

~19~
Malley's Plan

THREE roads crossed the way of Tag Enderby. Three lucky queries put him right. He came with the end of the day to the foothills, and in the purple of the dusk he saw the lights of a little town. It was cupped in a gorge. Ragged, wild walls of rock stood up on either side of the village. A stream went roaring down the center and the noise of that river was mixed with all the talk that ever would be in the place. In the house or in the open street, the voice of the river was always present, dim or shouting.

Tag looked for a tavern or hotel and he found one on the very verge of the stream, where it seemed that the flimsy wooden walls of the building were always shaking with the uproar as though with a heavy storm wind.

He went straight back to the stable behind the hostelry, and in the stable he found a pinto which matched the description of the horse which Ray Champion had ridden out of Grove City.

So Champion was there. But in all the rest of the stable, among a dozen other horses, there was no sign whatsoever of a bay or sorrel with one long white stocking on the near foreleg and a white blaze on the forehead.

However, Champion was there, and that was more than half of the goal that Tag Enderby rode to seek.

He put up his own long-legged gray, and as he was coming out of the stable, had a glimpse of a figure turning the corner of the barn. There was a skulking haste about the form, and Tag, turning about, ran through the open sliding door of the barn, the length of the stalled horses, and out again at the farther end. He turned the other corner of the building in time to encounter the skulker, and he saw before him one Sam Doran, a fellow he had seen several times in the Malley camp.

The profession of Sam Doran was pocket picking, which he varied with crookedness at cards; and he was an expert shot—when he stood "behind" his target!

He stopped with a shock when he saw Tag Enderby. Then he forced a grin to his face.

"Why, hullo, Tag," said he. "I'm surprised to see you up here."

"I'll bet you are," answered Enderby. "That's why you were spying on me and the gray when I went into the stable, isn't it?"

"Spying?" said the other. "Now, why should I be spying on one of our own, will you tell me?"

"Yeah, I'll tell you that," said Tag. "Malley told you to."

"Dan Malley? Great Scott, old son," exclaimed Sam Doran. "Why should he tell me to spy on our best man?"

Tag smiled upon him through the dusk, and there was evil meaning in that smile.

"Sam," said he, "you could tell the truth and save yourself from the devil. Come out with it. Malley told you to draw Champion up into the hills."

The other blinked, and swallowed hard. Then he nodded and grinned in turn, as well as he could.

"Of course, he did," said he. "And I suppose that he sent you along to make sure that—"

"He'll never send me anywhere again," said Tag. "I'm through with him and with the lot of you."

"You're a wise fellow to break loose," said Sam Doran, with a pretense of heartiness. "The fact is that it's a dog's life, workin' for Malley. We get livin' expenses, and he gets all the main profits. You're wise to get clear away from him, and when I get my nerve up, I'm goin' to do the same thing."

"Where'd you leave your horse?" Tag asked.

"He's in the stable there, of course," said Doran.

"He's not," said Enderby.

"Why not, Tag?"

"Your horse has a white stocking on the near foreleg, and a white blaze on the forehead. As sure as his rider has a limp in the left leg!"

He nodded at the partially crippled leg of Sam Doran. The man had been twice shot through that leg, and he never had fully recovered from the torn nerves and tendons.

"Oh, that one," murmured Doran. "Well, I've got it hid out there in the woods."

He blinked again at the taller man.

"What's the matter with you, Tag?" he whined. "You look kind of hostile and mean at me."

"I'm not hostile and mean," said Tag. "That is, I'm not hostile and mean if you tell me what Malley has planned for to-night."

"How would I know that?" asked the other.

Tag Enderby laughed softly.

"Listen to me, Sam," said he. "D'you think that I value you too much to pass a knife between your ribs and drop you into the river?"

Then he paused, and listened to the panting of the sneak thief.

"Whatcha want me to say, Tag?" said the other. "I dunno nothin'. I'd have to make something up, just to please you!"

"You won't have to make anything up," answered Tag. "I'll break your neck for you if you do. I've wasted enough time on you, too, you rat. How far away is Malley?"

"Malley ain't here," said the other.

"You lie," said Tag. "He's here. I want to know where."

The other groaned with fear.

"Ah, Tag," he said, "have a heart, will you? You know Malley's here, so why ask me? I know he's here, but I don't know where. That's the only reason that I said that he wasn't."

"Go on," said Tag. "I know enough to check up. It's the last time I'll call you a liar. The next time, I'll simply break your neck. What's the plan for to-night about Champion?"

"It's a child's plan, it's so simple," said Sam Doran. "Champion's a fool. He's half blind. He's down there in the dining room, right now, sitting where he could be shot through the window. But that ain't the plan. While he's down there, Tucker has picked his lock. Tucker's waiting for him with a riot gun in his room. When Champion unlocks his door and goes in, he'll be a good, easy target against the light in the hall, and Tucker will pick him off.

Tucker'll have a rope from the window to the water, and he'll slide down that rope, and hop onto a horse that's waiting for him at the edge of the gulch. That's all there is to the plan. It's pretty simple, ain't it?"

"Yeah, it's simple and it's pretty. Malley's plans are mostly simple and pretty, like this one!"

"Malley's got a good working kind of a brain," declared Sam Doran.

"Now tell me what Malley told you about me?"

"You? He wouldn't say anything about the best—"

Tag took the man by the throat.

"I told you I'd snuff you out!" he said savagely.

"Hold up!" gasped Sam Doran. "You know everything, anyway, so what's the use of askin' me? Malley just passed the word around that we was to take a slam at you, if we saw the chance. You mean some money to him, it seems like."

"I know that," lied Enderby. "What's the price for me, now?"

"Five grand," said Sam Doran. "Not that I'd touch any dirty blood money that was laid on the head of a pal of—"

"That'll do," interrupted Tag. "He'll pay five thousand for me, will he?"

"Yes, he will. He's started in hating your heart, he talks like."

"Yes, he hates my heart," agreed Tag. "He always did, but now it's in the open. I was always too free-handed with coin and horseflesh to suit Malley. Come back here with me into the brush."

"Tag," breathed the thief, "whatcha plan to do with me, anyways?"

"I won't hurt you. I'm going to keep you quiet for a little while. That's all. I'm going to tie you, Sam. Otherwise you might meet your friend Malley, and feel like having a chat with him. You seem to be talkative, to-night."

So he took the other into the pitch darkness of the brush. He held him with the wrists gathered into the grip of one hard, bony hand. Then he tied Sam Doran, not with many lashings, but securely, so that he could hardly move a muscle. A small gag, which permitted breathing but prevented sound, was tied into his mouth.

Then Tag went back to the hotel.

He still did not enter. To a loiterer on the window-lighted front veranda, he said:

"What's the police in this town, brother? I've dropped a wallet."

"Sid Locksley is a deputy sheriff," said the loiterer. "He'd be the man to see. Where'd you lose it?"

"In the daylight," said Tag Enderby. "Just around the corner of the evening. Where's the deputy sheriff live?"

"Follow your nose to the first crossing and take the street you live on," said the other, with an equal pertness.

But Tag laughed. He did not mind brisk returns.

A few steps up the street he inquired again, and in five minutes he had located Deputy Sheriff Sid Locksley in a busy little barroom. He drew him aside and said:

"I have a job for you down at the hotel. Will you come along with me?"

"What sort of a job?" asked the deputy sheriff.

"Murder in the making," answered Tag Enderby.

The deputy looked closely at him, seemed to like the fit of his clothes, and nodded.

"Where'd you get the tip? Friend of yours?" he asked.

"You might call it a tip from a friend," said Tag. "Shall we start now?"

"Yeah, we can start now."

They walked down the street briskly.

"Who is it?" asked the deputy.

"You'll see the whole plant when I lead you up to it," answered Tag. "The dead man is eating dinner now, in the dining room of the hotel. I hope we get there before he steps into his grave."

"I hope so, too," said the deputy. "You in the Federal service, maybe?"

Tag laughed.

"Not yet," he said. "But I'm trying to qualify."

"Why laugh?" asked the other.

"Maybe you'll hear the reason before long," said Tag Enderby.

At the hotel they paused in the lobby.

"Ask for the second key to Champion's room, and somebody to show us the way," said he.

The room clerk looked wide-eyed at the man of the law. It was plain that Sid Locksley had built for himself no small reputation. He was a burly man, with bulging jaws, and very small eyes under battered brows. He was in the law, it seemed, for the fighting he could get out of it.

He got the key at once, and the pair of them followed the clerk up the stairs.

20

Ready for Murder

I N the upper hall, Tag Enderby halted them. He said to the clerk: "I'm going down the hall to the room. Which is it?"

"Right there at the end. The door at the end of the passage."

"When I get there," went on Tag, "I'll turn the key in the lock and signal you with my left hand—so. Take that lamp down from the bracket. There you are! Hold it in your hand. Stay here. When you get my signal, blow the lamp out, and stand tight. Locksley, you come behind me. As soon as the lamp goes out, I'm throwing the door open. You crouch there in the dark. If a man comes through on the run, you salt him down. Don't ask any questions, but sock him with a chunk of lead where it'll do him the most good."

"Who's the man?" asked the deputy sheriff, more than a little doubtful of this procedure.

"A sneak," said Tag, "and a murderer, if I have him right. It's Champion's room. Champion's downstairs. What would any other man be doing in there, skulking in the dark?"

"That sounds right," admitted the sheriff. "But look here. I'll go in first and—"

"And get your head blown off by a riot gun, eh? That's the tool the fellow in there is holding."

Sid Locksley protested no more. There is no more harmful weapon in the world than a sawed-off shotgun at any distance. There is nothing half so deadly at close hand. Light is not needed. The riot gun sees by its own sense of touch, so to speak. So the deputy sheriff held his peace and became docile.

Down the hall went Tag, motioning to Locksley to tiptoe, while he himself moved with a bold, noisy step. When he came to the door, he fitted the key into the lock, turned it, and at the same time moved his left hand as he had promised. Instantly the hall was solid with the blackness of night.

He turned the knob, flung the door open, and leaped straight into the room as far as he could bound.

An instant later, he wished that he had slid in on hands and knees, for in mid-air he crashed into a chair and toppled with stunning violence to the floor. At the same moment the shotgun roared like thunder. He heard the rush and rattle of the shot as the charge tore through the wall just above him, but apparently Tucker had been too bent on firing at a form in the doorway. He had not planned to change his aim to the side, and therefore the bullets went wide.

Tag, gathering himself on the floor, saw half of a head and one shoulder outlined against the opposite window. His gun was in his hand, and he knew that he could find the heart with a shot. But that was not what he wanted. Dead men could not talk. He wanted to hear what Tucker could tell.

Therefore he set his grip on the chair over which he had fallen. One barrel of the big-mouthed riot gun still remained undischarged while Tucker, no doubt, peered to pick out a target in the darkness. And that gave Tag time to grasp the chair and hurl it with all his might.

He heard it crash. The head and the shoulder disappeared from the dim square of the open window, and the other barrel of the gun belched fire and thunder.

As a ferret leaps for a throat, so Enderby crossed that room at a bound, leaping from feet and hands. Diving into the darkness he found his prey. A fist struck him heavily across the jaw. He hardly felt the blow; excitement and battle anger had anæsthetized his nerves against pain and shock.

He had both hands on the other now. The man was whining with animal terror and rage, but the oldest of wrestling tricks jerked him upon his face. Tag rested his weight upon him, the man's hands tucked high on the small of his back. A little extra pressure, and the shoulder joints and tendons would burst under the strain.

"You're tearin' me in two!" he heard a groaning voice complain.

"Now a light, Locksley," panted Tag. "There ought to be a lamp in here somewhere."

Locksley came in, scratched a match, and lighted a lamp which stood on a small table near the corner of the room. The glow of it showed his battered face, pale and set. It had not been easy to step into that room with the roar of the shotgun hardly dead in the air, and the acrid scent of the gunpowder swirling into the nostrils.

But now the lamp was lighted, and by the glare of it, Tag Enderby saw the profile of Tucker pressed against the floor.

Tag stood up, and forced the outlaw to his feet.

A big man was Tucker, with the eye and the jaw of a fighter, and the lean look of the hardened athlete. But, nevertheless, Tag's tigerish attack in the darkness had completely unnerved and paralyzed him.

He was still too shaken to be himself. He looked about

him in a bewildered way. Intelligent understanding of what had happened dawned on him only gradually.

Sid Locksley had handcuffs on the wrists of the big fellow before there was a chance for words. Then the door was closed. The three of them were alone in the room, while the uproar of the excited guests washed up the stairs and thundered down the hall. The voice of Locksley ordered the crowd away again, and inside of the room, they sat down to talk.

Locksley was as eager as a terrier to worry a confession out of his prisoner.

"You were waiting in here in the dark," he said. "You had a riot gun loaded and ready for murder. Murder in the dark! Well, Enderby pulled your teeth for you. You'll about hang for this, Tucker. But the best way for you is to confess. Tell us why you're here and who sent you, and all of that!"

Tucker looked straight before him, his jaws set so hard that there was a white spot bulging in either cheek. He said nothing.

Locksley added, enraged: "If the boys in the street know about what you've tried to do, they'll tear you to pieces. The jail couldn't hold you. You ought to know that!"

Still Tucker said not a word.

Tag broke in for the first time.

"I know why you're here," he said. "I know who sent you. I know the money you were to make for it. But we want it out of your own mouth. It'll be easier for you. Savvy?"

Tucker did not speak.

Several heavy footfalls came down the hallway outside and a hand beat roughly on the door.

"Who's there?" demanded Locksley.

"Some of the boys," answered a heavy voice. "Look here, Sid, Tommy"—that was the name of the clerk who had showed them up the stairs—"has been tellin' us about what pretty near happened in that room—a dirty murder. Now, Sid, we just wanta take a lot of responsibility off your hands. Indian Gulch has stood for a lot of rough stuff in its time, but it ain't goin' to stand for a thing like a dirty murder in the dark. Just open this here door, Sid, or we'll have to knock it in and take that smart boy away from you!"

"I'd like to see you try to get him," shouted the deputy, with fine courage and spirit.

"Don't say that, Sid!" called another from the hall. "You ain't got a chance against us, and you oughta know it!"

"Wait a minute," said Tag to the deputy. "What's the good of putting up a fight for the hide of this water rat? He won't confess. He's making everything as hard as he can. The boys out there will fight till they drop for the pleasure of stretching his neck for him. Well, why put up the fight? Make a protest, and let them come and grab this Tucker, if they want him!"

He spoke seriously, steadily, convincingly, with only a single quick flutter of an eyelid to give the deputy a clew to his real meaning.

"Give me a couple of minutes, boys, will you?" called Locksley.

"We'll give you a couple of minutes," said the spokesman from the hallway. "Then we want some action. Hurry it up, Sid!"

The deputy turned to Tucker.

"You see how it is, old man," he argued persuasively. "I

don't want to see you hung by the boys. I'd a lot rather see the law take its course, but I can't start in shootin' up law-abidin' citizens for the sake of saving your hide for a while. You see the way that it is? It's no value to me to save you—there's no profit in you, so far as I'm concerned, unless I get the whole confession out of you."

Tucker looked hard at Tag Enderby, not at Locksley.

"Tag," he said, breaking his silence at the last, "what the devil is Ray Champion to you? What made you horn in? What made you break in the first place?"

"Break what, Tucker?"

"Break with the boys. What made you?"

"Spit it all out," urged Tag. "That's the best way for you. Locksley wants to do something for you. But it'll be hard to manage anything, if you're going to keep your face shut. You can't expect him to risk his neck for nothing, but if you can give him some leads—why, I'll bet that he'll see you through!"

"He will?" asked Tucker, almost contemptuously, glancing at the deputy.

He turned to Tag Enderby again.

"What about you, Tag?" he said. "Suppose that I spill the beans, will 'you' give me a hand, old man? Will you see me through?"

Tag grinned.

"You nearly saw 'me' through," said he. "You nearly saw 'holes' through me, in fact. Well, it depends on how much you can tell."

"How much do you 'want' me to tell?" asked Tucker. "You know that if I begin at the start and go through, I—"

His voice stopped, rising on a dark insinuation.

"I don't know at all," said Tag.

"I could put you in the pen for life!" snapped Tucker.

Deputy Sheriff Locksley stiffened in his chair. His eyes bulged. He even cast a glance toward the door, as much as to say that he did not care to attempt to arrest that wild cat unaided.

"You can't touch me, Tucker," insisted Tag Enderby.

"Can't I prove that you were one of Malley's gang?" cried out Tucker suddenly.

Locksley started, with a groan of excitement.

"You try," said Enderby steadily. "What have you on me?"

"What have I? Why, I have—I have—"

The voice of Tucker trailed away. He concluded, with a growl: "Your deals were lone deals. I guess that you turned your tricks without any witnesses. I might 'a' guessed that you'd keep your own fur sleek and smooth, no matter what happened! That's why you never would take another man along to help fill out your hand! I see now. I was a fool not to see before! But I can prove that you were in camp, and that you—"

"Sure I was in camp," said Tag Enderby. "I was there as a sort of missionary. I was trying to reform Malley. That's all!"

He leaned back in his chair and smiled insolently, his bold eyes dwelling upon the face of Tucker.

21

The Mob

As for the deputy sheriff, his glance kept leaping from one to the other, trying to draw great deductions. Tag Enderby said to him:

"You see, Locksley, Tucker is trying to tell me that I've been a member of the Malley gang. I've just proved to him that I've visited the Malley camp only for the sake of reforming Malley himself."

He chuckled as he faced the sheriff.

"And that's where it stands," said he.

The deputy sighed.

"The man who rounds up the Malleys will be famous for life," said he. "But it'll take a whole herd of foxes to corner you, son, I'm thinking. Tucker, let Enderby be out of it. Are you going to talk for us or—"

He pointed solemnly toward the door, behind which the men were waiting, perhaps with watches in their hands.

Tucker's face was shining with a fine perspiration.

"Tag," said he, "d'you give me your guarantee?"

Tag shrugged his shoulders.

"I don't know why I should," said he. "But I'll give you my guarantee to keep you away from the lynching party, if that's what you want."

"I'll have your hand on that," said Tucker.

He spoke feverishly, his nostrils widening, and then pinching in.

"Here's my hand," answered Tag.

The manacles clanked as they shook hands. And then Tucker leaned back in his chair with a great sigh of relief.

"Hurry up, man," urged the deputy. "You know I got some impatient fellows out there in the hallway. They're liable to bust in at any time, and if they do, they'll take you away from us the way a river floats away a dead leaf!"

"Will they?" Tucker sneered. "You don't know Tag Enderby, son, or you wouldn't put so much of your money on the village boys. I ain't in any hurry now. I'll give you the truth and the whole truth, but I'll take my time about it. You can't rush the truth out of a man, can you?"

Mischief flickered in his eyes. The deputy sheriff cursed with a sudden anger.

"What sort of a game is this? And where do I figger in it?" he demanded.

"You don't figger at all," said Tucker coolly. "You never would 'a' been able to take me. You ain't man enough. I'd eat a gross like you, Locksley, and you know it. Enderby—he's a different kind. And if your little village cut-ups get through that door—he'll soon make 'em wish that they'd jumped into a kettle of boilin' pitch instead!"

"Shut up," said Tag. "Shut up, and let's hear you talk, will you?"

"I'll talk," agreed Tucker, settling himself back in the chair again. "I'm finished with Malley, anyway, after this. I'd about as well be hanged by law or lynched, as to be murdered by one of Malley's thugs, for not turning my trick to-night."

"Go on! Go on!" urged Locksley.

"Wait till I get a smoke started," said Tucker, as cool as could be.

And he made a smoke, speaking slowly at the same time.

"You know why I'm here, Tag. You know that I was sent

to get Champion."

"Why?" broke in the sheriff. "What have you against poor Ray Champion? Will you tell me that?"

Tucker looked at the other with open contempt. He seemed to hesitate, wondering whether or not that question were worth an answer, but at last he said:

"I didn't like the mug on him, for one thing. Is that reason enough?"

"I'd like to crack you on your sneerin' mouth!" said Locksley, thoroughly infuriated.

"You try to lay a hand on me," said Tucker, with a perfectly calm and indifferent air. "You'd better put a hand on a hornets' nest. No, no, son, I knew what I was about when I made Tag shake with me!"

"You fool," said the deputy, "Enderby was only playing with you; kidding you along!"

"You think so?" answered Tucker. "You talk like a flathead. Enderby don't know how to break a promise. It's a funny thing about him. Why, everybody knows that about him!"

"Go on, then, and get somewhere," said the deputy.

"Besides not liking Champion's mug," said Tucker, "there was one cold grand to put in my kick if I bumped him off. So why not? No reason not. I came down here to do the job, and I would 'a' done it, except that a dead man come in and spoiled the play!"

"Dead man?" echoed Locksley.

"Yeah, he's a dead man. There's five thousand hangin' on his head. He's no better than a dead man."

"Who's offering money on his head?"

"Malley, that's all." Tucker grinned. "You sock Mr.

Enderby, and you'll find five thousand lyin' on your doorstep the next day. I'm not a bad egg. I give you a tip, and there you are!"

"Drop Enderby for a while," said Locksley. "He seems pretty able to take care of himself."

"You've gone out and discovered something that hardly anybody knew about," Tucker sneered.

"What about Ray Champion? Why does Malley want him done in?"

"I dunno. There's a grudge between 'em. Champion's on the trail of Malley. Malley's on the trail of Champion. And there you are!"

"Is that all you have to say?" asked the deputy. "Is that your confession?"

"Sure. What else is there to confess? This Enderby—he knew about everything, anyway. He knew that I was in here, waiting for Champion. Tag, who tipped you off? Will you tell me that?"

There was a heavy knocking at the door of the room.

"Hello! Hello! Sid!" yelled the voices.

"Hello!" called Locksley. "Wait a minute, boys!"

"We've waited more'n enough. We want that killer! We want him quick!" shouted an angry voice from the outside.

"Now Enderby," said the unhappy deputy, "there's Hank Martin and Jeff Creek, out there, and those two boys mean business. They're goin' to have Tucker or bust. What about it?"

"Unlock the irons on Tucker," said Tag Enderby.

Such was the desperation of the deputy, or perhaps such was the dominance which Tag Enderby had acquired by his utter coolness, that Locksley, without another word, unlocked the shackles that held the wrists of the prisoner.

Tag, in the meantime, was leaning behind the chair of Tucker.

He said: "Tucker, I'll go through it with you. I'll trust you. Three days from now, you send in word to Locksley about where he's to pick you up. And then he'll take you off to the county jail. Is that fair?"

"Fair." Tucker nodded.

His eyes were bent in horror upon the closed door of the room.

"We'll shake on that," said Tag.

He held out his hand.

This time, the wrists of Tucker were free from the irons. He shook hands with a quick grip, and sprang to his feet.

"We'd better start, Tag," said he.

"There's the window," Tag said.

Tucker was already at it.

"It's fifteen feet to the ground," said he.

"That's easy," answered Tag.

As he spoke, he was stripping the blanket from the bed and drawing a knot in one corner of it. He held the knot and flung the other end through the window. It wasn't quite long enough but Tucker, in an instant, had slid down the blanket and dropped a mere foot or two to the ground.

"Hold this!" called Tag to the deputy.

The latter obeyed, muttering: "The boys are goin' to be pretty hot!"

But while he was still muttering, Tag was already on the ground.

"Hold on," said Locksley. "How am 'I' to get down? There's nobody to hold—"

"You're the law. They won't lynch the law of the town," called the cheerful voice of Tag Enderby from the darkness beneath. And he was already off down the side of the building, behind the racing form of Tucker.

With a mighty stride went Tucker, as a man should go when his life may depend upon his speed, but Tag was instantly beside him.

Above and behind them, they heard a crash, as the door of the room went down, and then the howling of human voices, like the cry of wolves upon a blood trail.

"You hear that?" called Tag.

The other panted out a groan.

They darted into the barn, and there Tucker jerked a saddle from a peg on the wall and flung it upon the back of a powerful-looking chestnut. Tag, with speed, jerked the bridle over the head of the gelding, and by the time he had buckled the throatlatch, the other was in the saddle.

For a moment, Tag held the reins with a hard grip, checking the dancing horse.

"You heard me, Tucker?" he said. "Three days from now, you send in a message to Locksley?"

"Are you going to hold me to that?" moaned Tucker.

"I'm going to hold you to that. Is it right?"

"It's got to be right, then. But, Tag—"

"If you don't come in, I'll take your trail, Tucker, and as sure as there's sky and water, I'll find you and make you wish that you'd gone to hell before you ever met me! Now get out of here, and get fast. Three days from now, Locksley is to have you!"

Tucker waited to bid no farewells or to express no thanks. From the hotel the roar of angry voices was increasing. He drove the slipping, stumbling horse out the back door of the barn and furiously away through the night.

Tag Enderby laughed as he watched the other rocketing away. Then he hurried out into the dark of the night and found in the brush Sam Doran, just as he had left him. He removed the gag and cut the bonds of the little man. Then he helped Doran to his feet.

"How does it go, Sam?" he asked.

"My head's spinning," said Doran. "What's happening around here? What's all the yapping about?"

"They've been wanting to lynch Tucker. Tucker's gone now. He may have a couple of words to say to you, though, if he sees you."

"Did you tell him that 'I' gave him away and—"

"No, but he might guess. If I were you, I'd grab my horse and just slide away, Sam, and keep moving till I had a couple of hundred miles between me and this neck of the woods. Tucker's a mighty angry man."

"Tucker? Great guns!" gasped Doran, and instantly darted out of sight into the obscurity of the darkness.

~22~
Wolf and Bulldog

TAG Enderby trailed back into the hotel. He found that all the excitement had centered about the figure of unfortunate Deputy Sheriff Locksley, who, all in a moment, found that his popularity was slipping away from him.

The inhabitants of Indian Gulch were a rough lot. No name was less pleasant in their ears than the name of

Malley, and the thought that a member of that detested gang had been among them drove them mad. Their appetites were high to destroy; they wanted a victim; and they were almost of a mind to seize upon the deputy and make him serve in the place of the man who had disappeared from Champion's room.

A dozen rough-looking fellows surrounded Locksley in the hall of the hotel, as Tag Enderby entered, and the air was filled with threats. It was not exactly fear that made Locksley turn to Tag, the moment that he saw the latter.

"There's the man!" he shouted. "Enderby—Tag Enderby! You've heard something about him! Enderby's the man who got Tucker. Enderby's the man who turned him loose and went surety for him! What're you talkin' to 'me' about?"

Attention swept suddenly to the new focus. Angry men really only want something upon which to vent their rage, and the figure of the slender stranger was more attractive than a fellow townsman who, after all, was the limb of the law.

One bearded man roared: "Let's have a look at Enderby. 'I've' heard about him! I've heard about his gun tricks and his gun plays. Nobody ever learns a gun that good without havin' murder up his sleeve. Don't say no to me! Let's take Mr. Enderby and have a look at him and maybe we could see him better in the jail!"

Several voices joined the clamor.

They wanted to learn what Enderby meant by securing the release of one of the dreaded Malley gangsters. Perhaps there had been more than a little listening through the door of Champion's room, for one voice shouted that he knew that Enderby was really a member of Malley's gang!

And that drove the crowd mad.

It was not a large mob. It was far more dangerous than a large mob. When Westerners gather for action, those who do not handle guns well are not apt to appear. This was a fighting unit of a dozen practiced handlers of weapons. Now they swerved straight across the hall toward Tag Enderby.

He did not wait for them to come. Neither did he flee.

He stepped straight to the first speaker, the man of the beard, and caught him by that beard, and twisted his hand in it. For it was a magnificently flowing stream of brown, curling and somewhat entangled. Huge mustaches thrust out from the upper lip of the man and dripped downward into the greater ocean of the beard.

He reached inside his coat for a gun, but though Tag Enderby did not draw a weapon of his own, his flashing hand found that of the bearded giant and gripped it in such a way that it forgot its original errand.

"You want to have a look at me," said Tag. "And here I am. Look hard! And after you've looked, will you tell the boys what you've seen?"

With that, he jerked the beard of the other twice, so that his head nodded to this side and then to that; and thrusting him suddenly away so that he stumbled backward for a considerable distance, Tag stepped past him through the group.

They made a way before him, drawing reluctantly back. Half of them would have been glad to follow any lead in flinging themselves at this insolent stranger. The trouble was that no one felt exactly like commencing the trouble.

Not a word was said.

And, as Tag walked calmly, slowly toward the dining-room door, his victim of the flowing beard stood at a little distance by himself, with a leveled Colt in his grasp.

Certainly if Tag Enderby had run, or stopped, or turned, a .45-caliber chunk of lead would have dropped him. But he merely sauntered on in unconcern. The dining-room door he thrust open, and it swung behind him, oscillating rapidly to and fro, like the blinking of an eye, letting in the greater light of the room beyond.

Not a one of the group moved to pursue this slim and fearless man. There was something in the power of a name which had rung in their ears before. There was still more in the cold indifference of his manner, the paralyzing speed of his hand.

Inside the dining room he glanced about him and saw, as a matter of course, that every table was empty—with one exception. That was a little corner place, and there in the corner sat a single diner.

It was Ray Champion, smoking a cigarette and finishing his coffee at his ease. He looked up and waved his hand as he saw Tag approaching.

"Thought I heard your name out there," said he.

Tag Enderby sat down in the opposite chair, his back turned to the empty room.

"They got a little excited," he said.

"What about?"

"Nothing much. They wanted to lynch Tucker; that's all."

"Who's Tucker?"

"Fellow who was waiting up in your room with a riot gun

to blow your head off when you went inside; that's all."

The Negro waiter came in. He came on tiptoe, his eyes enormous and rolling.

"And who found him there?" asked Champion.

"I did," said Tag, and to the waiter: "Give me everything you've got."

" 'You' did?" exclaimed Champion.

"Yes. I found the fellow that you've chased all the way from Grove City—"

Champion leaned forward. His calm was broken. His color changed. His jaw set in that bulldog fashion which Tag had seen before.

"Where is he now?" he asked. "He's one of Malley's men who framed—"

"He's riding away from Indian Gulch as fast as a good horse can take him, just now. A while ago, he was lying out in the brush, tied up, while I went into the hotel to see how much truth he'd been telling me. He'd told the truth, all right. Tucker was in your room. But after we'd nailed Tucker, the boys wanted to lynch him, and I hate lynchings. Don't you?"

Champion said nothing. He merely stared, his head lowered a trifle, as though he wanted to fight.

"Are you laughing at me, Enderby?" he asked.

"Not a bit. Why should I? Tucker promised me that he'd come back to Locksley and surrender, in three days. And nothing but a bullet will keep Tucker from coming. So that's all right. But when the boys learned that I'd turned him loose, they thought that it might be a good idea to switch the necktie party to my honor. That's why there was a little trouble in the hall, just now, but everything is simmering down, now, and every one will soon be happily in bed. How's that coffee?"

Champion cleared his throat.

"What are you doing here?" he asked.

"Looking after the truant boy," said Tag.

"Meaning me?"

"Yes—meaning you."

"What made you come?"

"Molly, of course."

"Of course?" said the other, his temper rising, while his voice lowered.

Tag Enderby smiled upon him without mirth.

"Keep a sense of humor," said he. "We both may have a big laugh out of this, before the wind-up. If our throats are not cut before the finish, as they probably will be."

"Tell me what I'm to laugh at?" asked Champion.

"You've come up here to be the boy hero and wreck the Malley gang," said Tag. "That's because you're brave. But I'd rather see a coward than a brave fool. You're a fool, Champion. You would have been dead, by this time. You would have been dead, and in bits!"

Champion cleared his throat again. A big bowl of soup was brought to Tag. The other watched him balance the clumsy thing on his three nicely pointed finger tips, while he sipped as though from a dainty cup.

"Maybe I would have been dead," said Champion. "But you've called me a fool, Enderby. You understand that I don't take that?"

"You'll take worse than that, I think," said Tag Enderby. "I've got to stay along with you and be lady in waiting while you blunder about and try to break your neck. That's to be my job, and I'll take the liberty of speaking my mind, now and then, in the meantime."

Champion swallowed hard. Then he took a sip of the black coffee.

"You say that Molly sent you?" he said.

"I'm making a campaign for Molly," said Tag frankly.

"I saw it start while I was at the Benton house," said Champion. "It'll do you no good. She's the soul of honor, and she's promised to me."

"Promises are nothing in my life," said Tag. "If ever I get the Champion idea out of her head, I'll have her away from you. You hear me?"

"You talk straight out," answered Champion. "It sounds to me as though we'd have a war about this, before we're through."

"That's the way it sounds to me, too," said Tag. And he smiled.

Looking at them, one might have said that it was wolf facing bulldog. And it would have been hard to say which was the more formidable of the two.

"But in the first place," went on Champion, "I have another job on my hands."

"You'll drop that job, if you have any wits," answered Tag. "You'll never catch Malley, but Malley will catch you. You think that you're doing some fishing. You're only the bait on a hook. You're nothing to Malley. Look at this. He pulls you out there, by drifting a rider past the window of your bank. He has a plant ready for you here in Indian Gulch, and you eat your dinner and get ready to go upstairs and die. But this isn't the only trick that Malley has up his sleeve. He has a lot more. You try to get some sense in your head, and go back to Grove City."

Champion nodded.

"So that Molly can hear how you've been the hero, and I've been the fool?" he asked.

"That's the main reason, for me," admitted Tag.

"I'll be likely to go back then," said Champion, with sarcasm.

"You'll see us both dead," said Enderby, "if you won't go back. But if you keep on the trail, I'm keeping on the same trail with you. Confound your stubborn soul!"

~23~
Blackberry Creek

WHEN Champion went to bed that night, his soul was filled with trouble. He lay awake, rigid in the bed, for hours, trying to think a way out of the difficulties.

On the one hand, he owed his life to the intervention of Tag Enderby. Before he went to bed, he had learned from the clerk the details of how Tag had flashed into the dark of the bedroom and tackled the man with the sawed-off shotgun. It was a grisly thing even to think about, far less to attempt.

On the other hand, Tag had been perfectly frank in admitting that he wanted to save the life of Champion merely to win the good graces of the girl. And when Champion thought of himself, his slow ways of body and thought, his short stature, his bulk of shoulder and length of jaw, he wondered how a girl could look twice at him when there was such a handsome picture as Tag Enderby near by.

No, the more hold he gave Tag upon his gratitude, the more he would be preparing the way for Tag with Molly. Tag had said as much. The very best way, all things considered for the future, was to return at once to Grove City, as Tag had suggested, settle back to work in the bank, and marry Molly before she had a good excuse for changing her mind.

He was confident of that, but there was in him a steady flame that burned up the good sense of his resolutions. And that flame was the hatred of Malley and Malley's works in this world.

Three years of hell Champion had spent in the State penitentiary. His name was blasted. Time had eaten into the very core of his being. And now he wanted his revenge. He had not known how desperate was the want in him, until he had seen the abhorrent outline of the hump-backed man riding past the window of the bank. But that sight had burst down a barrier and allowed vast emotions to rush out in a sliding tide. He could not stand against it.

One thing, at least, he could do, and that was to slip away from Tag Enderby and get to a distant point from which he could begin again the trail of Malley and Malley's men, without Tag's presence.

That, the more he reflected, seemed the wisest thing that he could attempt. Let Tag mull around for a time, in the vain effort to find him. Then let him go back to the girl and try to persuade her if he could.

But he could not persuade her, Champion was confident, before she had had a chance to speak face to face with the man to whom she was engaged.

And, when he, Ray Champion, returned, it would be as

the achiever of a great exploit, the vanquisher of a famous and dreadful enemy.

If the exploit were not achieved, he would simply not return, because he would be dead.

So it was that Ray Champion reasoned in the dark of his room, moving slowly from point to point, but sure of each detail as he came to it. And when he had reached his conclusion, he set his mind upon wakening at three in the morning, closed his eyes, and was instantly asleep.

At three o'clock, he awakened. He was very tired. Brain and body ached with a great fatigue, but he forced himself instantly from the bed, and then dressed, made up his pack, and went quietly down the stairs.

In the hall below, he found that the night clerk, as he had expected, was sound asleep. But being totally methodical of mind, Champion already had added up mentally every detail of his bill. So he put down the exact amount, and fifty cents over as a tip. This money he laid softly upon the open face of the ledger, picked up a pen, and scratched his name beneath the silver.

After that, he stole back through the dark hall, came to a rear window, worked it up without a sound, and dropped out into the outer night.

The damp, sharp cold struck through him at once, though there was no wind blowing. But he enjoyed the utter freshness of the air as he drew it to the bottom of his lungs.

He was glad that he had gone.

In the stable he found his hired horse, saddled it, glanced from it toward the beautiful gray of Tag Enderby with a touch of envy, and a shake of the head, and then strapped on his pack, and departed. He led the horse—to make sure of the stony footing through the winding street of the town—and did not mount until he was past its edge.

Then he went on at a sober pace. His horse was not one that could accomplish great distances at a considerable gait. But it could proceed with the steadiness of the true Western mustang, dogtrotting, or loping for mile after mile.

As for the darkness, he was not greatly troubled by it. He had hunted all through these hills when he was a youngster, and therefore he knew the trails with a great degree of perfection. The years between had not altered them greatly.

It was his goal to cross the high range of hills and get near to the town of Claybrick on the other side.

For rumor said that the chief hiding place for Malley and his men was in the rough country that lay in the high heart of the hills, between Indian Gulch and Claybrick, and to the north of the straight line between them. In Claybrick or its vicinity, he would be far from Indian Gulch, far from Tag Enderby, and at least in striking distance of the work which he wanted to do.

Steadily sticking to his labor, he found that the distance he made was very small per hour along the dark of the trails. It was dawn, and he had still a distance to cover.

So he gave the horse no rest. Patiently he wore away the miles, and before the midmorning, he came upon sight of the town of Claybrick, its eastern windows flashing against the face of the sun.

It was not the town itself which he wanted, however, but a good camping ground near to it, and then some luck for the finding of the scoundrel Malley.

As for the camping ground, there leaped into his mind a picture of a certain creek that flowed through good woods near Claybrick, woods in which there were many small openings where the grass grew tall and rich for the pasturage of cattle. On any one of those clearings he would be able to make his permanent camp while he angled through the hills for the proper trail to the Malley hide-out.

So he branched toward the north, found the waters of the stream near Claybrick, and followed them down toward the west and south to find the ideal spot that he had in mind. He came to one or two clearings, but they seemed to him rather too big for his purpose. They were so big that they might be known to other travelers. He wanted a mere hint of a meadow, to give the proper forage to his mustang.

And now, coming through the heavy brush of the timber, he was aware of a faint tint of wood smoke in the air, and he was pleased by it. For this was a stretch of country made after the heart of many an old prospector or trapper. How many old-timers were settled here and there among the hills, hunting for pay dirt, or having found it, sweating their hearts out over a "coffee grinder" to extract a dollar or so a day, doing five times a cow-puncher's work for hardly more than his daily wage?

Any one of these solitary fellows would be sure to give him a welcome and a hot breakfast. He could even camp with the man and extract from him, no doubt, the very information of which he was in such need about the exact whereabouts of the outlaws.

While he was gladdening himself with these prospects, the trees thinned out before him, and he had a glimpse of the white arm of the smoke rising up from the ground of a little clearing, just ahead of him. It was an arm of smoke thick and gleaming as smoke is when it rises from a newly kindled blaze, before the strength of the fire has had a chance to dry out some of the green firewood and throw up a strong natural draft. The flame itself he could next see, as it made a golden flickering through the middle of the smoke.

And he sighed with relief. He was very tired. He certainly had not been looking forward with any great pleasure toward the duty of making camp, cutting wood, cooking a miserable breakfast on this morning.

He was rather surprised, when he came closer, almost breaking through the last of the tree screen, to see that a tall gray horse was grazing in this clearing, but that surprise was as nothing compared with the shock which he received a moment later.

For, as his own mustang was stepping through the last of the brush and trees into the open, he had a glimpse of the face of the other camper in profile, and he was amazed to see that it was young Tag Enderby, already here, and so far before him!

He could not believe his eyes.

It seemed to him that this could be no man, but the devil himself. Or else, there was a real double of Tag. Surely, far, far behind him in the town of Indian Gulch, young Tag Enderby, the real Tag Enderby, was hardly more than through with his breakfast by this time, and yawning and stretching the sleep out of his body while he smoked the after-breakfast cigarette upon the front veranda of the hotel.

Ray Champion drew rein. His brain was spinning.

"Hey, Ray!" called the indubitable voice of Tag. "Fall off your horse and rustle me some more wood, will you? And what did you bring along in the line of chuck? I didn't pack the whole of a grocery store with me!"

Almost literally, Champion "fell" from his horse, dragged off the saddle, and went with his hand ax into the woods to cut more fuel for the fire.

His mind was not prepared for much thinking or deliberation, but he could not help wondering that Tag had found such green, smoking wood for his camp fire, when the woods were filled with brush absolutely dead and ready to answer the touch of the first spark with a burst of flames.

He came back with all he could carry and drag, and flung it down at hand. Then he started to break the good timber off in convenient lengths.

Still he had not spoken to Tag Enderby. He preferred to work out the problem, if he could, without asking questions, but he failed to solve the riddle. And his curiosity grew red-hot.

"Tag!" he broke out, at last.

"Ay?" said Tag, looking up from the fuming coffeepot.

"Tag, what made you think that I'd come in this direction?"

"I didn't think. I saw you lining out in this direction," said Tag.

"Did you sit up all night and watch?"

"No, but I paid the kid on night duty to pretend to be asleep when you came downstairs."

"The devil! How did you know that I'd come down?"

"Because I sort of thought that you'd find that I was crowding the game for you, a little. That was my idea, at any rate, and it seems that I was about right. After you got through the hills, I guessed that you'd strike for Blackberry Creek, and I just slipped around and came on ahead. But I burned enough green wood to call the whole Indian nation before you finally got the signal and arrived!"

~24~
Tag's Riding Job

T HE anger of Champion was mixed with an odd sort of despair. He did not speak again until he had a breakfast of greasy bacon and hard-tack, bolted down with a slug of powerful black coffee. Then, over his cigarette, he said:

"Enderby, you've got to see that this thing can't go on."

"What thing?" asked Tag Enderby.

"You know what I mean. This trailing of me around the mountains!"

"Why can't it go on?"

"I won't have it," answered Champion, without heat, but with much purpose in his voice.

"You'll have to pick me off the trail with a gun then," said Tag Enderby. "I've found my riding job, and I stay riding herd on you, Ray, until the job's finished."

"Until Malley's dead, eh?"

"Yes, or you, or both of us—which is a lot more likely."

Suddenly Ray Champion laughed, rather weakly, his sides shaking with the weary mirth.

"You beat me, Tag," he said.

"I'm only beginning to beat you," said Tag. "We haven't really started the play of our hands, old son!"

"Tell me," said Ray Champion. "D'you intend to help me erret out Malley?"

"Ferret out Malley?" exclaimed Tag. "Why, there won't

be any need of doing that. Malley will do the ferreting. He'll have his wasps buzzing all around our ears, before long. You can trust to that, if you trust to nothing."

"Well," said Champion, "you may know. I'm going to turn in and have a sleep, for one."

"Not yet," said Tag. "We'll match for the first sleep. The two of us don't sleep at the same time, on this trip."

Champion, nodding his head in gloomy surrender, obediently threw up his coin. It spatted down on the palm of his hand as Tag Enderby called "Tails," and Champion looked without surprise on the eagle design on the silver coin. It would have been a miracle, he decided, if Tag had failed to win.

First, Tag Enderby wrapped a blanket around some bits of brush, making the outfit resemble a man asleep near the fire. Then he retreated inside the brush, gave another blanket a twist around his body and lay down.

"You keep stirring through the woods, just in sight of the smoke of the fire," said Tag. "If you make any more sound than a snake, you're likely to be swallowed alive. That's all."

"How long do you sleep?" asked Champion.

He got no answer, and perceived then that his companion was already sound asleep.

He had a foolish desire to take his horse and press on again. But he checked that desire. Tag Enderby would find him once more, as he already had found him. Even if he took the long-legged dappled gray, he was not apt to get away from the cunning brains of the younger man.

So he took up his beat, stirring slowly, cautiously through the trees, putting down his foot each time with manifold care. For now that Tag Enderby was sleeping, it seemed to him almost as though an army of defense had been stripped away from him and that he had been left alone to meet great numbers.

There were plenty of sounds in the forest. There always are!

There is either the stealthy whisper of wind, exactly like approaching voices on all hands, or else there is a startling cracking, from time to time, as though a twig had snapped underfoot. The noise comes from some movement of the boughs, as a rule, and it is really different from the half-muffled crack of a twig underfoot. But to a lonely, attentive ear it seems almost the same.

Half a dozen times an hour, Champion looked at his watch. A whole day of agonized fatigue seemed to pass over him before two hours elapsed. And, at the end of that time, he felt something like a shadow behind him. He whirled about with gun ready. His forefinger almost closed upon the ready trigger, as he saw the silhouette of a man watching him, hardly arm's length away.

It was then that he recognized Tag Enderby.

"A real Malley man would cut your throat from behind," said Tag. "Go take a sleep, Champion."

Ray Champion did not argue or protest against the trick. He felt that there must be some truth in what was said, or otherwise Tag would not have been able to steal up on him in this manner. But surely Dan Malley did not have another in his outfit so cat-footed as this wild man!

Wrapped in his blanket, Champion slept soundly, not two hours, but half a dozen, and when he awakened, he found that the sun was well to the west past the zenith. On the edge of the clearing, near by, Tag Enderby was busily skinning a very small deer.

Champion stood up, rubbing his eyes in amazement.

"Why, I slept so confoundedly hard, Tag," said he, "that I didn't even hear your rifle when you shot that deer!"

"There wasn't any rifle shot," said Tag. "I knew that you wanted sleep a lot more than you wanted meat. But this little rascal came down for water, looking like a moving patch of dapple and shadow. So I just chucked a knife in behind its shoulder, and it dropped without a sound. Come here and cut it up, while I get back on the beat. The Malleyites ought to be pretty close to us, by this time. Because you're a great sleeper, Ray. You surely are."

Champion did not answer. It was not the first time that Tag had made a fool of him, and he suspected that it would not be the last. He cut up the deer and then stepped into the woods and patiently resumed his watch, drifting from tree to tree, sometimes glancing over either shoulder. For the first lesson which Tag Enderby had given him in stalking had not been altogether wasted upon him. He himself possessed a reasonable share of woodcraft, and he now used it all.

Inside the clearing, behind him, he could hear the flame of the fire crackling.

There was not a trace of smoke, however, appearing above the tops of the trees, so far as he could see, so very carefully was Tag selecting the dryest and the clearest wood for the purposes of his cookery. And the fragrance of the roast began to steal out to the nostrils of the watcher.

He had a chance to take his thoughts, now and then, from the work in hand in order to contemplate the manner in which Tag had apportioned to him three times as much sleep as Tag himself had enjoyed. And yet something told him that Tag had not wakened until he was really rested.

There were men like that in the world perhaps—men of steel and tough sinew. He realized that he never would be able to compete with them.

That thought had barely passed through his mind when, a little distance before him, he saw, or thought he saw, a shadow that slipped between tree and tree.

The mere sway of a branch had done that possibly. But he stepped far to the side—and then he had a glimpse of a man stepping lightly out of view, at that instant, behind a broad tree trunk.

He jerked his rifle to his shoulder and waited for a chance at a shot, but the other appeared again only by the merest trifling show of a shoulder at a greater distance. There was no opportunity for planting a shot, even if he took it for granted that this was one of the Malley men.

So shadowlike was the disappearance of the fellow, however, that he could not help being taken back to the warning of Tag Enderby. The trailing of a cloud shadow could have been more noiseless. At least, he was not bringing danger closer to the camp. He was slipping away from it with a cautious speed.

With that news, Champion hurried into the clearing to give word to Tag.

The latter merely moved closer to the fire the gobbets of meat which he had arranged upon a number of small twigs and splinters of wood, turning them so that they might cook evenly.

"What sort of a looking fellow?" he asked.

"I saw his back only," said Champion. "How could I tell by that?"

"Can't you?" asked Tag. "Well, I've known other fellows beside you, Ray, that have to look at a face before they know their man. And that's a pity. Because the face that you recognize generally has spotted you already, may have a gun already brought down on you. And that's the ending of a lot of good hunters!"

He began to whistle, as he tended the meat again.

"You know backs the way you do faces, I suppose?" asked Champion grimly.

"Why not? There's more to a back than there is to a face."

"You might as well say that there's more to a desert than there is to a mountain. But it hasn't as many features."

"Why," said Tag Enderby, "there's the line of the shoulders, and one is always higher than the other, a shade. And there's the angle of the head to one side, because it's never just upright. And there's the curve of the back, and the way the shoulder blades fit in or stick out, and the hollow in the small of the back, and the size of the hips, and the slope of the shoulders, too. There's the look of the hair around the nape of the neck, and how the hat's worn—which is never the same on any two men I've ever seen. Why, old son, a back's as clear as a face to read, if you'll only keep more than half an eye on it."

"We'd better get out of here, backs or no backs," said Champion. "We're spotted now, and we'd better move."

"On an empty stomach I hate riding," declared Tag. "That fellow who slipped away will have to find his friends, and then he'll come in and find that we've had breakfast and we're on our way, I suppose."

"And suppose he comes back before we leave?"

"That would be our bad luck, and maybe their bad luck, too. You have to take chances in this little old world. By the way, what was the look of him?"

"I'm no back reader," said Champion, somewhat angrily. "He was slimmish, though, and stepped like a cat, without a sound."

"Slim?" said Enderby. "Narrow all the way? Hips and shoulders, too?"

"Yeah, hips and shoulders, too. But I couldn't see—"

"It must be one of Malley's men," said Tag, "and the only one who looks like that from behind is Skeet Raleigh. If it's Skeet—and that's who it is—we'd better hurry just a trifle with this breakfast, Ray. Pour out some of that coffee. Here's some hard-tack and venison. Great Scott, how good that meat smells!"

And his mouth was already filled as he ended his words.

"Who's Skeet Raleigh?" asked Champion.

With shrugged shoulders, speaking with difficulty, the other answered: " 'Mucho diablo!' "

And he continued his breakfast with a hearty appetite.

~25~
Taking Chances

THEY wolfed down the breakfast rapidly, washing down hard-tack and venison with the scalding coffee. As they ate, Tag Enderby carried on a brief conversation with his companion. Champion was full of inquiries about "Skeet" Raleigh.

"Skeet," said Tag, "is what you'd call a handy man. He can crack a safe, read a mind, stack a deck, or palm the other fellow's watch. He's a bit of a penman and he's a snake in the woods. With a knife he's an artist and with a Colt he can do tricks that ought to be on the stage. That's where he'd be, but they can't afford to pay him the salary that he ought to get. That's Skeet."

"Why, it sounds to me," said Ray Champion, "as though Skeet himself would be enough to give us all the trouble that we want in the world."

"He would," answered Tag. "But see how it is? He's too modest. He doesn't appreciate himself as much as other people do. And that's a pity. If he had a heart as big as his wits, he would never have gone back for help. He would have cut your throat and gone on to shoot me in the back in the clearing."

"Cut my throat? I saw him!" said Champion.

"You saw him while he was going away," said Tag. "I'll bet before that he was close enough to touch you. But let that go. Skeet lacks imagination. That's his chief trouble. He's a No. 2 man, not a No. 1!"

Champion cast another nervous glance toward the trees.

"They're likely to be here any moment!" he complained.

"Don't you be nervous," urged Tag. "Skeet got close enough, of course, to see the pair of us. And when he saw me cooking, he knew that I'd eat what I cooked. They know that I like my chuck, and they're right. They're going to come in, taking their time. They want to get me badly."

"And me," said Champion.

"There's a thousand on you; there's five on me," said Tag Enderby.

"Five thousand?" exclaimed Ray Champion.

"That's the news."

"By thunder, you're the cool one!" said Ray Champion, opening his eyes. "I'd certainly head for the other side of the world if I were you."

"You know, Ray," said Tag, "that the faster you run, the quicker you're caught."

Champion grunted.

"And when do we start?" he repeated for the tenth time.

"Now," said Tag. "Now they're closing in on us. Now they're somewhere yonder in the thick of the trees, and it'll take 'em half an hour to soft-shoe their way to this spot. Pack and start, old son!"

In five minutes they were under way, Tag leading up the margin of the creek where the soft sand muffled the sound of the steps. Their horses they kept on a long rein.

For a few moments, they went on until they came to one of the larger clearings, and there Tag set the example of mounting.

"They can follow that back trail!" said Champion. "It's as clear and as big as a headline in a newspaper."

"They'll follow it, but they won't make our speed," said Tag.

He led straight across the meadow, and into the trees on the farther side, angling off to the left.

"Wait a minute!" called Champion in a guarded voice. "You're cutting back toward the place where the Malleyites must have come into the woods. They're nearly at the camp, by this time, no matter how slowly they've gone. And—"

He stopped speaking. Before them, he could make out

the forms of several horses standing tethered among the brush. Tag headed straight on until they were among the mounts, and there Champion counted seven horses, as fine as ever he had seen in one group together.

Tag was already hastily undoing the lead ropes by which the animals were fastened, and Champion followed the example.

He only gasped, in his excitement: "What made you guess that they wouldn't have left a guard with their nags, Tag?"

"Because I thought that they'd take every gun they had to try to grab me," answered Tag. "I had an idea that they wouldn't leave any reserve. And they didn't. You know, old son, that the lucky fellow is the fellow who takes the chances. Now let's string away from here. And let's string fast. I hear something coming through the woods behind us, and it's not a wind, either!"

He started off at a canter, leading four of the horses, tied head to head, and Champion followed with the remaining three. They broke from the brush, crossed a hollow, mounted a slope, and were crossing the rounded crest of this beyond, when they heard the clang of a rifle behind them, and a bullet sang between them.

They looked back as they urged their horses forward, and Champion saw three riflemen rush out from the edge of the brush, shooting as they came.

The rim of the hill rose and shut out that picture, while Champion groaned with relief.

"That was a near thing, Tag!" he cried out, as they went on at an easy lope.

"Worked out like a time schedule," said Tag. "There's

nothing worse than having to wait for a train. Here, old fellow. You'd better stop and change to one of those other nags. They've got longer legs, and we have some riding to do today."

Champion obeyed. A little later, since his tired mustang held up the pace of the party, it was cut adrift. And they rolled along at a slashing gallop that thrust the miles swiftly behind them.

Ten miles they covered in this fashion. Then they changed to a pair of animals which had not yet been ridden. The rest were turned loose, and they struck away more northerly through the hills.

"Where are we aiming?" asked Champion.

"We are aiming at two marks," said Tag. "The first one is Derbytown, across the hills. I think if the boys start following our trail, they'll make up their minds, after a few miles, that we're leading out in that direction. And while they're in that mind, they'll head for the nearest place where they can pick up horses to follow us. Oh, they'll follow hard. There's not a one of 'em, from Skeet Raleigh down, that wants to see old Malley face to face with a report like the one they have to give now. Malley loves his horses more than he loves his men. And they've chucked away seven of 'em in a lump!"

He laughed happily.

"They'll drive away for Derbytown, I think. And in the meantime, we've got a pretty clear road ahead of us. Even if they know where were heading, they're pretty far behind us."

"And what's in your mind now? Will you tell me?"

"Malley's in my mind."

"He's in mine too, night and day. But where are we riding now?"

"To Malley."

"Hold on! You know where he is?"

"Sure. He stays denned up, most of the year. He's there now, waiting for reports, or scalps. He'd rather have our scalps, though, than any reports."

"D'you mean," asked Champion, "that you're aiming straight at his headquarters?"

"That's what I mean."

"Are you planning to kill a dozen or so of those thugs in one swoop?" demanded Champion, turning crimson with his excitement.

"You've got too strong an imagination," said Tag. "He hasn't got an army working for him. Never has more than a dozen, as a rule, around him. Well, a couple of his men are likely to be delayed around Indian Gulch, for a spell. And there's seven more back there in the woods. Probably he's got some more out on the trail. And my way of counting is—if the chances are with us—that we'll find Malley alone with the cook. There won't be another soul in any of the shacks."

Champion cleared his throat. But he changed his mind and his speech.

"I'll tell you what," said he. "There's a grand chance for a finish, in this thing. You're all brass, Enderby. But the luck seems to be with you. I'd never think of a job like this. I'd never make this sort of plan, but perhaps you're right."

"What sort of plan would you have in mind?"

"Well, I'd find where the headquarters were, and then I'd lie low and wait until I had a chance to see Malley himself come out into the open, and then I'd have it out with him, man to man!"

"Would you?"

"That's what I had in mind."

"Malley's not a man. He's a beast," declared Tag. "But let that go. We're not far from headquarters, right now. In fact, I think we'd better stow the horses here in the brush, and go in on foot."

They put up the horses, therefore, in a thick grove, and then Tag dropped upon one knee, produced a pair of revolvers, and went over them rapidly. Champion, seeing that good example, followed suit at once.

Finally Tag stood up.

"Are you ready?" he said.

His voice had changed. There was a terse ring and snap to it, like a thrumming upon strings drawn to too high a pitch. Champion glanced aside at him in some wonder. It was a situation sufficient to make any man's nerves uneasy, but he had begun to feel that Tag Enderby was beyond nervousness.

The conception put new spirit in him. He had been badly frightened before, but now he was as steady as a clock. A warm thrill of pride went through him. Perhaps he, not Tag, would be able to cut the Gordian knot of their problem when the time came for the final action.

"I'm ready," said he.

Tag nodded at him, with a smile that came and suddenly went out again.

"You've got the real stuff in you," he said. "I thought so at the start, and the first hunch is the right hunch, every time."

He led on rapidly through the trees, which thinned, thickened, thinned again, and finally through the clustered trunks, Champion could see the bright sunshine of a clearing beyond. On the edge of this, Tag paused to take stock.

~26~
In Malley's Den

THERE were four small shacks about the clearing, three of them almost totally concealed in the brush and trees, and one, a little larger than the other, standing well out by itself.

"That's Malley's own den," said Tag. "He lets the boys come in and out sometimes. I used to bunk in there myself. But that's a special honor!"

He grinned.

"I was a star of the order, Ray," he muttered.

Champion said nothing. He was straining his eyes toward the shacks.

"There's somebody in that nearest one—there to the right among the trees," he said.

"That's where Ban lives," said Tag.

"Who's Ban?"

"The cook."

"Nobody else with him?"

"Nobody, except at mealtimes. Nobody would ever want to be in the same room with Ban, except at mealtimes. He's alone now, cooking."

"What about the other shacks?"

"You have eyes. Use 'em. I'd like to know the answer to that myself."

"I don't see a living thing, except the horses at the far end of the clearing."

"Five horses," counted Tag. "That looks as though there's not a soul here. You don't see a fat chunk of a man down there among them, do you? Malley spends a great deal of time patting and petting 'em. He's pretty nearly a human being—when he's with dumb brutes!"

"I don't see any man near 'em."

"Then we'll take a flyer at his shack. Can you walk soft? No, you can't, and he could hear a clock tick a mile away. Walk right behind me. Step in the prints that I leave behind me. He's probably sitting in the sun on the steps in front of the place!"

With that, he started out at once, and Champion followed, stepping exactly where the footfalls of the other had left an imprint in the grass. With small, dainty steps Tag proceeded, and so they approached the shack from the side. When they came to the corner of the little house, Tag stepped out wide of it. Two guns were gleaming in his hands.

And before Champion could step out into the same line, he heard a deep, gruff voice saying:

"Why, hullo, Tag. There you are, eh? I've been expecting you for quite a while."

Then Champion came into view of the squat, shapeless hulk of Malley seated in the sun and whittling rather aimlessly at a stick.

"And old Ray Champion, too," said Malley, and gave a smile and a nod to the last-comer.

Red rage covered the eyes of Champion with a film.

He could not speak for a moment, and before words

came to him, he heard Tag saying:

"Wouldn't want to keep you out here in the glare of the sun, Dan. Suppose that we step inside for a minute?"

"Sure," said Malley, and rose.

"Just walk a little slowly," said Tag. "I like the look of you better when you're moving slowly."

"Because you know that an old man don't look too good when he hurries," said the other. "You know that. You were raised, Tag.

"That's what you were. You were raised pretty good. You got nacheral manners, too."

He lumbered up the steps as he spoke, and Tag Enderby and Ray Champion entered closely behind him into the house. To Champion, it seemed that a miracle had been worked. Far away on the plains, in Grove City, it had seemed a hopeless task, looking up toward the blue mountains and thinking of Dan Malley, and the power of men and of distance that surrounded him. But doors had been opened by magic, in between, and here they were, face to face, and with their guns carefully covering the celebrated outlaw.

Dan Malley had not lost color. Neither did his smile seem in the least forced.

"Why the guns, boys?" said he. "You wouldn't be here at all if Skeet hadn't got to you with my message."

"Hold on," said Tag. "Did Skeet go out with a message to us?"

"Skeet? Why, of course he did," said the other. "Who would I send but Skeet when I had a tricky pair of boys to spot, and a message that needed delivering?"

"What was the message, Dan?" asked Tag, in the most

friendly of voices.

"Why, it was just that I was tired of having a merry-go-round with you, Tag. You meant too much to me. You and me, we been too close to fall out about nothing. About Champion? Well, I was sorry for Champion, too. I didn't blame him for being pretty hot at me. But what would you have a desperate man do, Ray? You know how it is. Rough men take rough ways. Now you're out, and I'm glad you're out. Maybe I wouldn't 'a' cared whether you were friends or not, except that you got Tag along with you. But that was too much. I had to have Tag back. First, I was pretty wild at him. I put money on the head of him. Would you believe that, Tag?"

"That's hard to believe," said Tag, shaking his head.

"It's true, though."

"How much?" asked Tag.

"Five-thousand-dollars!" said the outlaw.

He sighed.

"Imagine how I was feeling about you, Tag, when I done a thing like that!"

"Imagine!" said Tag.

"A fellow gets excited," explained the outlaw.

"Yeah, that's it," said Tag. "A fellow gets excited."

"Skeet didn't even want to go. I guess he told you that."

"I didn't see Skeet."

"What? You didn't see Skeet? Why, old son, you mean that you really understood, without seeing him, that there was no sense in having a war with me?"

Tag Enderby suddenly smiled, and the sight of his smile wiped the pretended pleasure from the face of Dan Malley.

"I didn't see Skeet, but Ray Champion did. He saw Skeet

sneaking away through the trees. 'Away' from us, Dan."

"Don't know what could have been the matter with Skeet," said Malley. "Can't imagine! He's smart, but he ain't got real nerve or real brains. He's just tricky, like a trained dog, or a monkey."

"There was nothing the matter with Skeet," insisted Tag. "We finished breakfast in a bit of a hurry after Champion had seen your hound on the trail. We rode around the boys, and while they were stalking our camp, we got to their horses and rode off with 'em. They came back from the trees just in time to see us go over a hill."

"You shouldn't have ridden away," urged Dan Malley, with much earnestness. "You should have stayed right there and chummed up with the boys. They only meant friend-ship—"

"That's exactly why they stalked us so carefully, I guess," said Champion.

"That's why they shot at us, as we went over the hill," added Tag Enderby.

Malley shrugged his fat shoulders.

"Well," he said, "they shot at you, did they?"

"But you tell a good lie while you're about it," answered Tag.

"Ray, just step up and shove a gun into his stomach. I want to take a look at that safe."

Champion willingly leaned the muzzle of a Colt on the bulge of Malley's stomach. Tag went to the safe.

"You know, Tag," said Malley, "that there's no use throwing yourself away. Sure I've lied to you. But the reason that I could lie so good was that the moment I clapped eyes on you, to-day, I really was glad, in spite of the guns you held on me. I was glad. I saw that your proper place was back here with me and the boys. I didn't feel mean about you. I just wanted you back."

"I'll bet you did," murmured Tag Enderby, already on his knees before the safe and fingering the combination.

"If you rob me and the boys, son," said Malley, "they'll never forgive you. They'll trail you to the end of time. You know that?"

"Shut him up," said Tag to Champion. "If the old goat keeps on blatting, knock him over the head. I have to do some listening in, just here."

He pressed his ear close to the combination, and began to turn the disk slowly, delicately. Champion saw shining sweat roll down the face of Malley.

A light metallic click came from the little safe, and then the soft groaning of hinges.

"Tag!" muttered Malley, out of great anguish of heart.

Tag was dumping on the floor the contents of a canvas sack, the total which the safe contained.

"Yes, Dan?" said Tag.

"Are you going to rob us, Tag?" gasped Malley.

Tag looked up with a grin.

"Rob you, Dan?" he repeated slowly.

Then he went on with a rapid counting of the money, which consisted of a quantity of gold and silver, plus many small sheafs of paper money, and bound with brown-paper wrappings.

"Tag," said Dan Malley, "there's the savings of years and years in that safe! There's the money that I've thought for and rode for and planned for and fought for. Are you actually going to rob me of that?"

"You know, Dan," said Tag, cheerfully, "that you've never done a lick of 'honest' work for the whole caboodle."

Malley groaned.

"It's mine, Tag," said he. "It's my honest share, that's what it is. I've never beat any of the boys out of their parts of the loot. And everything in there is what really is mine. I ask you as a man, Tag. You're a brave boy and a wonderful boy. You're going to make a fortune any time that you want to. But remember that I'm old. I ain't going to be able to make a new start. That's my 'life' that you're adding up so free and easy, passing under your fingers there!"

"It's a fat life and an easy life," said Tag. "There's two hundred grand in there, and even more, old son!"

"That ain't much," protested the sweating Malley. "Put that out at interest—I'm going to retire, pretty soon—and it wouldn't be more than eleven, twelve thousand a year. Just enough to run a pleasant home. You know that! And—well, you'd always find a room in that home for you, Tag. What's that money to you? You'd blow it in a year. It'd be dead leaves on the wind, to you. To me, it's everything, and—"

"There's enough," said Tag, "to make you afford the five thousand bucks that you put up on my head. I can understand that, all right."

"Listen, Enderby!" broke in Champion. "What's that outside?"

For a sound of voices was drifting across the clearing toward Malley's shack.

~27~
A Bright Pair

T AG swept the contents back into the canvas bag, threw it against the wall near the door, closed the door of the safe, and whirled the combination.

Malley, his face a strange green-gray, looked steadily toward the sack. He seemed to have no thought of life, but only of his money.

"Watch that fat sucker, Ray," urged Tag. "I'm going to step out and have a chat with the boys."

"They'll shoot you!" exclaimed Champion.

"It's a chance. We've got to take the chance, I think, if we want Malley's money, and his scalp, too. Watch him, though. If he lets out a yip from in here, shoot him dead as a cold shrimp. Then jump for the door and try to give me a hand, because I'm going to be working pretty hard and fast out there. They'll have the drop on me from the start—"

As he spoke—and still speaking—he walked through the door and down the steps. A startled cry broke out from one of the two men who were walking across the meadow.

"Enderby!"

"It's Tag!" exclaimed the bigger of the two.

And the pair of them produced long Colts, ready for action.

"Hullo, Grey," said Tag Enderby. "Hello, Stew," he added to the larger.

They were both mere youngsters, in their later teens, withal hardy specimens as mountaineers.

"Look at him!" said Grey, the smaller youth. "Calm as you please! Go on and roll a cigarette, Tag, and show how much you're at home."

"I've just finished a smoke," said Tag, with much good nature. "What's the matter with you boys? D'you think that the war's still on between me and Dan Malley?"

"Yeah, I think there's five thousand dollars' worth of war still on between you," said Stew, grimly. "And I mean to get that coin. What say, Grey?"

"I'm saying just that," said Grey.

"I see," said Tag. "You kids haven't grown up yet. You think I'd be here, walking around and taking the air, and still having my little war with Malley?"

"You can talk," said Stew, "but you can't say all that's in the mouth of a Colt, Tag! You stand still and say your prayers!"

"Hold on," said Grey. "Let's have Dan's word on this. It's kind of funny to see Tag walking around here on the green."

"Tag's always doing something funny," insisted Stew. "That's his way! Fresh, is what he is."

"I'm going to yip to Dan, anyways," said Grey. "Hey, Dan!"

There was no answer.

Tag Enderby measured a hundredth part of a second in his mind, wondering if he could get out his guns and at least die fighting.

"Hey, Dan!" called Grey again.

Still there was no answer.

"Go on and yell again," said Tag Enderby, forcing a grin. "You keep trying and you'll get an answer, after a while. You'll get a boot chucked at your fool head, spurs and all!"

"What's the matter with Dan then? Is he dumb?" asked Stew.

"What's generally the matter with him?" asked Tag. "What's generally the matter when he has to split up a haul, and figure out how much he can keep for himself, the old hog?"

"You've made a haul, have you?" asked Grey, his eyes glistening.

"Yeah. Why else would I be here?"

"He's made a haul," said Stew. "Dog-goned if he don't look pretty satisfied, too. How big a haul, Tag?"

"Oh, just a couple of hundred thousand. That's all!"

"Great guns!" groaned Grey. "Two-hundred-thousand dollars, you say?"

"It ain't possible! said Stew. "The whole mountains would be filled with the noise of an explosion like that!"

"There hasn't been time. The cat's not far enough out of the bag, boys," said Tag Enderby. "You'll be hearing the details before long."

"Where'd you get the coin?" asked Grey, keen with curiosity.

"Out of a safe," said Tag.

"Come on and loosen up," urged Stew. "Where'd you get it?"

"A mighty short ride from here," said Tag.

"Over at the Crossing!" exclaimed Grey. "I'll bet that was it."

"I'm not talking," said Tag. "The chief can talk, when he feels like it. I'm a fool to have come back here with the loot, though. Two hundred thousand would be enough to last me."

"Not you, Tag," said Stew. "You'd have it all blown in a year. I've seen you chuck the long green away."

"Go on and give Dan another call," said Tag, yawning. "He'll be glad to hear your sweet voice, Grey, right in the middle of his figuring."

"I'd rather look at the new moon over my left shoulder than call to the old pig while he's adding up loot," admitted Grey. "He'll beat you out of something, Tag."

"He always beats everybody out of a little," answered Tag. "You know that!"

"Playing your kind of a lone hand," said Stew, "it's a funny thing to me that you keep playing with Dan Malley. Why d'you do it?"

"Because Dan has a brain, and he gets the fat jobs all staked out for me," answered Tag.

"This one? Did he have it ripe for you?"

"I just shook the tree, and the plums fell down," said Tag, smiling at the thought. "It was the easiest haul that I ever made."

"You took some big chances though, I guess."

"Sure, I took some chances. You've always got to take chances, though."

"You're always taking the long chances," said Stew, shaking his head with a wisdom graver than his years. "And one of these days, you're going to get it in the neck, in the soft bend of the neck, at that. You mark what I'm telling you!"

"I'll mark, and you keep telling," said Tag. "Well, I'm going to slope back inside and see what's coming to me."

"Don't you let him hand you anything less than forty per cent," said Grey.

"Fifty, you oughta have, working the game all by your-self," said Stew. "Otherwise it's a dog-gone robbery!"

"It's a robbery already," answered Tag. "Forty to me, forty to the rest of the boys. And twenty per cent to the chief. I suppose that'll be the way. It usually is."

"It's hard on you, Tag," said Grey. "But it's pretty sweet for us. Great Scott! That's eighty thousand to split in the gang, and that's about six-seven thousand apiece! This is a mighty clear day for the rest of us, Tag!"

"Yeah, you oughta remember this day," commented Tag. "I'll go on in now, and see what's what. You boys coming on in, too?"

"And get our heads chopped off by old Dan? I guess not." said Grey, and he grinned broadly.

"I'll be seeing you later then," said Tag.

"We'll see you as you scoot for a party," said Stew. "I know your habits after you've made a haul, Tag!"

He laughed, and Grey joined him. Then the pair saun-tered away across the meadow, and Tag, drawing his first deep breath in some moments, went back toward Malley's shack.

As he came up the steps, he heard a murmured cursing that flowed from the lips of Dan Malley.

"You heard those bright boys?" asked Tag, as he stepped back into the house.

"That was a great play, Tag!" breathed Ray Champion. "I thought you were cooked, for a minute!"

"The blockheads!" groaned Malley. "The wooden-headed, hollow-brained idiots! Five thousand dollars right under their guns, and they couldn't pull their triggers! I got a parcel of fools when I got the half-baked lot of saplings that I'm working with now! Halfwits—and robbers!"

He glared at Tag.

"If I'd been out there—" said Malley, through his yellow teeth.

"You would have socked a chunk of lead right between my eyes, Dan," said Tag, "and that's what we're going to do for you."

"Fire a gun in here, and your jig will be up," said Dan Malley, his teeth clicking. "The boys will sure know that there's something wrong, and they'll nail you!"

Tag nodded.

"See any way out of this mess, Ray?" he asked. "We can't shoot him without giving a regular alarm."

"I don't know," muttered Champion, staring bitterly at Malley. "All I know is that he has to die to-day!"

"Youngsters are always bitter," sighed Dan Malley. "There ain't much forgiveness in young men. I'll tell you why—it's because you boys ain't lived long enough. You ain't seen the ups and downs of life. You ain't seen the truth. Life's a fairy story to you still, and it's full of golden princes, and full of old wizards and witches. But the real world is a mixture. Everybody's part good and part bad. You've seen mostly my bad side, Ray. But Tag, here, he's seen a lot of my good side. I'm kind of surprised about you, Tag. I wouldn't 'a' thought it of you, to tell you the truth!"

"I'll bet you wouldn't," agreed Tag.

"No, I wouldn't 'a' thought it!"

"It'll be a knife between the ribs for him," suggested Tag Enderby. "That's the medicine for Malley!"

"Murder?" gasped Malley.

He stared from one of them to the other.

Ray Champion was shaking his head.

But Tag Enderby was smiling. A pleasant thought had suddenly come to him.

"I've seen the Canucks in Canada," said he, "work out a pretty good system. Two fellows grab by the left hand and hold fast. Then they fight with knives in the right. Ray, you want to see the old boy dead. Now's your chance. You wouldn't want to take advantage of your faster footwork. Just grab him by the hand, and fight it out the way I said. That suit you?"

Champion and Malley gazed fixedly at one another. In the eyes of Malley there was a rising glimmer. And Champion suddenly thrust out his combative chin.

"What do you say, Malley?" he asked.

"Why not?" answered Malley.

"That's what I say," answered Champion.

"If I win, what do I get out of it?" said Malley. "A fight with you afterwards?"

He glanced at Tag.

"Not unless you ask for it," said Tag.

"I don't ask to die—not that easy," said Malley. "You let me go if I win, Tag?"

"That's it."

"Then it's a go," said Malley. "Champion, stand up!"

~28~
A New Pack

THEY went about the preparations in perfect calm. Each man rolled up the sleeve of his right arm to above the elbow. Each was equipped with a large, long, and heavy hunting knife, razor-sharp. And beside them stood Tag Enderby, ready to superintend the fight.

He said to Champion: "Mind you, Ray—it's a fair fight."

Champion nodded.

To Malley, Tag added: "No foul cuts, Dan."

"What's a foul cut?" demanded Malley, scowling at his antagonist, not at the speaker.

"A slash at the left arm of the other fellow, for instance."

"Is that foul?" said Malley bitterly.

It was plain that he had contemplated exactly such a stroke to begin the fray!

"But, outside of that," said Tag, "you can pull and haul and trip and stab when and where you please. Only when the other fellow drops, you stand back. That's the rule of the game. Two rules won't choke you, Dan."

"I'd rather be without 'em," said Malley.

Suddenly he licked his lips.

"Stand up here, Champion!" he said.

A brutal fury was in his face. His lips kept moving, lifting a little upon the upper teeth. His eyes blared. His face was crimson.

"He looks like a butcher, Ray," said Tag. "But mind him—he's older than you are, and his reach isn't as long. Yet he can move his hand as fast as a snake strikes. Watch him hard. He may be a butcher, and he may do the carving to-day, too!"

"He may carve me," said Champion gravely. "And if he does, you'll have no more trouble—down there?"

He nodded in the direction of far-off Grove City.

"If you drop," said Tag Enderby, "that's the end of you with her, I suppose. If you drop, I'll have to wait a little longer for her; that's all. But not so very long, at that, I think. She's tired of you already," he added cruelly. "She'll forget you pretty fast, Ray!"

Champion stared at him with a rather dull eye.

"If I die," he said, in his quiet, deep voice, something like a growl of a dog, at a distance, as it works up its temper and suspicions for a fight, "Malley will die with me. He may carve me, but I'll cut his throat for him, and split his heart, before I die."

He extended his left hand.

"Here's my hand, Dan," he said.

They gripped hands.

"Wait till I give the word," broke in Tag.

"We'll wait," said Malley, his mouth still working with passion. If there were fear in him about the result of this savage battle, he dropped all show of it, at once. The exultation at the thought of bloodshed swept him away.

Said Champion, his deep voice a little louder:

"I've waited for three years of prison, thinking about the time when I'd square up to you, Malley. Now the time's come. And I thank fate—and Tag Enderby, who brought me here!"

"I'm ready and waiting," said Malley. "Are we going to hold off all day long, for talk?"

"Are you ready, too, Ray?" asked the other.

"I'm ready, too," said the other.

"Wait half a second," said Tag.

He raised his head. He stood stiff, looking up, fastening all his effort in the attempt to hear at a distance.

"You hear that?" he asked.

Only then could the duller organs of the others perceive,

far off, a sound like the thrumming of drums, a vibration in the air, without resonance.

"Horses!" gasped Champion.

"Aye, horses, and coming lickety-split," said Tag.

"Give the word! Give the word!" exclaimed Malley. "We can have this here finished off in a couple of seconds, no matter who comes after that. I've wanted to have the slicing of your bull throat, Champion. I dunno why I hate you. I just do, and that's a good enough reason for me. I'm going to stick you like a pig, and see you kick on the floor, and bleed, and choke, and your eyes pop out while you try for just one more breath."

He drew in his own breath deeply, with a whistling sound.

"Give the word, Enderby!" he repeated with a savage insistence.

"Steady, partners," said Tag, shaking his head. "There's a new pack for this deal—and no one knows what the game will be. It hasn't been named yet, but I think that it's a Malley deck!"

As he spoke, the thrumming of the hoofs drew nearer, and then broke out with a heavy hammering across the meadow. Tag sprang to the door and saw seven riders sweeping in, and the leader was the narrow-shouldered form of Skeet! Skeet saw him at the same instant, and tried a snap shot that neatly lifted the hat from Tag Enderby's head as he leaped back and slammed the door with a crash.

Malley, rocking back on his heels, as though overwhelmed by a wave of joy, uttered a long, whooping cry of triumph.

Then he exclaimed: "The boys are here! I might 'a'

knowed that Skeet would pick up the trail and get fresh hosses pretty fast. He oughta be a general, he ought. He's general enough to suit me! You get down on your knees, Tag, and you, Champion, and you start praying to me for mercy now, will you? And then see me kick you in the faces, the way you've been kicking me!"

Champion, overmastered with blind rage, struck full at the face of the outlaw, but Tag knocked the blow to one side. The next instant, he had pinioned the arms of Malley behind his back with a length of rope.

"You fool!" shouted Malley. "Are you still going to try to make a fight of it? Don't you feel the lead already slamming through your bones, breaking 'em like straws?"

"I feel that we've still got you inside our hands," answered Tag. "And that's about enough for me!"

He turned to Champion.

"Watch that window at the back of the house. Watch from it, but don't show your face at it. They're scattering around, and those boys can shoot. Believe me when I tell you that. They can shoot like the devil, and they'll pick you off if they have only a fast glimpse at you!"

Champion nodded.

From the outside, there was a chorus of war whoops that rang through the air, Indian cries and yells that curdled the blood of the two defenders in the house.

Malley, sitting down, regardless of his helpless position with his hands behind his back, began to laugh heartily, rocking from side to side in an ecstasy of mirth and complacent expectation.

"Look here, Tag," called Champion, from the rear window. "There's a fellow coming, walking behind two horses, and showing a white handkerchief on a stick. What about that?"

"Flag of truce, eh?" said Tag. "You see, Dan? They're thinking about your own neck. They want to know if it's broken yet! That's what I call a pretty considerate family of boys that you have."

"They're going to eat you," said Dan Malley, shaking with fury as he looked back at Tag. "They're going to swallow you whole. D'you hear me say it, Tag?"

"Maybe they will," said Tag.

He added: "Knock the window open, will you, Ray?"

This was accordingly done, and standing well back in the room, so that its shadow would protect him while he looked the more easily out into the brilliance of the sunlight beyond, he shouted:

"Who's there?"

The flag of truce waved violently.

"Skeet!" came the rather shrill answer.

"All right, Skeet. Whatcha want?"

"I wanta know if Dan Malley is still in there with you boys?"

"I'm here—safe and sound!" roared Dan Malley. "Burn 'em out! Cut their throats for 'em! I'm going to make you rich, Skeet! I'm going to be a father to you!"

"He's there, all right," said Skeet. And though he did not speak his thought loudly, it was audible inside the shack.

"Shall I gag Malley?" asked Champion of Tag, looking gravely at their captive.

"Every good stroke you do for me now," said Malley, "is going to get the two of you off a lot easier. And every bad stroke that you do for me now is going to cost you yards of hide, peeled off slow, and burned!"

"You'd be a good cook, Dan," said Tag. "I always knew that you'd shine at a job like that—toasting people. I think you've done it before, haven't you, to make 'em tell where they'd hid their money?"

"A white man gets white treatment out of me," Malley growled. "But if you boys try to make too much trouble now—"

"Let him alone," said Tag Enderby to Champion, "but if he shouts again, just bash in his face with a gun. That's all."

He spoke gently, almost tenderly. He actually smiled upon Malley, and the latter, under the influence of this voice, shook his head, blinked and straightened. He looked like a man who has suddenly sobered himself by a plunge into icy water.

But some of the beast had gone out of his face. He reined himself in, and muttered, yet none of his words were audible.

Outside, from the shelter of the horses, Skeet was calling: "Tag!"

"Well?" said Tag.

"Turn the chief loose, and we'll make a good deal with you."

"Will you make the deal after I've turned him loose?" asked Tag.

"Sure," said Skeet. "We've got the upper hand here. We've got a right to dictate terms, I guess."

"Well," answered Tag, "you'll have to think again, old-timer. I figure that I'm still on top of the deck here."

"You think again," cried Skeet. "We can burn you out of there like nothing at all."

"If you roast us, you roast Malley," said Tag.

"Maybe we will," said Skeet. "But we're sure going to get you, young feller. You thought you'd made a fool of us today. You didn't know that we'd spotted a second string of hosses back in the country, did you?"

"You're a smart fellow, Skeet," said Tag.

"I'm smart enough to trim your beard for you," shouted Skeet. "Turn Malley loose!"

"Not much," said Tag calmly, and slammed the window shut, to indicate that the negotiations were ended, for the moment at least.

~29~
The Powwow

SKEET they could hear withdrawing. His retreat could be followed as the course of a bomb is known by the smoke that splutters from it in the air. The smoke in this case was the hot language of Skeet. Inside the shack, Dan Malley had slumped down into a chair and was sneering and snarling—but in utter silence. Ray Champion stood in a dark corner, his eyes fixed upon the hated face of the outlaw. But Tag Enderby was busily rattling at the stove, as he built up a fire and turned his attention to cookery. There was the usual great iron pot of beans, at the back of the stove, and the lid of this he lifted, and sniffed at the contents.

"No garlic in that," he said. "Can't eat beans without garlic, Dan, you know."

"Go and choke yourself, for all of me," said Malley. "You're the bright, and sleek, fancy young feller, ain't you?

Well, you've got yourself collared and bogged down now, and I wanta sec you get yourself out of the mess."

"Do you?" said Tag. "Where's the bacon, Dan?"

"Not on 'your' ribs!" cried Malley.

"That's because I've thinned myself and dieted myself, Dan," said the cheerful Tag, "to be lighter, and all for the sake of your horses that I've been riding. That's why I keep myself so lean. All on account of your horses, which is another way of saying on your account, Dan. Because I suppose your horses mean more to you than you mean to yourself. Am I wrong?"

He had found the bacon, by this time, and he was slicing it with long and slashing strokes of a carving-knife. It was a big knife and a sharp one, but still the skill with which Tag made use of it was so remarkable that the outlaw chief looked on amazed and almost aghast, seeing the thin, translucent slices fall one upon the other.

"You like yourself," said Malley. "You're proud of yourself. You don't see that you've always been a fool. You've worked hard, and I've got all the real profits out of your work. It's me that's profited. You've blown your own. And now I hold the sack!"

He chuckled with satisfaction.

The other was slicing cold boiled potatoes into a frying pan, and laying the bacon in strips around the sides of the pan. He talked as he worked.

"You know, Dan," said he, "that I never knew you were such a short sport—such a tinhorn sport—before this. I'm a good deal surprised!"

"What do I care about your opinions?" asked Dan Malley. "Tell me that, you skinny question mark, will you?"

"What about taking a look around, Tag?" asked Ray Champion.

"We don't need to yet," said Tag. "The boys are off there talking things over. They're having a confab. In another few minutes, they'll be back. We can have lunch in the meantime, I hope."

Malley went back to his talk. He was taking a great pleasure in taunting his captors.

"I was saying, what does your opinion mean to me? Nothing, Tag. And it never 'did' mean anything. I've fed you along with flattery. I've praised you up a lot. But all the time I was laughing at you. You thought you were free. You were only a slave. A slave of mine. Working at the risk of your neck to fatten that canvas bag for me!"

The frying bacon and potatoes began to hiss and steam in the pan. The coffeepot was muttering over the fire.

"You're not a little shortsighted, are you, old son?" asked Tag Enderby of the outlaw chief.

"Shortsighted about just what?" asked Malley. "I can see through you, my smart boy!"

"That's the way you see it," said Tag cheerfully. "You don't understand that you've simply been a banker for me, all the time?"

"Me?" said Malley. "Me—your banker?"

"Certainly," said Tag. "Everytime I spent a dollar, I did it with a free conscience. You know why?"

"Because you're a nacheral fool," declared Malley.

"No, no," said Tag. "But because I knew that you had laid up here two dollars for every one that I was spending. And so it was a real pleasure to do the spending, while I knew that you were doing the saving for me."

"Saving for you?" shouted Malley. "I never saved a penny for you, and I never would 'a' saved a penny. My plan was to keep you riding wild—in between jobs. Sooner or later, you'd break your neck. I didn't much care when. I got tired of your lip, if you wanta know the truth!"

"Well," said Tag, "you could be a little politer. But I can't complain about you. Not really, when I see what you've done for me."

"What have I done for you? You tell me what I've done, except to show you where you could go and risk your head stealing?"

"That's what you've done for me," said Tag, as he slid the crusted mass of potatoes and crisped bacon onto a platter.

And he pointed with the iron fork he was holding toward the canvas sack that lay beside the door.

"I've done that for you, have I?" said Malley. "You'll never see a penny of it! Never! It's mine, my boy. It'll be mine when you're stretching a rope on one of them trees, outside there—unless I choose to say a good word for you to the boys. You ain't too popular with 'em—you never was, with your fighting ways and your sassy talk. It'll take a lot from me to save you. I dunno that I can do it!"

"Sit down, Ray," invited Tag Enderby. "You sit on that side of the table and I sit on this, and I'll beat you to the center of the platter. What say?"

They seated themselves, Champion uneasily looking about him toward the door, and then toward the window.

"It's all right," said Tag. "I know these boys. They're having their powwow now. They're like Indians. They can't go on the warpath till they've talked themselves out.

Eat hearty, Ray, because we're going to have a long ride ahead of us this afternoon. Malley here has some good horses for us to ride, and we'll have to burn 'em up regardless. Riding is hungry work, the way that I've found it."

He was eating as he talked.

"As if," put in Malley, "you was going to get away. You're kind of batty, Tag. But then, you always was, for that matter!"

"Oh, we'll get away," said Tag, as he and Champion polished the platter with chunks of pone, and then finished off their first cups of coffee. "We'll get away," he added, tilting back his chair and making a cigarette. "I'm only waiting till your boys come back to snoop around the shack, and then I'll tell them what's what. They'll let us go, fast enough."

"Go on," said Malley. "You tell me how you'll get away. You're going to take the money along with you, too, I suppose, by your way of thinking the thing out?"

"Yes, we're going to take that along with us, too," said Tag.

"You'll be in hell before you take that," said Malley.

"Hush!" murmured Champion, starting up from his chair.

Outside, they heard the snort of a horse close by.

"See who it is, Ray," said Tag lazily, as he lighted his smoke.

"It's a pair of horses in front of the house, and a pair behind it," said Champion.

"Men behind 'em?"

"Yes."

"The fools don't know we could shoot the horses, and then the men behind 'em. You have a bright lot with you,

Malley. But then it takes a fool to work for a fool. They haven't even sense enough to use you as a banker, Dan. For my part, I always intended to have the lining of that safe. I always aimed at it, and now it's as good as mine."

Dan Malley grunted with rage and disdain. Tag had stepped close to the front door.

"All right, boys," said he. "You've come just in time. I've finished lunch. What d'you want?"

"You can't come it over us like this any more, Tag," said the angry voice of Skeet. "We've got you, and you know that we've got you."

"And I've got Malley," said Tag.

There was an angry roar from Malley. Tag Enderby turned on him and said slowly, softly:

"If you open your mouth again, I'll shoot the words off your face. Remember that!"

The mouth of Malley closed like a trap. Unspoken rage, unuttered ideas swelled in him and turned his face purple and red, in spots.

"I wanta talk to Dan," said Skeet.

"Dan's not talking," answered Tag. "I'm doing the talking just now. I'm ready to make the bargain with you."

"Why should we make a bargain?" demanded Skeet. "We got you, ain't we?"

"You fool!" said Tag, with cold scorn. "What makes you think that you have us? We can wait till night, and cut Malley's throat, and slip away in the dark."

"We'll surround the cabin with bonfires!" said Skeet, his voice sharp and high.

"We'll shoot the heads off the men who tend the fires," answered Tag Enderby.

"You're going to make it a show-down, are you?" said Skeet.

"I'm making it a show-down now," answered Tag. "The game's in my hands. You fellows have to have Malley to keep you together. You and the rest have just been talking things over and you know what a lot of wrangling there was."

"Who told you about that?" demanded Skeet, with a falling voice.

"Nobody. I knew it. I know what a lot of saps you are. Now then, you need Malley. And you can have him. I wanted to bump him off, but now I can use him as a ticket for a getaway. I'm going to leave here, and take Malley with me to the edge of the woods. If you open up on me, on the way, I shoot a dose of lead into Malley. You understand?"

Malley writhed in his chair. He looked like a man dying of suffocation.

The woeful voice of Skeet called from outside: "It ain't any good trying to bluff you, Tag. I told the boys that you'd make a bargain, using Malley against us. And now you've gone and done it. You can go, Tag, but you leave Champion behind."

"Say that again," said Tag.

"Look here!" cried Skeet. "Don't be a hog! You can't have all the best of everything. You go clean, but we get Champion."

"We go together or not at all," said Tag Enderby.

"All right!" groaned Skeet. "I knew the way it would be. Dan Malley, you're a blockhead. You've spoiled everything!"

Leaving the Camp

D AN Malley, when he heard this insult, arose from his chair and seemed either about to scream out an answer or burst with emotion and pent-up speech.

He did neither. He slowly collapsed into the chair again, and emitted a hissing sigh. His head dropped upon his chest. He seemed to shrivel, like a punctured bag of wind.

Tag Enderby was making the final arrangement through the door, briskly and calmly. In ten minutes, he and Ray Champion and Dan Malley would leave the cabin in a group. They would then walk to the edge of the woods. None of the band must be in hiding. Ban, the cook, and nine other men were expected to be gathered in a group in the meadow. That would assure Tag against treachery. At the verge of the woods, he would turn Malley loose. Then the gang was as free as the wind to do all that it could to overtake the fugitives.

"You say that you'll turn Malley loose," said Skeet. "You always come clean when you was part of the gang. But how'll we trust you now, Tag?"

"You'll have to take that chance," said Tag. "I never lied before. Why should I start now?"

With that answer, Skeet appeared fairly well satisfied. They could hear the steps of retreating horses, then a sharp whistle sounded in the distance.

"You can talk a little now," said Tag almost kindly to Malley. "Only don't yell."

But Malley did not talk. He merely rolled his eyes, like

one in the grip of a vast agony that has sealed the lips. Screams were working in his throat, but they did not issue at the mouth. A repulsive picture he made as he sat there in the chair.

But he submitted passively to everything. It was now upon the canvas bag that he fixed his eyes, and he never glanced toward the human faces around him. From the distance, after a few moments, came the sharp, high voice of Skeet, wailing: "All right, Tag!"

Tag threw the door open. There they were, gathered in the center of the meadow, ten men, screened partially behind ten horses.

Said Tag, as he looked out on them:

"That would be sharpshooting for you, Ray—to clip off the legs of those fellows under the bellies of the horses. We could make them hop pretty fast to get out of that place, I tell you. But we've made the deal and we'll stick to it. Ready?"

He took the canvas bag under his arm. The muzzle of his revolver he laid in the small of Malley's back, and so, with Champion at the shoulder of the outlaw chief, they left the shack in a compact group and headed off toward the point in the wall of trees which was nearest to the spot where they had left their horses.

There was not a shot behind them; there was not a sound. The brightness of the flood of sunshine seemed to have frozen the very wind to stillness.

"From the edge of the trees," said Tag, "we have nearly a hundred yards to the spot where we left the horses, and after old man Malley is turned loose, they'll come for us on their horses like so many arrows off bowstrings. I'm going to carry this sack. It's heavier than you think. Pay no attention to me. Carry straight ahead and sprint like the devil all the way to the horses. When you get to them, loose the tie ropes, jump into your saddle, and have your rifle at your shoulder ready to take a few cracks at the boys on horseback, if they press in too close."

"I'll do everything you say," said Ray Champion.

They came to the edge of the trees, and Tag looked back. The ten men were ready, their reins gathered, prepared to leap into the saddle and bolt after the fugitives the moment that Malley was turned loose.

"Now, Dan," said Tag, "if I were your cut of a man, I'd put a slug through you, and turn you loose that way."

Malley looked blankly at him. At least, there was no fear in his face.

"But I'm not that cut of a man, as you know," said Tag. "Good-by, Dan, and thanks for the careful banking. All that I miss is the interest on the money."

Without replying, Malley turned slowly away toward his gang.

The other two were instantly off through the trees, leaning well forward, like true sprinters.

Champion had the speed which many stocky men possess—a great driving power for a short distance. But though he ran with all his might, Tag was very little behind him, in spite of the encumbrance of the sack of money. By the time Champion had loosed the horses and gained his own saddle, Tag was in his.

And it was his rifle that spoke first, fired not from the shoulder but from the ready position.

In answer, from the crashing line of riders who were

sweeping now through the brush and weaving among the trees, there came a loud scream of fear and of agony. A scattering of alarmed yells followed. They could see the horsemen split to the right and to the left. Then the pair, whirling their own mounts, were off.

Again Champion was in the lead, and his horse was fully as fine as that which Tag was riding, but the cunning jockeyship of the latter quickly put him ahead. He it was who showed the straightest way through those familiar trees, and then into the open. So thoroughly had the other riders been checked, that a full furlong of green, gently rolling ground was between the leaders and the pursued by the time the latter came out of the trees.

The Malley men were riding hard, flogging their horses to the fullest speed. For a mile or more they struggled. Then Tag, though the others had not gained, turned in the saddle and fired twice with his rifle. No one fell, but the center of the line was in confusion. Several of the riders pulled up their horses, and swerved to the right and the left. The whole group split in two; speed was lost. And a few moments later the chase was abandoned.

Tag instantly dragged the horse down to a walk. And Champion followed that example. He had formed the habit of looking constantly to his companion, in every emergency. And Tag accepted the responsibility without the slightest indication of annoyance.

He began to sing now, and when he finished his song, he was whistling.

"Where away now?" asked Champion.

"I don't know. Why not back to Grove City? That's home, Ray."

The other shook his head doggedly.

"Why not?" asked Tag.

"You've filled your hand with a fine fortune, Tag," said he. "And I'm glad of it. But this day's work means nothing to me, except to give me more appetite and less confidence. I don't know how I'll come out against Malley and his crew. But I'll never give up the trail till I've salted Dan Malley away. He's no man, Tag. He's a brute. He needs to die. He deserves to die!"

Tag Enderby nodded. "He needs to die, all right. But why not let him slide, Ray? You saw how it was. Killing him would not be much to Malley, now that his money's gone. This is his heart and soul—here in this sack. And you get a fifty-fifty split of it."

"I get a share of that?" said Champion surprised.

"A share? Of course you do. A full half."

"What did I do to gain the share?" asked Champion curiously.

"Why, man, you were there with me all the time!"

"I was lead around your neck," answered Champion. "You know that, and I know it. I was no help. You did everything. You did the acting, you did the thinking. You did the talking, too, and talked us out of the pinch. Don't tell me that I rate a share of that money!"

Tag frowned at him.

"You want to split straws, Ray," he declared. "But that's not the way that I've learned to do business. You get half of what's in this sack."

"Not a penny," said Champion. "I wouldn't have it."

"Soiled money, eh?"

"I'm simply not having any of it," said Champion.

Tag gaped at him, utterly amazed.

"What difference does it make to you where the money came from?" he demanded. "You take it and put it to a good use—that's all that you have to do!"

Champion suddenly smiled.

"Look here, Tag," said he. "When I work a month, hard, I get a pay check—a hundred dollars, say. Well, that money is mine. I've worked for it. It's really mine. But I haven't worked for this. I don't know anything about it. It's not mine. And I won't have it."

"Suppose that you found some buried treasure?"

"That wasn't buried treasure," answered Ray Champion. "That's thieves' money, and you know it!"

Tag flushed. He sat stiffly erect in his saddle, staring at the other, and Champion, gloomily frowning, looked straight back at him. There was not the slightest flinching in his gaze.

"You're making a fool of yourself," said Tag. "Here's money that will make you practically rich. A hundred thousand dollars, for your split! You can buy a ranch, and a mighty good one. You can marry. You can raise a family. You can live very comfortably and raise your children in style, too. That's the possibility that's in this sack, for you. And you say no to it!"

"I say no," repeated Champion.

"It's good enough for me, but not for you, eh?" said Tag Enderby, snapping out the words.

"It's good enough for you," answered Champion. "And it's not good enough for me."

"Great thunder, Champion," said Tag. "I've never taken anything like this before, and I'm not going to take it from you now!"

"You can leave it or lump it," said Champion, as terse as impolite. "I've said my say."

"I've half a mind—" exploded Enderby.

But he checked himself.

"Go on," said Champion. "Say it! Or if it's not saying, but shooting, start that. I'm ready. I've been ready from the start. You've done some pretty wonderful things. I've owed my life to you, and not one time only! You've kept me from prison, from murder twice. But I tell you that my hands are too clean to touch thieves' gold. It's all right for you, if you say so. You're used to taking chances. You can take this one, too. But it's not for me!"

"Molly wouldn't like it, eh?" said Tag.

Champion looked at him without anger, almost in pity.

"Tag," said he, "you're a child. You don't know the mind of Molly any more than a child knows the mind of the Almighty!"

And suddenly, with a cold and empty sense of loss, Tag Enderby knew that his companion was right!

~31~
At Indian Gulch

THEY went back to Indian Gulch, traveling slowly. As Tag pointed out, there was no use remaining around the vicinity of Malley's old headquarters. Now that the gang had been smoked in that place, they would be drifted on to a new place by their chief. And though Champion was desperately eager to stay right on the trail and come to grips with Malley, to wreak his old grudge to the full, still he could not help realizing that Tag was right when he advised moving to a distance and making a fresh start.

"We know his trail now," said Tag, "but he's got a dozen experts to put on 'our' trail. The best thing for us is to lose ourselves in a town, and then hit out again. We can send in the law to beat up the old headquarters, and the law may be able to do something worth while."

So finally Champion submitted to the new plan.

When they got to Indian Gulch, excitement swept out from around them as a storm center. The events of the other night, when Tag had bearded half the town and captured Tucker, were not, of course, forgotten. And the excitement had been redoubled on this morning for, the third day after his capture, Tucker, the outlaw, had lived up to his word and had come straight into the town and surrendered to Deputy Sheriff Locksley.

It was an incredible thing. There was something romantic about it that softened all hearts, and men gathering in the streets, in groups, no longer talked about hanging, but suggested the necessity of clemency in the law for men who were not so bad as they might have been.

The news from the new arrivals, Tag Enderby and Ray Champion, brought the excitement to a fever point. For they went straight to Locksley and told him where the hang-out of the Malley gang was situated.

As Locksley said: "It's going to be a long chase for nothing. I can swear in twenty good riders and good shots, and we'll go where you found those thugs, and when we get there, we'll harvest nothing but trouble. Malley won't stay put there."

"I'll tell you what," said Tag; "a gang is like an army.

You drive them far enough, and they lose heart. And if you keep that lot rolling, for a while, half of 'em are likely to get tired of the trail. Keep them rustling, and see what happens. You may pick up one or two, and even one or two would be a pretty fat reward for the ride, Locksley."

The deputy sheriff finally agreed. He invited the best men in the town and from the vicinity around it to join him, and within two hours a well-appointed body of nearly thirty riders had galloped out of the streets of Indian Gulch.

Tag watched them going with a broad grin.

"Old Malley is going to love us for this," said he. "You know that he's been lying up at ease there in the hills for so long that he's just about forgotten that there's such a thing as the law. Nobody's bothered him. And he likes comfort almost as much as he likes money and life!"

They were on the veranda of the hotel, as they watched the dust flying up into the air, dissolving on high, and leaving a thin mist between the houses down the street. Two or three loungers were near by, sunning themselves in the presence of the two new celebrities, when, up the street, came a dusty figure on a little rusty mustang.

When he was near enough so that the flopping brim of his hat did not mask the upper part of his face too much, they recognized Henry Benton. And he, recognizing them at the same instant, waved his hand and pulled up his horse. Then he dismounted, tethered the animal, and came slowly up the steps.

"He's got something pretty heavy on his mind," suggested Tag.

"He's got no mind to bear any weight," answered Champion, in contempt. "The infernal old bluffer! What makes you think that he has anything on his mind?"

"Because he's acting so nonchalant, and sticking his thumbs in the armholes of his vest and chewing on that toothpick so steadily. If he didn't have something important, he'd be more hurried. He acts as though he had a commission from the president to be a first-class fool!"

Mr. Benton drew near, unaware of the uncomplimentary nature of the remarks which were being made about him, sotto voce. He waved his hand jauntily to the pair. Then he shook hands with them, and took the nearest chair.

"Have a drink?" asked Tag.

"Why," said Benton. "I don't reckon that I will."

There was a muffled exclamation from Champion. He had started violently in his place, hearing this refusal, the first which he could recall from the lips of the older man.

"Liquor," said Benton wisely, "is all right when a man's got the leisure for it. But when a man's got his hands full, he don't want to be drinking. You know how it is."

"Your hands full, sir?" asked Tag.

"Yeah, they're tolerable full," said Benton.

"How come?"

"What with riding and worrying, and fretting and stewing, my hands are pretty full."

He shook his head.

"Riding and worrying, and fretting and stewing," said Tag, "are enough to fill anybody's hands. Only—what's brought you all the way up here to Indian Gulch?"

"Why, to tell you the truth, son," said Benton, "we got some stories drifting around, down there on the flat around Grove City, about how you was up here opening Indian Gulch wider than a tomato can in a tramp jungle. There was a lot of talk that came in every day, and every day's talk was louder and longer than the talk that had gone before. You know how such things are!"

"I know that it's easy to make talk out of nothing," said Tag.

"And I came up here to find you, finally," said Benton.

"You're a good trailer," said Tag. "You've come right smack onto me, as a matter of fact!"

"There was a time," said Benton, wagging his gray head with much content, "when I could trail like an Injun. I was known for it. When they got up a party to go snooping through the hills after robbers or hoss thieves, they always had me along. There was better riders, and there was better shots. But when it come to trailing, I didn't take my hat off to no man."

"Good for you," said Tag. And he added the charitable lie, "I think I've heard something about you on the trail."

"Have you?" said Benton, with an indubitable note of surprise in his voice. "Well, facts is facts, and they won't down. I was a good hand on a trail. Though it wasn't no trick to find you here, no more than to find a calf that gives you the light of its own bawling to steer you to it in the corral."

Tag Enderby smiled again.

"Well, here we are together," he said expectantly. "What made you want to catch up with me, Mr. Benton? Just curiosity?"

"There was a letter that I had for you," said Benton. "And though it wasn't a very fat letter, there was something about it that made me think that maybe you would want to see it pretty pronto. I mean, considering all of the things that had gone on before it was delivered at our house."

"I'd like to see it," said Tag, holding out his hand.

Benton removed an envelope from his pocket, but he did not surrender it at once. He made the most of the remaining circumstances. He said:

"It was delivered, but it wasn't no postman that brung it. It was delivered, but it wasn't delivered by day. Right during the night it was shoved under the door, and taking all of them things together, I thought that maybe you would want to see it pretty bad."

He tapped the envelope on his thumb nail for another moment, as though striving to find other elements worthy of remark, but discovering none, he finally handed the letter over to Tag with a sigh of regret.

Tag ripped it open and found within a fold of paper on which was scratched a single word:

Sorry!

There was no address, no signature. But that single word sent a chill down Tag's back, for he recognized the hand-writing of none other than the great Dan Malley!

He crumbled the letter, smoothed it again, stared at the single word, and then replaced the letter in his pocket.

Henry Benton observed his consternation with a delighted eye.

"Glad to get it, ain't you, son?" said he.

"I'm glad to get it, since it had to be written," said Tag. "Now, I'll tell you what, Benton, something makes me think that you're keeping things back from me."

"Me? I wouldn't do that."

"Nothing happened around Grove City that I'd be interested in?"

"You? Interesting to you?" murmured Benton thoughtfully.

He shook his head.

"No, nothing much," he decided.

"You're sure?"

"Dead sure. More interesting to Ray here, I'd say, then to you."

"What would be interesting to me?" snapped Champion, speaking for the first time.

"A thing, son," said Henry Benton, "that ain't easy for me to talk about. A thing that I'd better go off and talk with you alone about, if the facts have got to be stated."

"You can talk in front of Enderby," said Champion. "I've no secret in the world from him." Then he added: "Is it about Molly?"

"Ay," sighed the father, "Molly's no more—"

The two youths rose suddenly from their chairs.

"She's dead!" said Enderby, the only one to speak.

Benton nodded gloomily.

"Likely dead," he said. "As likely dead as not. Why not? But what I meant, first off, is that Molly ain't no more at home!"

Champion leaned forward. His voice was deep with huskiness as he said:

"Will you try to tell us exactly what happened?"

Benton made a gesture of surrender with both hands.

"What happens when salt dissolves in water? First you see it, and then you don't," he declared. "And the same way with Molly. Along comes the dark of the night. We hear her singing in the front room, and then we don't. We go to fetch her, but her voice is gone, and Molly's gone, too—soaked up in the middle of the night."

"Is that all you know?" Tag asked.

"It ain't much," said Benton, "but it's all that I know. It's a kind of a shock to me, now that I'm—"

"How does your wife take it?" asked Tag.

"Hard. Hard and silent, and white in the face," said Benton. "That's how she takes it."

"You're a great trailer, Benton. Did you find any sign around the house to start you thinking?"

"No, sir, I didn't find any sign around the house to start me thinking. I done my share of looking."

"You told the sheriff?"

"Sure I told him. I rode right into town and I told him all about her, beginning with the singing and winding up with the silence."

Tag threw his letter to Champion. And, as the latter stared down at the single word, Tag explained:

"It's Malley. I thought that there was no danger. How he could know that I'd be hurt in that direction, I can't tell! It's a mystery to me! But he guessed, and his guess was right! It's Malley!"

"D'you mean," said Champion, "that to knife us, he'd harm—"

"Not murder, old son. No, not that. Not that yet. He's simply holding up his hand and warning us to hold off. If we push on in, he'll finish—"

"Malley?" said Benton sharply. "What has Malley to do with all of this?"

Tag turned on the father.

"You tell me, Benton," he said, "what you think is the reason for Molly's disappearance, will you?"

Benton smiled and then stroked his mustache with some complacence.

"There is girls and girls," he said. "There is some that don't mind grubbing and slaving. There's some that do it, and don't say nothing, but the bitter is inside of 'em, working. And Molly's one of them. She's been a slave the most part of her life. My ship ain't come in. She ain't had a chance to live right. And her ma has always been nagging, keeping her at work, you see?

"Well, I ain't saying nothing—I wouldn't wanta hurt the feelings of Ray here. Only—young Mays, the son of the banker, he come home the other day, and he was right fetched by Molly's pretty face, like he'd been before this. Well, Mays, he goes right out of town again, the next morning—and that same night Molly has disappeared. I ain't saying nothing—only it wouldn't be a big surprise to me if I heard that the pair of them was married and hopping off for Paris, or St. Louis, or some other place!"

He could not help smiling, though he maintained the frown of regret upon his brow.

Champion looked in disgust toward Tag, but he was surprised to see neither anger nor impatience in the other's look. For Tag regarded the older man with a sort of gentle sympathy; at the same time it was plain that he studied Benton as a scientist might study a strange specimen.

"Perhaps you're right," he said to Benton. "Perhaps it's Mays. She'd make a wife for a banker, at that!"

"Ay, and wouldn't she, though!" cried Benton, slapping a hand upon his knee. "Would she be the makings of a fine banker's wife, I'm asking you?"

He turned with an air of apology to Ray Champion.

"Not that I'd wanta see you broke up none, Ray," said he.

Champion, his face like iron, said not a word.

"In a carriage, behind a pair of fine high steppers—with a fox fur around her throat—I guess Molly would look pretty well like that, Benton, wouldn't she?" persisted Tag Enderby.

"Wouldn't she though?" cried Benton, beaming. "Ah, there was always a light in her that I could see shining, but the glass was smoked with mean poverty; other folks, they couldn't see what I seen in her."

"I have to speak to Champion a moment," said Tag, drawing the other aside.

"The old fool!" said Champion, muttering through his teeth.

"Partly old fool, and partly old father," said Tag. "He's not so bad. I rather like him. Malley's the fellow we have to think about now, though."

"We should have finished off Malley when we had him there in the cabin," declared Champion, his jaw thrusting out in the familiar way. "We should have killed the devil and taken our chances in getting away in the dark, as you suggested."

"We never would have gotten away," answered Tag. "That was all bluff on my part. Those fellows are wild cats. They see in the dark, every one of them. It's easy to look back at the pinch and see how we might have done better, but when the time came, all we could think of was how the pinch was hurting."

"I don't complain of you; I complain of myself," said

Champion. "There's the truth for you. Now what's next? 'Is' there any next?"

"We have to put our heads in the lion's mouth," said Tag. "He's inviting us to keep clear away—or else to follow the trail into the trap that he's set for us. And that's what we've got to do."

"We might as well jump off a cliff," said Champion. "He'll be ready for us, the old fox!"

"He'll be ready," admitted Tag, "but you and I have to take that chance. Everything is chance, anyway. Keep Benton here while I try a scheme that I have in mind."

"Keep Benton here?"

"Yes."

"I'd rather talk to the wind."

"Maybe. But keep him here. Head him back for Grove City if you can. I have a job on my hands."

"What sort?"

"I'll tell you afterwards, if it works."

Champion grunted assent, and Tag, leaving the hotel, hurried to the jail. Since the deputy sheriff was not in town, the jailer himself was the highest authority. This one was an old sourdough whose wooden leg kept him from prospecting any longer his beloved distant reaches of the mountains. His disposition was far more ruined than his leg. Gloomy and set of face, he glowered upon Tag.

One hand grasped the knob of the jail door, which he had opened only a few inches.

"Whatcha want?" he asked, after sweeping Tag with an unfavorable glance.

"I want to see Tucker," said Tag.

"You can't," said the jailer.

He closed the door.

Tag knocked again. This time the voice called from within: "Without no order, you can't see him, and the deputy ain't around to give no order. Don't bother me!"

"I want to see Tucker," Tag repeated.

"Say, who are you?" roared the jailer, in a rage.

"My name is Enderby."

The door was jerked open.

"Him that took Tucker in the hotel? You lie!" said the frank old sourdough.

"I'm the one who took Tucker," said Tag.

"You're Tag Enderby, are you?"

"Yes."

"You don't look it," said the jailer.

"It's not much to look, after all," said Tag.

Suddenly the jailer grinned.

"Well," he said, "I guess that you're him. Come on in."

He widened the door, he even shook hands, and grinned again.

"Name of Peters," he said.

Tag said that he was glad to meet Peters.

"Now whatcha want to see Tucker about?" asked the jailer.

"I want to pass the time of day with him," answered Tag. "And I want to ask him a few questions."

"About what? I gotta know. It's my duty."

"I know that. You can come right along and listen. Tucker's down now. He's turned into a bad one. But I used to know him when he was all right, and we were friends. I want to give him a good word, and that's all."

"Is that it?" asked Peters. "Aw, you got a heart in you,

lad. You go back there and talk to him then, if you want to. I gotta do some odd jobs in the office. I reckon that you that took him wouldn't be him that'd turn him loose."

"No, it's not likely," said Tag. "You never can tell, though."

Peters chuckled.

"That's a true thing for you," he said. "You never can tell. The best of 'em turn into the worst, and the worst turn into the best, same day of the week. Well, you go on back there. He needs some cheering up, I reckon. Hanging is all the to-morrow that he's got in front of him, poor man. And that ain't quite so good as Christmas!"

So Tag was left alone, his greatest wish granted—to speak with Tucker.

~32~
A Talk with Tucker

I N the small room, there were four cells, often crowded to overflowing during the round-up season of the year, but now quite empty except for Tucker, in a far corner. He was not manacled. The heavy steel bars and the lock upon his door were trusted to keep him inside the hand of the law.

He sat on his bunk, his head suspended, and resting on his doubled fists, and his elbow, in turn, planted upon his knee. He did not look up when Tag came near.

"What trail are you riding?" asked Tag.

"The out trail, Tag," said Tucker, but still without looking up.

"Not as bad as that," answered Tag.

"Ay, the out trail," said Tucker. "It's a short one, too, but it'll get me to hell, all the same!"

"Have they framed you?" asked Tag.

"No. It's not framing. But they've got me."

"I never knew that you were a killer, Tucker—not till the other night."

"The other night I was a fool," said Tucker. "That's the only really dirty game that I ever was mixed up in. I'll tell you something about it, too. The old man wanted me to blow Champion's head off and give him no chance. But I wasn't going to do that. When he came in through the door, I was going to sing out and give him a fighting chance to pull a gun and make a fight of it. You won't believe that, I guess?"

"I'll believe it. Why not?" said Tag. "I always found you a white man, Tucker."

The latter looked up, amazed.

"What's all this about?" he asked. "You ain't come here to laugh at me, have you, Tag? You was always a cut above dirty work like that!"

"No, I haven't come here to laugh at you. But what have they got on you, Tucker—outside of the play in the hotel room?"

"Three, four years back, I tangled with a big redhead of a Swede."

"Redhead, eh?"

"Yeah. Red as they come. You'd 'a' liked the color of that hair!" Tucker forgot his own troubles long enough to smile at Tag's well-known dislike for redheads.

"I don't blame you for anything that you may have done to a redhead," declared Tag.

"It was a fair fight," said Tucker. "I mean, it started unfair. Because he come at me from behind, with a knife. I managed to dodge and sink a bullet through him. But when they found him dead, his knife was lost in the long grass. His hands was empty. There was no gun on him. And so it was murder, you savvy?"

"Yeah. I understand. They could make murder out of that."

"Yeah. They could hang me for it, and that's what they're going to do."

"Lawyers might help you, Tucker."

"Lawyers won't help me in this neck of the woods," answered Tucker firmly. "The boys know that I've played in Malley's gang, and any jury in the mountains would hang me for that. Maybe they're right, anyway. I dunno. I've been doing a good bit of thinking since I landed inside of the bars here."

"Thinking is a pretty dry diet," answered Tag.

"As dry as they come," replied Tucker.

"Tuck," said Tag, "suppose that somebody walked into this jail to-night, and unlocked the doors, and let you out. What of that?"

Tucker looked steadily at him.

"You ain't building me up for a fall, are you?" said he.

"I'm just telling you and asking you. What of that?"

"Ask a dead man if he'd like to come back to life!" exclaimed Tucker.

"I'll cut it short. I want a job done. What about that?"

"Anything up to jumping off a cliff. You name the job, and I'll name the man that'll do it, or bust himself trying!"

"That's all," said Tag. "I hope to come back to-night. Lie

down and get some sleep. You'll have some riding ahead of you when you wake up."

"Tag," said Tucker, suddenly stepping to the bars, "I dunno what to say to you."

"Don't say a thing. Just rest here and wait for me. I'll surely come for you inside of the next two nights."

"I've got your word for it?"

"You have my word."

"By thunder!" said Tucker softly, through his teeth, "I'd rather have your bare word than any other man's Bible oath! Tag, Heaven bless you—and so long till you come for me! I know your hand—there ain't any locks in this place that'll be more than thin air to you!"

Tag Enderby went back to the hotel, and on the veranda he found Champion listening in an agony of boredom to the clatterings of Henry Benton. The younger man stood up at once.

"News?" he asked, lifting his brows at Tag.

"Not yet," said Tag, and went into the hotel.

He rented a double room for himself and Champion, and going up to it, he treated himself to a sponge bath, and then lay down on the bed to think and to smoke.

The day was dying. Already the color was clouding the west, and the voices from the street arose to him with a dreamlike distance. He closed his eyes. For he could see with a mortal clearness the bedroom in the Benton house, and the couch where he had lain under the window, the couch upon which the mottled shadow of the oak leaves was always falling.

He thought of that room, and he thought of Molly Benton, and this world appeared suddenly to Tag Enderby a place of infinite sweet and of equally infinite sour.

It was the apparent futility of all his labors that depressed him. For, no matter what he did, Champion was the obvious man to win her in the end. No matter what she had said about following him, Tag, to the end of the world. If she went with him out of gratitude for what he had done for another man—then he would be a fool if he held her to her contract!

He felt that, and he was sunk in a greater gloom than before.

And then it seemed to Tag that there was a cruel justice in the situation in which he found himself—a justice in that he, who had flaunted through life so cheerfully, like a bird on the wing, living as he pleased, totally regardless of all things except his own pleasure, should now be the slave to such circumstances as these.

But still the thought of the girl struck through him with a vital pang. Her name was a sound in his ears, as though a musical tongue were pronouncing it. Her courage, her steady frankness haunted him like a ghost of surpassing beauty. Yet, somewhere, he felt that there was evil in her, a thing revealed not even to herself.

Or was it no more, perhaps, than the unforgettable copper gleam of her hair?

He dozed. When he wakened, Champion was in the room, sitting by the window, smoking. His silhouette showed strongly against the stars beyond, the bulldog silhouette, with the outthrust of the chin.

"How long you been there, Ray?" he asked.

"Three, four minutes. You were sleeping like a baby. I didn't want to wake you up. But it's close to dinner time.

What about it?"

Tag sat up with a groan.

"I feel like an old man," he said.

"Speaking of old men, I'll tell you a funny thing."

"About Benton, maybe?"

"Yeah. He shut up. What do you think of that?"

"I think that he'll choke. That's what I think."

"He's shut up, and he's not starting back for Grove City right away. And he wants to see you—and he wants to see you bad."

"He needs some money, and he's heard about the roulette games in Indian Gulch. That's what he wants to see me about."

"I don't know. But he wants to see you. He wants to see you so bad that he stopped talking about everything else. He has a room right down the hall. No. 14, if you want to see him. I wouldn't, if I were you. He's been silent for so many minutes now that he's pretty sure to swamp you. He'll break the dam, and he'll drown you with words. He'll certainly wreck you, old son."

"I'll go see him, anyway," said Enderby. "Meet you down in the dining room."

He went down the hall and tapped at the door of No. 14. It was opened at once, with a promptness that seemed to indicate that Benton had been waiting, prepared for a caller.

He motioned his visitor inside, and when Tag was within, he closed the door, turned, and set his shoulders against it. He faced Tag grimly.

"All right," said Tag Enderby. "I won't jump out the window, anyway, Mr. Benton. What's up?"

"That's what I want to know," answered Benton.

"Tut, tut," said Tag. "You're getting excited about some-thing."

"I am."

"Well? What is it?"

"I been thinking about that letter you got."

"So have I," said Tag.

"What did it have in it?"

"Just a word. It was a joke."

"Just a word?"

"That's all."

"What sort of word?"

" 'Sorry!' That's all it said."

" 'Sorry'?"

"Yes, that's all."

"Sorry for what?"

"Oh, I don't know. It was just a fool joke, Mr. Benton."

"Who was sorry? Who wrote that letter?"

"I don't know. There wasn't even a signature."

"Then there wasn't any signature needed, because you knew who wrote the word."

Tag looked at the other out of narrowed eyes. He was amazed by the insight which Benton was showing.

The older man went on: "Look here, Tag, I got to thinking. I got to thinking when I was talking to Ray. He gives me lots of time for thought. He don't appreciate me much, and he gives me a lot of time for thought. He don't bother to answer me, very often! And, all at once, while he was setting there silent, and I was chattering, I seen that you boys had been holding something out on me. What is it?"

"You're dreaming, Mr. Benton," said Tag.

"I ain't dreaming. I seen a shadow go over your own

face, just now."

"I was puzzled by what you said; that's all."

"Tag Enderby," said the other, "that word in the letter meant something about Molly!"

Tag started—literally gasped.

"What makes you think it was about Molly?" he asked.

"Something that went over your face, and Champion's face, when you talked to him afterwards. Tag, was it Molly?"

And Tag, after a moment's thought, said gently: "Yes, it was Molly."

He saw the eyes of the older man wink suddenly shut, as though a stroke of pain had pierced him.

"It was Molly!" whispered Benton.

He opened his eyes again.

"And what was it?" he said.

Tag went to him and laid a hand on his arm.

"What it was," he said, "I've an idea, but I'm not dead sure. That's about all I can tell you."

"You'll tell me no more?"

"I can't, Mr. Benton."

"And what's to be done about her?"

"That I don't know. I'm fumbling in the dark. I can only tell you one thing—that I'm going to do what I can, and so will Ray Champion."

"Ah, Tag," said Benton, "a bright day for all of us, when you came into my house."

"A bright day?" answered Tag bitterly. "I'll tell you this. All the trouble that comes on her now is because men that hate me are trying to get at me through her."

Inside the Jail

IT was an hour after this that Tag Enderby left the hotel. It had not been a pleasant hour for him. He had spent most of it in the dining room, eating supper with Benton and Champion. A crushed and absent-minded Henry Benton was this who sat with the two younger men. Ray Champion was abstracted also, and all that Tag could do was to be aware of the numbers of men who filed into the room and took their places at various tables, all striving to take places which faced toward him.

They had heard enough about him to whet their appetites to learn more, and they stared at him with a hungry interest. The proprietor lingered near by, ready to be of help, full of smiles. He saw the possibilities of a suddenly expanded trade, through the presence of this youth, and he wished to make the most of it. But Tag Enderby was miserable.

His living depended, to a vast degree, upon the veil of mystery with which he could surround himself, and that veil was being snatched away. The battery of eyes now fixed upon him would never forget his features. He hated them all. He hated them as though they had been red-headed, every man.

And, in the meantime, two hundred thousand dollars were packed away upon his person. The gold and silver were discarded, and certain bulky packages of bills of smaller denominations. Those of the larger kind still made a considerable bulk, but he knew how to place them so that their lumpishness would be least apparent.

Two hundred thousand dollars of what Champion chose to call thieves' gold was on him. He might as well have carried a dozen flasks of "soup." Sooner or later, he knew, that treasure was likely to be the death of him.

Then a thought came to him that perhaps the great Malley would be willing to give up the girl for the return of the coin. That was possible.

He brooded over it during the supper. It clung in his mind afterwards when he left the hotel and the main street, and worked around to the rear of the little squat building which was the jail.

He had to prowl about the place, at first, to make sure of what he had before him.

His gray, and the Malley horse which Champion had ridden down from the mountains, Tag had placed in a thicket not fifty yards from the jail. He only needed to get two seconds' start from the place with Tucker in order to see the latter safely mounted. Then, if need were, he would ride the gantlet at the side of the outlaw. His hope, however, was that he might be able to arrange the matter without further exposing himself, if only the jail delivery could be accomplished.

By climbing to two lighted windows, he finally made out Peters, the jailer. He sat in what was probably the sanctum of Locksley. The old jailer was biting his lips with profound concentration as he stared at the pages of a magazine. His coat was off. His sleeves were rolled up and exposed the big, red, hairy forearms, one of them marked with the blue picture of a ship under full sail.

Where had Peters been in this wild world of adventure?

He slipped down from the window. Peters could not be

in a more favorable position, from Tag's viewpoint. So the latter went at once to the rear of the jail and tried his picklock there. It was a small task, as he had expected. The door opened before him almost at once, and pushing it carefully, he finally had it wide without having made the slightest sound.

Then he stole to the cell of Tucker.

The latter stood erect, in the farthest corner. He did not move or speak, when he saw Tag Enderby. It gave Tag an odd feeling that the man hung from the ceiling, lifeless. Except that the head was stiffly erect!

Upon his knees, Tag worked at the lock upon the cell door. This was a different task. For the lock was of a new and a complicated model. It resisted the little solving movements of the picklock. And when Tag had worked for a few minutes, the sweat was standing on his forehead.

Then a door opened, and a broad shaft of light washed down the corridor, between the cells.

Tag could have groaned aloud—for he had left the rear door of the jail open!

What could he do?

He retreated, crawling like a cat, to the mouth of the open doorway. He reached out, caught the edge of the door, and drew it slowly shut.

Peters, carrying his swinging lantern, as an addition to the one small lamp that burned to illumine the cell room, was making his rounds, and naturally he came straight to the cell of his solitary prisoner.

He held the lantern over his head.

"Well, Tucker?" he said.

"Well?" answered the prisoner.

"How's things?"

"Fair."

"I'll tell you what," said Peters, "Enderby cheered you up a good lot, didn't he?"

"Oh, the devil with Enderby," said Tucker.

"That's what you say, because he put you here. But Enderby's all right."

"He's the hanging of me. That's all," said Tucker.

"Well, you never can tell," said the sourdough. "There's some that hang for one man, and some that hang for two. You've had your hard luck. A gent that has to hang for the shooting of a redhead of a Swede, I feel kind of sorry for him. I remember once that I had a run-in with a big Swede in a mine down in Arizona. I got a crowbar, and I bent it over his head. It knocked him flat, and I thought he was dead. But he wasn't. He reached out and kicked the legs from under me, and he grabbed me when I dropped, and he sure about swallered me alive. I wasn't the same man for a month. I was kind of all in pieces. Now, if his skull hadn't been an extra-plated Swede skull, that might 'a' been the finish of me. I might 'a' hanged for that. The same as you'll do!"

"That's a pile of comfort for me," said Tucker.

"You get comfort out of the small things, son," said Peters. "Well, I'm for turning in. But where's the draft coming from, in here?"

He raised the lantern above his head and looked curiously around him.

"I dunno," said Tucker. "There's a wind leak in the roof, I'd take it. I been feeling it for some time over my head."

"I'm going to take a look in the morning," said Peters. "I'll just have a flash at the back door, and then I'll turn in."

"It's the roof," said Tucker. "The way that them that call themselves carpenters put on shingles, these days—"

"Ay, it's a crime," said Peters. "When I was a boy, I would 'a' made 'em look sick, nine times out of ten."

"You would, I reckon," said Tucker. "You got an eye in your head. That's what you've got. You got the eye of a mechanic."

"I can hammer a nail and saw to a line," admitted Peters, with some pride. "Well, I'll be turning in."

He moved, and Tag waited tensely. He had not dared to pull on the back door so hard that the latch would snap shut. And if the old man came near, he would not dare to expose himself. He could drop a younger and more athletic opponent, but he knew that he could not raise his hand against this kind-hearted old veteran.

But he was immensely relieved to see that Peters had turned down the corridor between the cells. Presently the door to the office slammed shut, and the cell room was left to the dim radiance of the single lamp.

Then Tag went back to the lock on which he had been working in vain. It now, as though his first experience of it had been a sufficient trial, instantly gave way, and the door fell noiselessly open against his hand.

Tucker glided out into the aisle, but instead of following his deliverer, he paused and grasped one of the strong bars. Tag stepped back to him, amazed.

"Hurry, man!" he whispered.

Then he saw that Tucker was shaking from head to foot in the grasp of a powerful ague.

Tag had seen the thing before. He had heard of it often, too. Tramps and criminals know it as the "prison shakes."

It is a testimony to the sudden breaking down of nerves which may have resisted the most terrible friction for a long time. Then, unexpectedly, they give way, and the man is helpless, unable to move.

Tag, grinding his teeth with horror and rage and disgust and pity, caught the big man under the shoulders and drew at him, but the convulsive grasp of Tucker still was locked upon the steel bar, and would not give way.

In the desperate face of Tucker could be seen the struggle as with all his will he strove to master himself, strove to force himself away from the place to which he was anchored. He tried to speak. But his teeth merely rattled together as loudly as castanets.

He could only shake his head at Tag, in a motion which deprecated the catastrophe.

Then, in a moment, the fit left him, and, exhausted, he was able to walk with trailing feet from the jail, one hand resting for support upon Tag's shoulder.

They passed out. The door was closed and locked behind them, and a moment later they were beside the horses in the grove. There they paused, and Tucker said gloomily, grimly:

"You see how it is with me, Tag. I'm no good. I'm done!"

"You're only starting, Tuck," answered Tag. "You're going to be twice the man that you think you are. I'm betting on you. You hear?"

"You were always the one for chances," said Tucker. "But when a fellow has the prison shakes—"

"Listen to me," argued Tag. "You're going to tackle a tough job for me. I've got your promise; I'm going to hold you to it, because I know you can do the thing if you'll once tackle it."

"Tell me what you want," said Tucker. "Heaven knows I'm willing to try."

"I have a couple of hundred thousand dollars," said Tag. "I took it from the chief. You go tell him that I'm willing to make a trade—the two hundred thousand in exchange for the girl. He's got Molly Benton somewhere."

"The devil he has!" Tucker scowled. "He can't do that. Not even Malley's own gang would let him do a thing like that!"

"Oh, he's treating her well enough, I suppose," said Tag. "When you spot the gang, you'll probably find out that they're treating her like the Queen of the May. Anyway, you get to Malley, and tell him that I turned you loose, and that the reason I did it was because I wanted to make the exchange. You hear?"

"Two hundred thousand," said Tucker, with a new quiver of emotion in his voice, "is a pile of coin."

"It's what Malley has stacked up," answered Tag. "He's taken mighty few chances to get it, but he's collected it from the boys. His share is always a pretty fat share. You know that."

"I know," growled Tucker. "Two-hundred-thousand-dollars!"

He groaned suddenly.

"We've been fools!" he declared. "He's been bleeding us to the white!"

"Never mind that," replied Tag Enderby. "You understand, Tucker. A lot depends on this. You spot the gang. It'll be easy for you to get to them; it's eating bullets, if Ray Champion and I try that trail. Tell your chief that I'm offering him the exchange."

"And suppose that he doesn't want the exchange?" suggested Tucker.

"Ay, I've thought of that, too. And if that happens, then I'll have to get up to him. If he won't see my money, and turn the girl loose, then I've got to get at him. Tucker, it'll be your job to slip word back here to the town and let me know where I can get at Malley."

"That's a tough assignment," muttered Tucker.

"It's a tough assignment," admitted Tag. "And the minute he finds out that you've been helped by me, he's going to have you under suspicion. But what else is there to do?"

"I know," said Tucker softly. "It's a matter of that or nothing."

He stretched out his hand, found that of Tag, and gripped it hard.

"Look, Tag," said he. "I've been a hound. I know it. Now I'm going to try to make a cleaner break for myself. I'm going to try to pay you back. I dunno. Maybe my nerve is no good. Maybe my nerve will clean break down. But I'm going to try!"

~34~
A Hard Ride

THERE was still no sign of an alarm from the jail. And big Tucker rode quietly out from the town, and steadily on through the darkness. He stopped at the wretched shack of a shepherd and banged at the door with a revolver. A groan from the interior darkness answered him.

"Joe!" called Tucker,

"Ay? Who's there?"

"Tucker. Where do I find Malley?"

"How should I know?" said Joe. "Get out and leave me be, will you?"

Tucker hesitated. Then something that had been in the voice of the man came back into his mind, and he shrugged his shoulders. Probably Joe did not know.

So he rode on.

He had before him a narrow pass. Through the pass leaped a wind with a fine, whipping rain in its arms. He had no slicker, and the rain cut through him to the bone. He was very cold, chilled from facing that wind.

In the middle of the pass he came to a shack hardly larger than the first, but behind it was the looming bulk of a barn that seemed fairly prosperous. He could see, very faintly, the tangled shadows of corral fencing.

Upon the door of this house he pounded. Twice he had to repeat the summons, and then he heard voices inside, a woman and a man speaking together.

"It's me, Bill," said Tucker. "It's Tucker."

The door was pulled open a trifle.

"Hello, Tucker," said the voice of Bill. "Thought you was taking a rest in the Indian Gulch jail?"

Tucker did not even answer the question.

"Where's Malley holing up?" he asked.

"I dunno," said Bill.

Tucker dismounted. He felt stiff and weak from the exposure.

"I ain't got much room for you in here," said the man

of the shack.

"I don't want your room," said Tucker, in disgust at this inhospitable treatment. "Give me a tarpaulin or an old slicker, will you? It's wet as the devil."

"Ain't got a thing like that handy," said Bill, in a more surly voice.

"You go right on up the line, Mr. Tucker," said the nasal voice of the woman. "Tom Bitler, he'll fix you up real comfortable for the night."

"Bill," said Tucker, "I want to know where Malley is. You fool, d'you think that I've broken with him?"

"I don't know anything about Malley," complained Bill.

Tucker thrust out his hand. In the darkness he found a coat collar and jerked the coat and the wearer of it out into the whipping drizzle of the rain. But he found a gun thrust into his stomach.

"Quit it!" snarled Bill, "or I'll let the light through you, you jailbird!"

Tucker was fairly staggered by the quickness of the draw, but he answered in the largest way he could manage:

"You're talking like a fool. I've got to get to Malley. The air's full of money for him. I've got to get him word, and I guess you know his trail. Put up your gun. What's the matter with you?"

The woman screamed in a sudden rage from inside the house: "Don't you tell him a word. If you got the drop on him, shoot him. There'll be a reward on him, Billy!"

Her husband waited for a moment that was one of the longest that Tucker ever stood through. Finally Bill said:

"Shut yer face, Maggie. You, Tucker, you may be all right, I dunno."

"How long have I been with Malley?"

"You been with the jail since then. You been on the other side of the fence, and maybe you wanta stay there. Tag Enderby, he's on the other side of the fence now."

"Enderby's the one who got me into jail. Would I be on his side of the fence? You're loco, Bill."

"Never mind that. I dunno. I guess you're all right."

"Of course I'm all right."

"Leave go of my collar."

"Not till I get the direction out of you."

"By thunder, Tucker," said Bill, "you're taking your chances, ain't you? Well, I'll tell you. He's up on Goose Mountain and—"

"Bill, you're a fool!" shouted his wife from the shack.

"Which side of Goose Mountain?" asked Tucker.

"I dunno, and I don't care. Take your hand off my collar. I'm telling you for the last time!"

His voice rose to a shrill whine of rage. Tucker released him at once, feeling that he had learned all he could and, remounting, he faced again into the whipping of the rain.

It was a bitter hard ride. The horse began to shudder under him, for the work was not sufficient to keep it warm. But presently the dawn commenced. He saw that he had been going all through the night at no more than a snail's pace. By daylight he could have made the journey in less than half this number of hours.

Then, on his left, he saw the broad, black shoulders of Goose Mountain looming through the dark. The day increased. He saw the white rain mists draw like lace about the peak, which soared above them.

Bitterly cold, he cursed his luck, and Bill. It was a huge

mountain, and he might have to wander for hours through those black, dripping woods before he came upon Malley's crew. But he could do nothing except turn the horse into the woods and drift on, rather aimlessly. He remembered a high shoulder of the mountain across which a small stream ran at most seasons of the year. That might have been chosen as a camping spot by Malley. There was the wreckage of a miner's hut on the place.

Toward that goal Tucker aimed. The water dripped steadily from the trees. Now and again he brushed against a branch which let down a sudden, icy shower of rain upon him. But at least the wind did not comb through these trees. Yet he began to feel sick at heart—fear was colder in him than the fingers of the wind had been.

He found the stream of which he had been thinking, and up this he urged the horse, keeping to the easier slopes near the water. The shoulder at which he aimed was now not far above him when, looking up, he saw that the clouds had parted. Lower down, they were sheeted across the sky; but at this altitude, they broke, and he could look up to brilliant patches of blue, with white clouds blown across the heavens.

This raised his heart. A sharply challenging voice, a moment later, made him rein in the tired, shivering horse.

"Hold up there, stranger. Hey, if it ain't Tuck!"

Between two rocks appeared Stew Bender, his young face shaggy with uncropped beard, a big overcoat swathing him, a rifle in his mittened hands.

"Hullo, Stew," said Tucker. "I've had a rotten ride."

"Better be riding in rain," said Stew, "than in fire, I reckon! I'm glad to see you, Tuck. We all thought you'd walk on air before we ever laid eyes on you again. Come on up. The chief'll be glad to see you, too. He's been cursing a good deal, but I guess he'll be glad to see you, too!"

As Tucker rode on beside the creek, Stew Bender walked at his stirrup.

"How's the lay?" asked Tucker.

"It ain't like the old camp. But it's only temporary. It's only while the folks down below are so heated up. They got about four posses riding for us now. And so we lay low and take things easy. Who steered you this way?"

"That mangy Bill Rider."

"Yeah, he's a hound, all right. D'you see Ma Rider and get some of her tongue?"

"I got some of her tongue, all right. She wanted Bill to put a slug through me and collect the reward."

"She'd want that. She's that way."

"How's the chief?"

"He's changed a lot. He's got young."

"Young?"

"Yeah. You'll see when you meet him. He's different. It's all Enderby now."

"Yeah. He wants Tag's scalp, I guess."

"He dreams about it," said Stew Bender. "So do I. You know the way that he made a fool of me and Grey?"

"No."

"The boys'll tell you. I wouldn't spoil the story for 'em. But we'll get Enderby. That's sure. There ain't anything else in the world that I'm sure of, but I know that Enderby's a dead one. He took his last chance, when he come up to headquarters!"

"He had his nerve with him," answered Tucker.

"He's all nerve. But he was a fool to step on Dan's toes that way. Robbing him that way. He'd better 'a' murdered him. A lot better!"

"I hear that there's a girl up here somewheres?"

"That's a funny thing, ain't it?" said the youth. "She's here to bait Enderby. You wouldn't think that he'd come to that kind of a trap, would you? She ain't so pretty. She's kind of cold. She's kind of like a man. But the chief has it worked out that Enderby's crazy about her. And that's why he's keeping her. She don't mind much."

"Kind of a lark for her, maybe," suggested Tucker.

"A lark? I dunno. She don't talk much. Sort of good natured and cold and quiet. Looks at you like a man. Funny thing about her. She's got red hair. How could Enderby ever fall for a girl that had red hair? Tell me that?"

"You know," said Tucker, "You never can tell about a man and a girl. What they fall for is mostly surprising. Here we are, eh?"

They came up through the trees to a small clearing. Backed against the upper slope of Goose Mountain was the old wreck of a hut which Tucker had remembered. Not very far from it stood a shelter which was in part a tent and in part a windbreak and a lean-to, made of boughs very crudely thatched across.

"Here's our happy home," said Bender. "The boys are getting pretty damp and soggy up here. It's raining mostly all the time. There's Brownie bringing in some wood. We burn up about ten cord a day."

"What for? To show the posses where you are?"

"They'll never come toward a smoke as big as ours.

They know that a smoke like that goes up from some ten-derfoot camp. That's the way that Malley figures it, anyway. And there's Malley himself."

For the chief of the band now appeared at the door of the shelter tent, yawning and stretching his arms.

~35~
Malley's Price

TUCKER could see, at once, that there was much in what Bender had told him about the change in the chief. It seemed as though he had grown young, and the flabby folds in his cheeks had diminished. His eye was bright. His step was more alert. He stood straight as a boy. And now he waved cheerfully toward Tucker.

When the latter came up and dismounted, Malley grasped him warmly by the hand and welcomed him "home."

"This ain't much of a place. This is only camping out, Tuck. But things will get better than this. I thought that there was sure to be a necktie party for you, Tuck. I was arranging to go down and raid the jail."

Young Grey came out from the entrance to the shelter.

"Yeah. You believe that," said he. "Dan's been saying that he hoped you'd choke slow and painful. He's been saying that a blundering fool like you deserved to hang, and he hoped you would. What a liar you are, Dan Malley!"

He covered the insults, in a sense, by the breadth of his grin. And then came a flash, an explosion from the hand of Malley. The hat leaped from the head of the youth, and he found himself covered by the weapon which was held negligently low in the fingers of the chief.

"Take off your sombrero when you talk to your elders," advised Malley cheerfully.

Young Grey, rather white, but with fury in his eyes, glared back at his chief.

"I'm going to remember that!" he said.

"Yeah, you remember it," said Malley. "I been a woolly lamb, with all of you boys. I've took a lot of lip from you, but I'm not taking it no more. There's going to be a change around here. Any time that you wanta remember the way that I knocked that hat off your empty head, you come and tell me about it. Why not remember right now? There's my gun, stuck away safe and sound. Here's my arms folded nice and high on my chest. Now do your remembering, Grey, and go for your gun, if you got the nerve to do it!"

Grey, for a moment, whiter than before, stared at his chief, but he found something unendurable in the blazing eye of the older man. He turned, and without picking up his hat, he walked away into the dark of the dripping trees.

"That kid will never forget," said Tucker truthfully.

"I don't care if he don't," answered Malley. "I don't want boys around me that ain't got the courage to stand up and fight. Even to fight me. I been lying around like a calf. I been a woolly lamb," he repeated, the phrase evidently tickling him profoundly. "But now I'm going to show the boys that I'm their master. I'm going to make 'em or break 'em! Come in here, Tucker, and peel off those clothes. You're soaked. Here, Ban. You put up Tuck's hoss for him, will you? That's the boy. Get that fire going. Here's Tucker, all blue goose flesh."

He was the very heart of hospitality. No matter how much truth there may have been in the remarks of young Grey about Malley's attitude to his jailed gunman, the chief now chose to be entirely cordial. The wet clothes were stripped away; fresh ones were donned from the pack of Malley himself, for he always kept an ample supply of wearing apparel for his crew.

When Tucker was dressed, Malley went on: "The boys fix up their own chow, and Ban cooks for 'em in the open, but I've got a special cook over there in the cabin. You come along, and we'll have a breakfast there. I got a cook that'll make you blink a couple of times, and then you can tell me what you think!"

He laughed cheerfully as he spoke, and led Tucker across the clearing to the shack. He knocked at the door, and the voice of a woman, rich, low-pitched, called out. The door was thrown open by Malley, and Tucker saw the dingy interior of the cabin, and the fuming of the little stove, covered with cooking food, and near the stove a girl with her sleeves rolled up, and a big iron fork in her hand, and coppery hair coiled sleekly about her head.

That was Molly Benton, he knew.

Somehow it gave his heart a new sort of a jump. He had seen prettier women. Bender was right in that. But the heart of Tucker leaped as he looked into the rather flat, expressionless eyes of the girl.

He went in, stepping rather gingerly.

"Here's Tucker come along for breakfast," said Malley. "You don't mind?"

"Why should I mind?" said Molly cheerfully. "Hello,

Tucker. Deal another plate and cup onto that table, will you?"

Tucker obeyed. The table was composed of two planks laid over a pair of homemade sawhorses.

"What's for chow?" asked Malley, approaching the stove and leaning into the steam that arose from it.

"Venison steaks, and stewed berries, and coffee, and biscuits—and plum jam, and honey, and some bacon crisped to go with the venison. And here's a pan of trout. Can you make out on that?"

"Not more'n barely," said Malley, grinning. "You're feeding a man now, Molly. You ain't feeding one of them stable-raised plainsmen. You got a mountaineer to feed. And Tucker's another of my own breed."

"I'll feed you," said the girl. "Tucker, I thought you were cooling yourself in jail? You're the fellow who tried to kill Ray Champion, aren't you?"

"I'm the one," said Tucker.

He knew what Ray Champion was supposed to mean to the girl. But so much had flowed under the bridge since that first night in the hotel room that he looked back at Molly without even a ghost of shame.

"I'm glad you're out," she said, "You don't look like murder in the dark, to me. I guess it was orders straight from Malley that sent you down to Indian Gulch?"

Tucker did not answer, but Malley said:

"Speak up and tell her 'Yes.' She knows all about me now. She's hard-boiled, too. Tell her that I sent you down there, and that you didn't like the job. I don't mind. And you sure 'did' the job as though you didn't like it!"

"Anyway," said Tucker, "Enderby blocked that play for me."

The girl nodded.

She was placing the food on the table.

"Sit down, boys," she said. "Get that steak while it's red-hot. Dan, you look as though you've had a good night's sleep."

"I sure have," he answered.

"That's because you've got a clean conscience, I guess," said she.

The table was loaded with food. She stood by, looking over the feast.

"Sit down, Molly," said Dan Malley.

"No, I'll stand. When I've got two men to feed, I prefer to stand around and be the waitress."

"You'll get stale, cold chuck," said Malley.

"I'm only a woman," she answered. "That doesn't matter to us."

So Malley and Tucker sat down.

"You picked the lock?" asked the girl, of Tucker.

"Enderby picked it," said he.

He looked across the table at Malley, hardening himself, and he was in time to see the green light of suspicion flame for an instant in the eyes of the other.

"It's Tag again, is it?" said Malley.

"Yeah. It was Tag. He faded into that jail and out again as though he was carrying the keys," explained Tucker.

"Friend of yours?" asked Malley.

"No. But he wanted me to do an odd job for him."

"Like coming up here and finding the trail for him, eh?" asked Malley fiercely.

"Look here," put in the girl. "If you're going to start wrangling, get out of the cabin, will you? I don't care if you cut each other's throats. I hope you do. But get out of the cabin. There's more elbow room for you in the clearing."

The evil nature disappeared instantly from the face of Malley. He grinned at the girl.

"Listen at her!" he said to Tucker. "That's the lingo she has. Gentle, ain't she? Yeah, gentle like a buzzsaw. She'll murder us all, one of these nights, and take our hosses down and sell 'em at public auction, and collect the rewards on our heads, and use the hard cash to marry her pet bulldog, Champion. Or is it Enderby now, Molly?"

"You're letting those steaks get cold," she warned them.

"Enderby wants to buy the girl from you. That's why he sent me. That's why he pried me out of the jail. He thought that I could find the trail and get the message to you."

"He wants to buy her, eh?" repeated Malley. "Well, for a girl like that, the price is high. How much does he offer?"

He turned toward Molly.

"Listen to it, Molly, See what sort of a price he puts on your head."

"Two hundred thousand dollars," said Tucker, looking at the girl, also.

He was amazed to see that she showed not the slightest alteration of expression.

Neither did Malley appear surprised.

"That's nothing," he said. "That's the money that he stole from me."

"It's the money that you stole first," said the girl. "It looks to me like a pretty fat price for one girl, height five feet six, weight a hundred and twenty-five."

"Is that all the size you are?" asked Dan Malley. "Well, it ain't the weight. It's the quality that counts. A hundred and twenty-five pounds of diamonds and rubies and emeralds. I wouldn't sell you for a couple of hundred thousand."

"Well," said Tucker, disappointed but striving not to show it, "I've done the job. I've found you and given you the message. It's up to you, chief."

"You ain't under bond to go back to jail, if you miss?"

"No, he didn't ask that."

"You was so honorable that you done that once before." Malley sneered.

"He's given me my life twice," said Tucker. "I guess he's getting used to it. But it's sort of a surprising thing to me that you rate her higher than two hundred thousand. Just what is the price on her?"

"It's a price you likely wouldn't guess, Tuck, you being so good-natured. You wouldn't guess the 'kind' of a price."

"What kind then?"

"No dollars, old son!"

"No? What else then?"

"Blood!" said Malley, leaning across the table with a savage joy. "If he'll pay that high in cash for her, he'll come himself to get her, later on. And when he comes, I'll be waiting. Molly, inside of two days, I'll show you handsome young Tag cold as a stone. You can say the prayers over him when we tuck him under the ground!"

Molly's Advice

I T seemed a remark sufficient to give any conversation pause, but there was no delay here, as the girl said: "You're getting over-confident, Dan. That's the spoiling of a lot of bigger men than you are!"

"Over-confident? Because I've taken so many tricks from that kid?" asked Dan Malley.

"Because you hate him so much," she replied, "that you can't see how you can fail to clean him up, one of these days. Isn't that the way you feel?"

"I've had my share of bad luck," declared Malley, scowling over his food.

"Oh, and you'll have more," she went on. "He's a cut too high for you to tackle, Dan."

"You'd have me lay down and take the money, eh?" said Malley.

"I would not," she replied. "You turn down the money, and then he'll come and get me away without paying down a cent."

"What would you bet on that?" asked Malley.

"Not a penny with you, Dan," she answered. "Because you'll be dead as a board when it comes time to pay up."

He gathered his coffee cup toward him and grinned at her again, with a hearty admiration in his eyes.

"Listen to her," he advised Tucker. "There ain't anybody else like her in the world. Been like a daughter to me all the time I've had her, ain't you, Molly?"

"I've given you a lot of good advice," she declared.

"Ay, a lot of good advice," said he. "And I been grateful,

too. I ain't seemed grateful, but I've been."

She poured herself a third of a cup of coffee and began to sip it, looking over the brim thoughtfully at Malley.

"Now what you thinking about?" asked Dan.

"I'd better not tell you."

"Yeah, you go on and tell me."

"I was thinking of a fight I saw once. A dog had cornered a bobcat. And the bobcat turned and jumped the dog. And the dog turned and scooted, but he couldn't get those red-hot claws out of his back. I'm thinking of the way you'll run and yell, when Tag gets at you!"

"Run, eh?" asked Malley, thrusting out his jaw.

"Yes, you'll run."

"I may die," said he. "I won't run."

"That's what you think now," she assured him. "But when the pinch comes, you'll cut loose and run like a good one! I know! You're brave. You forget the look of him, and the thin fast hands that he wears. He'll paralyze you, Dan. I'd really almost hate to see that fight!"

Malley no longer smiled. He was scowling instead.

"Do your own thinking," he advised her. "Don't you try to think for me. There ain't a day in the year when I'm afraid to meet Tag Enderby alone, man to man!"

She pointed to Tucker.

"You send Tuck back down the valley with that word to Tag," she suggested. "He won't be long away from any place you name!"

Furious red stained the face of Malley. He swelled with his passion.

"Oh, you'd like that," he answered. "You'd like me to chuck away all my winning cards. But I ain't that sort of a man. I'll meet him. But I'll play every card to win that game. And my cards here are about a dozen boys who shoot straight."

She sighed.

"I was almost beginning to think you were quite a man, Dan," said she. "But now I see that you're not. You're a cheap quitter. However, that's your business."

He glared at her. His two fists were hard-gripped and rested upon the edge of the table.

"You're a devil, Molly!" he told her huskily.

"Hold yourself in," she warned. "Bad temper like that spoils digestion. Ruins it. You haven't tried a scrap of those biscuits yet."

"Damn the biscuits," he answered. "Now lookit here—"

"I'm looking," she said. "You're not pretty just now, to tell you the truth."

"What do I care for looks?"

"You got a pretty fair start," she answered. "But you've let booze sag you a lot, Dan. It's a great pity, too."

"Molly," he said, "take your claws out of me, will you? I'd face guns sooner than your chatter."

"Not Enderby's guns," she replied.

The answer jerked him out of his chair, with a snarl.

"Enderby?" he shouted. "I've half a mind—"

He checked himself.

"Half a mind to be the hero and fight him like a man, eh?" said the girl. "No, it's less than half your mind, Dan. You'll never fight him. You'd rather fight the devil than to have Tag Enderby alone with you, even if his right hand were tied into the small of his back."

"Bah!" shouted Malley.

She smiled at him.

"Be honest for a change, Dan. It's not so very shameful to be afraid of Enderby. Everybody knows that you're getting old and slow with your guns."

"It's a lie!" he cried.

"Come, come!" she said. "You're getting so old that you boast like a child. But don't be ashamed of being afraid of Tag. You oughtn't to be, you know. You're at least ten years too old to be brave, Dan."

He took a great breath.

"I know one thing now," said he.

"What is it, Dan? I hope you know one thing. I hope you know that we understand how afraid you are of Tag."

He grunted with pain and rage. But he went on:

"You're kind of half mad about Tag, ain't you?"

"About Tag?" said she, turning up her eyes toward the ceiling. "Yes. A little more than half."

"Ay!" he snarled. "That slickster—that card sharper—that hoss thief—that yegg and safe cracker—that sleight-of-hand artist—but you're pretty crazy about him!"

"I'm crazy about him," she replied calmly.

"You turned down Champion for him!"

"I haven't turned down Champion," she said.

"You will, though."

"Yes, perhaps I will. I don't know."

"I tell you, Champion's worth ten of Enderby. Tag's no good. He's wilder'n quicksilver!"

"He'll be too wild for you, Dan," said the girl. "You've been lying around so long that you've turned into a rheumatic old house dog. You're tame. No wonder you fear a wild one like Tag!"

The outlaw chief glared at her for another moment. He vainly tried to find words. Then, whirling about, he rushed from the house, and slammed the door behind him.

The girl, undisturbed, slipped onto a stool, and began to eat her breakfast.

"He's going to explode. He's so hot that he's hissing like hot iron in water," said Tucker, looking at her in mingled admiration and doubt. "What d'you gain by teasing him like that?"

She looked calmly across the table at him.

"Why do you think I'll answer your questions, Tucker?" she asked him.

He glanced sharply around toward the door. Then he leaned forward a little, and his voice was a whisper.

"Because I belong to Enderby!" he murmured. "He's bought me, body and soul!"

For the first time he saw a flash in her eyes, a wild, bewildering gleam of light that dazzled him with its possibilities, with the profound and burning depths of soul which it suggested.

"I believe you!" she answered, in a voice no louder than his.

And he felt somehow as though he had been crowned as a king of men by her belief.

She raised her voice instantly, with a knowing nod at him.

"It's the same way, every mealtime. You see, he comes in here to enjoy the good cooking. And it's always this way. Before he finishes his second cup of coffee, he's so wild that he runs out of the cabin so that he can curse in the open air."

"But what d'you gain by that?"

"It's fun to torment him," said the girl. "I suppose that he's almost the blackest devil in the world, and it's fun to make a real devil twist and writhe a bit. Don't you think so?"

"Maybe," he said dubiously. "He might touch a match to the cabin sometime, though."

She murmured very softly:

"What will they do—Tag and Ray Champion?"

"I don't know. I guess Tag will come on here. I don't know about Champion."

"He'll never stay out of it," said the girl. "He's not that kind of a man."

"Maybe not. And my job is to get away from here and bring back word of the trail to 'em. To Tag."

"That'll be risky business, won't it?" said the girl. "I mean for you to go near Indian Gulch again?"

He shrugged his heavy shoulders.

Then he said simply, earnestly: "I've been no better than dead two times. He's pulled me through. All I could do now would be to die for Tag once."

He saw a wrinkle of pain appear and disappear between her eyes.

"I think you mean that," she said.

"Yes, I mean it," he answered.

"God bless you, Tucker," she said. "Tag's bad enough, I suppose, but what is there about him that gets so much good out of people?"

Inspiration came to Tucker.

"Because the rest of us are mean and bad by nacher. But Tag's only a kid. It's all a game to him. And he plays it as hard and as clean as he knows how. Only I suppose there's a few rules that he doesn't know. You could teach them to him, Molly!"

It wouldn't do for him to stay too long in the cabin alone with her. He left her sitting with a bowed and thoughtful head, while he went outside.

Malley was sitting in front of the lean-to, and he waved to Tucker, who went over to him.

"Tuck," said Dan Malley, "I guess you're all right. But I've told the boys to keep an eye on you. This here's a pretty good, big clearing. You're all right if you stay on it. Try to get off, and they'll shoot you dead. That's all!"

~37~
The Chestnut Horse

T HE dilemma pinched Tucker to the quick. He did not doubt the willingness or the ability of Malley's men to shoot him to shreds, but he was drawn almost irresistibly by his loyalty to young Tag Enderby.

So he sat yawning in the sun—for he was very tired, very sleepy—and strove to find a thought, but found none whatever. Dan Malley, hunched on a rock, squinted his eyes and stared through the dazzle of the sunshine.

"You've still got a good herd," said Tucker. "Those horses look as fit as any I ever saw the boys handle."

"Fitter," said Malley, touched on a tender side of his nature. "Mighty lot fitter. No cold cayuse blood in that lot. Look at the little gray there. No bigger'n a mustang, but all hard-hammered iron, I tell you. That filly, she could jump over the moon."

"She's got a set of legs," agreed Tucker, losing some of his own worries as he gazed at the beauty of the mare.

"But that chestnut gelding, he's the trick," said Malley.

He pointed toward the farther side of the clearing, where a brilliant chestnut was grazing, the sun glimmering along its silken flanks.

"That's a 'hoss'!" said Malley.

"Yeah, that's a hoss and a half," said Tucker. He added: "Sixteen two, if he's an inch."

Malley glanced askance at the other, opening his eyes a little.

"You know a hoss from a hand-saw," he said. Sixteen two is just what he is. There ain't no padding neither. He's a hoss and a half."

"He could move, I'll bet," said Tucker.

He was rather glad to talk himself somewhat deeper into the good graces of Malley.

"Can he move? He 'can' move," declared Malley. "I'll tell you what. His grandpa won the Louisiana Derby with a hundred and forty pounds in the saddle. That's what he done. His pa was a steeplechaser, and he was one of the best. They used to put a ton on him, the handicappers did, but they couldn't anchor him. He was always in the money. His ma, she burned up a mile in one thirty-six and some-thing. That's how 'she' could move."

"What did they go and geld that chestnut for?" asked Tucker. "Why, out of stock like that—"

"Well, it's like this," said Malley. "You take a racehoss owner, and he don't figger on what a hoss can do in an all-day run, or wrangling through soft sand, or twisting through rocks. All he cares is up to about a mile and a half of sprinting on a track, as smooth as a table top, or over the brush for a few miles with fine turf under them. That's all he cares about. He wants a set of watch springs, regular Swiss movement, or else he don't want nothing. You take a hoss that can't move his mile in around one forty, what good is he on a track? Only good to eat his fool head off. But that there chestnut, that Jerry hoss, though he ain't got the foot, he can run all day. And that's the sort of hoss that we want, ain't it?"

"It is," agreed Tucker devoutly.

"At that," went on Malley, "he can run away from everything else we've got, even in the first mile, except that scared jackrabbit, that filly, little gray streak of devil. But the second mile he catches her. And the third mile her head is bobbing, and he's just loafing along wondering how long it'll take himself to get warmed up."

He stopped talking and began to chuckle a little.

"Where'd you get him?" asked Tucker.

"Well, I'll tell you. There was a big sale about ten days back, and a lot of fine stock was sent under the hammer, and I went down and had a look. They had a fine show of hossflesh."

"Have to pay high for this one?"

"I paid pretty high," answered Malley. "I paid by sitting up mostly all night till the Negro in the stable went to sleep. There was a barking dog that bothered me some, too."

"What did you do to the dog?"

"Caught him by the throat and choked him till he was limp. Then I took the chestnut. It was quite a ride I had, at that. The dog woke up in time to make some racket; they seen me sliding away through the moonlight, and they made a good try for me. But the chestnut, he turned 'em into fools! A nice hoss! And gentle as a lamb. You take that hoss, he'll stand for you, the minute that you call his name. And when you hop on his back, you don't need no saddle or bridle—unless you mind the sweat stains on your pants."

"Just press him on the neck?" asked Tucker, growing strangely interested.

"That's all. Or you don't even need to do that. He guides like a cutting hoss from way back. Give him a nudge with your knee, and that's enough."

"Wouldn't buck, I guess."

"Him? He's all silk. He thinks every man that gets on his back is his uncle. He wouldn't know how to buck, even if he wanted to."

"I'd like to try him," observed Tucker.

The other grinned.

"Sure you would. And maybe you'd like to send that chestnut flash out of the clearing and right down the valley yonder, and get back to Indian Gulch, and tell Tag Enderby how things is going, and how this place could be rounded up. You'd like that pretty well, too, wouldn't you?"

"Wasn't even thinking of that," said Tucker.

"You keep away from the hosses," said the chief sternly. "I dunno, Tucker. You may be all right. But I got my doubts. I ain't taking any chances."

He rose, growling like a dog, and went into the lean-to.

For a moment, Tucker sat basking in the sun, but he was no longer sleepy. The idea was mastering his mind. The chestnut, to be sure, looked all that had been spoken of it—swift, gentle, and strong. And, once on the back of that powerful runner, was there not an excellent chance that he could dash down the bank of the stream without being overtaken by pursuit?

If there was a watcher ahead of him—well, that might be handled, too. For he had a revolver at his hip, and he could shoot as well as the next one.

He would have vastly preferred, of course, a bridle and saddle on the runner. But it would be too difficult to make these arrangements.

He rose and began to wander, keeping along the edge of the clearing, under the shade of the trees.

Suddenly Skeet Raleigh stepped out, with a rifle over the bend of his arm. He appeared from among the trees.

"You know the orders from the chief," said Skeet, looking rather hungrily at big Tucker. "If you try to slide out of sight into the trees you get a slug of lead."

"I know," said Tucker. "I'm going to live a long time, though, Skeet."

"I was just telling you," said Skeet sourly, and stepped back among the trees.

But he looked very assured, and Tucker paid no heed to him from that moment. He was reasonably confident that Skeet Raleigh would not have hair-trigger suspicions about him for a few moments.

In the meantime he drifted around the edge of the clearing until he was close to the chestnut. It had stopped grazing now and stood in the shade where a golden dappling of sunshine fell upon it.

"Jerry!" he called softly.

The chestnut lifted its proud head and stood alert. It turned a little and looked at the man out of bright, fearless eyes.

Tucker glanced about him.

Yonder was the lean-to, with not a man in sight in front of it. And straight ahead was the opening from the clearing down the shelving banks of the creek.

If this horse could move as he had been told, two seconds after a rider was on its back, it would be below rifle range down the slope of the valley. There would then be only the danger of the guard ahead—he would trust his revolver to meet that danger—or of pursuit from behind. And against that pursuit he could match the vaunted speed of the gelding.

There was danger, but Tucker was not new to danger. The horrible tremor that had come over him in the jail at the moment of his deliverance was now far from his nerves, for this was the open theater in which he was accustomed to live and to work.

So he made up his mind. He stepped closer, gathered in his hand a twist of the gleaming mane, just above the withers, swung back, with his shoulders almost touching the long neck of the gelding, and then stepped forward and leaped.

He shot up high, and, while he was still in the air, his blurred eyes saw a picture of none other than Malley himself stepping at this luckless moment into the doorway of the lean-to.

Malley himself!—and yet, for all that Tucker could see in the flash of that instant, there was no weapon sparkling in the hand of the chief, and he seemed, in fact, to be laughing.

Down came Tucker with a firm grip upon the shining back of the gelding. The next moment, he felt that he was cleaving through the upper firmament. For the chestnut bounded straight up, arrowlike, with ears flattened, and came down like a true sunfisher on stiffened forelegs.

It almost jerked Tucker from his seat, the first maneuver.

He called out softly to the horse, but his voice appeared merely to madden the brute more. Around that clearing they tore in a frantic, zigzag circle. Other men came running out to see the show. Well was Tucker known for his brilliant riding, and never did he stick to his post more skillfully than on this day, but he understood now the laughter of the chief, and the delighted whooping of the other outlaws. He had been sold—sold just like a fool and a tenderfoot, and he would pay with his life for his folly!

Twice they shot around the clearing, and then with a final whip snap, the chestnut shot Tucker into the air.

He landed heavily on his head and shoulders. The world flashed from fire to black.

When he wakened, a boot heel was jabbing him in the ribs, and the harsh voice of Dan Malley was ordering him to wake up.

He pushed himself up on his hands. His head was still reeling, but one glance at the black face of Malley was enough to clear his brain again.

The chief was saying, slowly and coldly:

"Pull him together, some of you boys. We been needing an example set, around here. We been needing it for a long time. The boys have been slipping out of my hand, and now I'm going to gather 'em in again. It ain't the first day that I've killed a man, and it ain't likely to be the last day. Get Tucker on his feet, and tell him to start his prayers!"

Fame for a Lawman

I N Indian Gulch, Tag Enderby had turned in, after the freeing of the prisoner from the jail, and he slept the round of the clock, arose, dined heartily, walked up and down the street a turn or two, and then turned in and slept the clock around again.

It was a time of fearful uncertainty and suspense for old Benton and for Ray Champion, but for Tag Enderby, it was a time of sleep, and he stored up strength like a hibernating animal. When he wakened from that second long sleep, he doused himself with cold water, shaved, dressed, and came down after the middle of the day with a question in his mind.

He saw old Benton on the veranda of the hotel, with a haunted look in his face, and of him Tag asked:

"What's the news?"

"No news," said Benton. And he looked fearfully at Tag.

"No news is bad news, just now," said Tag. "We'll go in and eat and then—"

"Eat?" exclaimed Benton. "I can't eat, man."

"Come and watch me," answered Tag. "It may give you an appetite."

So Benton went in with him and watched Tag eat like an Indian just in from a warpath.

"Tucker is stuck somewhere," said Tag. "That's the feeling that I have about it, anyway."

"D'ye think so, Tag?" asked the other, with sorrowful anxiety.

"I think so," said Tag.

"He may have simply gone on a long ride to find Malley It ain't so easy to find a fox like Malley, not even for one of his own tribe, if he's hiding out and holing up."

"It's not easy," said Tag. "But Tucker can find him. Tucker's an old member of the gang. And I don't think that he's gone so far. Malley would be pretty near."

"The posse have combed every inch of ground for fifty mile around Indian Gulch!" exclaimed Benton excitedly.

"A posse never really combs anything but its own hair," answered Tag. "You know how it is. Twenty pairs of eyes are worth one-twentieth of one pair. I'd rather have one man like you on the trail than any twenty posses, Benton!"

"Well, I've been on a trail, at that," said Benton. "There ain't any doubt of that. Man, man if we could pick out the trail of poor Tucker, and where he's gone!"

He had learned of Tag's plan with frightful anxiety, and now dismay stared out of his widened eyes.

"Tucker's hung up," said Tag. "That's plain to me. I feel it in my bones."

"He may have turned back to the gang," suggested Benton.

"He may," agreed Tag. "I could only take a chance on him; that's all. I want to finish this cigarette and another cup of coffee. You go find Champion and saddle the horses, will you? I have a thing to do after I get through with the meal, too."

"Are you going to let me go along?" asked Benton eagerly.

"Would you want to?"

"Would I? More'n life I'd want it."

"Then you'll come," said Tag. "I'm only a fair hand at

reading sign. And Champion's not much good, either, I think. It'll be mostly on your shoulders, Mr. Benton. You get Ray Champion, will you? I'll be ready to start in about half an hour."

When Benton had left the room, Tag was not long behind him. He paused at the hotel desk to pay his bill. Then he went straight to the office of Deputy Sheriff Locksley. The latter was groaning over a set of badly smudged finger prints. He looked up with a sigh and a smile toward Tag Enderby.

"There's no news, Tag," he said. "There's no news at all! Malley's faded out. But I've got the country stirred up, and we'll be having word before long, one of these days."

"I've got something from Malley for you," said Tag.

And he began to take from his pockets sheaf after sheaf of bills in brown-paper wrappers. The deputy sheriff, as he counted them, allowed his eyes to grow larger and larger. Before he had finished, he was pale with excitement, and looking alternately at the window and then at the door.

"Man," muttered Deputy Locksley, "here's a fortune to make half a dozen men rich!"

"It is," answered Tag. "Now, Locksley, it's up to you to use it the right way."

"It's from Malley, you say?"

"Yes, it's from Malley."

"How shall I use it?" asked Locksley.

"You know there are plenty of ranchers, here and there, who have gone against Malley, and he's raised the devil with 'em in consequence."

"Yes, I know that."

"And fifteen or twenty small banks that have been

cleaned out of a few thousand dollars apiece?"

"Ay, that's true."

"Well, then, take this coin and spread it around the coun-tryside. You don't need to tell 'em where you got the coin. That is, you can leave me out of it."

"It's a big job, Tag," said Locksley. "There's a lot of people that'll hate me for not giving 'em as much as they want for their share."

"I tell you," insisted Tag Enderby, "that by the time you've finished off passing out this coin, you'll have the county in the palm of your hand. You can run for sheriff at the next election, and the job's yours. Don't you see that? Before you get through, you'll have a hundred men and women, to say nothing of the kids, all ready to fight for you! This ought to make you the biggest fellow in the range, Locksley. It's going to make you famous!"

Locksley, slowly lifting his head, stared out the window as he visioned the golden picture which Tag was drawing for him.

Finally he nodded.

"You're right, Tag," said he.

He got up, locked the money into the safe which stood in a corner of the room, and returned to face his visitor.

"Tag," he said, "you got that money from Malley?"

"Yes."

"Swiped it, eh?"

"I took it," corrected Tag, "with Malley standing by. That's one reason why he's so fond of me."

The deputy sheriff grinned.

"Ay, fond enough to poison you, all right."

Then he added: "What made you do it?"

Tag shrugged his shoulders.

"I don't know exactly. But I'll tell you this much. There's times when a fellow specially wants to have his hands clean."

"I know," said Locksley, looking hard at the other, as though seeing a stranger for the first time.

"I've come to one of those times; that's all," said Tag Enderby.

Locksley followed him to the street.

"Tag," he said, "there's a queer look about you—a sort of do-or-die look, if you don't mind me saying that!"

"No, I don't mind," answered Tag.

"Is there anything that I can help about? The whole town's behind you. You certainly ought to know that."

"I know," Tag said. "But the job that I have on hand is too ticklish for that. I have more hands than I can use already. It's now nothing but the long chance that I have to take."

"And a hard chance, Tag?"

"Yes," admitted Tag, "it's hard enough. Good-by, Locksley."

They shook hands, and Locksley watched the other turn down the street. For a long time, he stared after him, remaining steadfast in his place. Strange thoughts came over him; and the thoughts were not all for his own future, which was locked up, behind him, in the safe in the corner of his office. Yes, there would be fame for him, no doubt. But what about the man who had brought that huge fortune to him, to spend undoing the evil wrought by the bandit?

A sauntering puncher stopped near by.

"Hullo, Locksley," he said. "What's the Malley news

today? What you looking at, man?"

"Tag Enderby," answered Locksley.

"Well, he's worth seeing, too. But sometimes he's a flash that the eye can't follow so very easy. What's he up to now?"

"He's going out to pull old man Death by the chin whiskers," said Locksley. "That's what he's going to do."

"Well, I wish him luck," said the puncher.

Locksley made no reply, but turned back into his office gloomily. He felt that the savor had been suddenly snatched from existence and that he himself was a worthless figure. Those who were worth while were like Tag Enderby, ready to throw away life for a mere idea.

~39~
Reading Sign

I N the grove behind the jail stood Tag Enderby with Benton and Ray Champion. Tag was saying quietly: "Here's where I left the horses. Here's where you find the trail of Tucker's horse as he rode away. There it is. There was a rain that day—a good sprinkle. Look here where he hit a soft spot. There's the track of all four shoes. But, confound it, they look like ten million other tracks to me!"

Ray Champion and old Benton were bending over the tracks. Champion eventually shook his head.

"It's no go," said he. "Goodish-sized tracks, all right, but they're no bigger than a thousand other horses would make. Nothing funny about the shoes, either. No bars, no calks, even. You might expect to find some calf traces, in a horse shod for the mountains! I can't make anything of this muddle."

Old Benton stood up from his examination, tying the last of several knots in a string which he had taken from his pocket.

He leaned against a tree then, and filled and lighted his pipe. From under his bush of gray brows, his eyes were twinkling.

"Mr. Benton, you've got something," said Tag Enderby. "Let us in on it."

"I ain't got nothing that ain't there for you boys to see," said Benton. "But still, it's enough for me. I'll foller that hoss to the end of time—so long as he leaves a print on the ground every hundred yards or so."

"How'll you follow him? What's the sign?" asked Tag. He could hardly believe that the older man might prove useful; it was a mere instinct that had induced him to include the other in the relief party.

"Well," said the other, "I'll tell you. There's a lot of hosses with feet about this size, but there's darn few feet 'exactly' this size. And the hoss that has the same rounds as other hosses for the front hoofs won't have the same ovals for the hind hoofs. Then these here shoes are smooth and light, and wore sort of thin. Look at how low the frog comes down, and leaves the print of itself good and deep in this soft place. Look here, too. Those shoes are pretty old, and hoofs have growed out a little beyond the iron. You see that ragged little line around the good, clean print of the shoes? Then there's the length of the step. A hoss mostly steps along just one length. I've got the measurements—the width and the length of every hoof, and the length of the

walking step, too. Later on, I'll get the trotting and gal-
loping length. But right the way it is, I reckon that I could
follow that hoss clean across a continent, so long's he'd
leave me a print now and then."

Ray Champion looked at the other with interest.

"You know," he said to Tag, "I think there's luck in the
number three. And here's three of us to tackle this trail. Tag,
let's start!"

"We'll start," said Tag. "It's a late start, anyway. But what
could I do till I began to have the idea that he was held up,
somewhere—Tucker, I mean to say?"

They mounted their horses and followed steadily along
through the woods to the point where Tucker had entered
upon the street. And here all signs of the hoof marks were
dissolved, lost in the stream of hundreds of similar mark-
ings which had flowed up and down the way in the interim.

So they struck out beyond the edge of the town, and
presently, as he skirted along the side of the road, Benton
called out. He had found the sign again, and now he followed it, bending a little to one side from the saddle and
never taking his glance for an instant from the ground.

He led them straight to the shepherd's shack. A brawny
woman came to the door and eyed them.

"Who're ye, and whatcha want?" she demanded.

"Not a thing," said Benton, waving his companions back.

He pointed down to the ground in front of the door, as he
led them away.

"Tucker didn't sit his horse there long enough to leave
even a double set of tracks," he explained. "We'll get
nothin' there. Here's a stretch of gravel. You boys try to
follow the sign through it. I'll cast ahead to the other side

onto the smooth again."

He cast ahead. In the hard gravel the tracks presently, to the eyes of Champion and Tag Enderby, disappeared. But the cheerful call of old Benton brought them forward once more. He had found the proper sign, and, without once being in doubt, without once dismounting, he went on to the next halting place, far higher up among the hills.

"It's like a fairy story," said Champion to Tag. "The old boy reads the mind of those tracks and finds out where they're going."

They came now, under the guidance of old Benton, to a wretched, down-at-the-heel shack with a large barn behind it, and the usual tangle of sheds and corral fencing. Tag squinted at the place and then nodded.

"I've seen it before, and the place has seen me," he said. "We'll take a look here. This is just the place Tucker may have asked the way. 'I' would have asked it here, if I'd thought to come this way from Indian Gulch."

He kicked at the front door, as he spoke, then reined his horse back.

The door was flung open instantly, and a red-faced woman appeared, bawling out:

"Who's banging at me front door? Where was you raised? Ain'tcha got no manners whatever?"

Tag Enderby lifted his hat to her with a flawless gesture.

"I'm lookin' for Bill," he said gently.

"You're lookin' for Bill, are you?" said she. "Well, you ain't goin' to see him. Bill's layin' down and restin'. He ain't goin' to be disturbed."

"Hullo, Bill!" called Tag.

"Shut yer face and back out of this!" advised the woman

savagely. "If Bill comes, he'll come out with that that'll start you away a darn sight faster than you come here! You can trust to that!"

And suddenly the hairy face of Bill appeared in the gap of the door. His soiled shirt sleeves were turned up; the red flannel of the undershirt, however, was exposed, hanging in tatters about the wrists. He was a little man, with a hanging head and red, horrible eyes, like the eyes of a bloodthirsty ferret.

"You want me, do you?" said he, barking out the words. He had his right hand behind him.

Tag smiled down at him.

"Don't move that right hand, Bill," said he, "or you'll die five times in a row."

Bill blinked at him.

"Listen to the loud-mouthed braggart!" shouted the woman. "Go and trim him down a little, will you?"

Fury worked in the face of Bill, for a moment, but his right hand did not appear.

"Who are you?" asked he.

"I'm a poor traveler asking the way," said Tag.

"The way to what?" asked Bill sourly.

"The way to Malley."

"Close the door, ma," said Bill, aside.

He added aloud: "I don't know, and what's more, I don't care where Malley is!"

The door slammed.

Tag dropped to the ground from his horse. He struck the door lightly with his hand.

A new voice—though it came from the throat of Bill—now roared with a beastly violence from inside the house:

"Get away from the door, or I'll blast you with a buckshot. You hear me?"

"I hear you," said Tag. "Now you hear me. I'm Tag Enderby. If you don't open that door for me, I'll open it for myself, and you'll wish that you'd taken my first advice."

There was a stunned moment of silence.

"Maggie, it's Enderby," they heard Bill mutter huskily.

"You jackass!" gasped his wife. "Didn't you know him?"

"I didn't rightly look at him. I didn't have all the sleep out of my eyes, but it's Enderby, all right!"

"Go talk to him. But don't say nothin'. Keep your face shut or I'll—"

The rest of the sentence was lost behind the door. Then Bill stood before them, nodding, ducking his ugly head.

"Why, hullo, Tag," he said, "I didn't rightly get my eye on you."

"Oh, that's all right," said Tag. "I know how it is, Bill. Faces slide out of a fellow's mind. I was just asking you the way to Malley."

Bill blinked.

"Malley? Sure!" said he. "Malley's down in Watterson Creek down in the canyon, there. You'll find him in Watterson Creek, and you'll—"

Tag glided close to him, his nostrils quivering.

"You lie!" said he.

"So help me!" gasped Bill. "That's where I last heard—"

"You lie!" repeated Tag. "I'll give you one more chance to tell the truth."

"Tag," whined Bill, "you know how it is—I been pretty close to Malley—I'm dog-gone sorry that you fell out with him. Malley's up on Goose Mountain. I kind of didn't want

~ 267 ~

to tell you—"

"Where on Goose Mountain?"

"Up on the high shoulders, to the south, and—"

"That's enough," said Tag.

He remounted, waved farewell to Bill, and as he rode off with the other two, he heard the loud, barking voice of Mrs. Bill as she soundly berated her husband.

"How did you know that he was lying the first time?" asked Champion. "I'd think that Watterson Creek would be a more likely place to find Malley than Goose Mountain."

"He blinked," said Tag. "And then there was a sort of flash in my mind. I don't know how it was. Just sort of a flash. I took the chance, and the chance turned out."

Old Benton was wagging his head and grinning.

"Ah, but they fear you, Tag, my boy," said he. "There was a time when I was young that they feared me, too. Some of them did. I had a kind of a name for myself."

"You're the fastest trailer that I ever rode with," said Tag. "You ought to have had a name for that. But this Goose Mountain business, what d'you think of it, Ray?"

"I know Goose Mountain, and I've been on the south shoulder of it," answered Champion. "There's an old wreck of a miner's cabin up there. Somebody sank a bit of a shaft a long time ago. I know that shoulder, well enough. It'll be a hard place to reach."

"We'll have to try it," answered Tag.

"And when you get there, boys?" asked old Benton. "Then what, when you get there?"

"When we get there, we'll take our chances, again," said Tag Enderby.

"It's always chances that you're taking," complained

Benton. "But I'm with you to the finish. There's Goose Mountain yonder, poking her head into the sky. And there's my girl, most likely. And there's death, too, I reckon, for more'n one man this day and night. All I pray is that it don't come to one of you boys!"

He spoke with such an obvious sincerity, and so from the heart, that Tag looked sharply across at him.

"Listen to me, Mr. Benton," said he. "You've done yourself proud in getting us this far along the trail. There's no use trying to go any farther with us. The job that's ahead of us now is a job for younger men, if you don't mind me saying so."

"I don't mind you saying so," answered Benton cheerfully, "but I'm with you so far, and I'm going to stay to the end. I know what you think about me—but maybe you'll find that bad eyes, even, don't altogether ruin a man's shooting, sometimes. I'm going to stay along with you both."

Tag Enderby thoughtfully shook his head.

"It's no good arguing," he said. "We have to get on. It's nearly sunset time, and we have a good many miles to go from here, before we hit the top of the mountain. You can see that. Mr. Benton, you'll have to turn back!"

Old Benton looked at them wistfully.

"Is that final, Tag?" he asked.

"Yes, that's as final as anything can be."

"I'll back up then," said the other. "I suppose that I'll have to back up, but it's hard to go. Tag—Ray—good-by, lads. More power to you. I'll be prayin' like a fool for you, every minute!"

On Trial

T HE cabin in the clearing upon the high southern shoulder of Goose Mountain had become a sort of tribunal. The members of the court were Skeet Raleigh and Dan Malley.

The man on trial was Tucker.

The spectator was Molly Benton.

It was an old-fashioned trial, and it had now reached the moment when torture is applied.

The torment was applied in the following manner:

Malley, seated, faced Tucker, who was opposite him at the rough table, being securely tied to his chair. Skeet Raleigh stood by with a pair of revolvers weighting down his hands. There was no real reason, perhaps, why he should be displaying the weapons, when the prisoner was totally disarmed and securely bound. But the guns he had, and he seemed to be comforted by his official position as sergeant at arms.

"I've laid you up for a whole day and more," said Malley.

Tucker nodded.

He had changed a good deal since his arrival at the camp. His cheeks were furrowed and sunken; his eyes were set off with huge, purple-black circles.

"And why did I lay you up?" asked Malley.

"You wanted to give me a chance to get more scared," said Tucker.

The girl stood back against the wall, by the stove. Her strange, dull-blue eyes rarely shifted from the faces before her, gathered around the lantern on the table. Steadily her glance went from one to the other, or occasionally lifted to the form of Skeet Raleigh, almost lost against the wall on the farther side of the room.

"I wasn't trying to scare you," insisted Malley. "I was trying to give you a chance."

Tucker said nothing.

"What I mean to say," said Malley, "is this. You deserve dying, don't you?"

"Ah, Malley, try to be a man, won't you?" asked the girl, from her place by the stove.

Malley turned and grinned at her without mirth.

"You don't like it, eh? Well, you'll stay right here and see how a man acts. And if he don't act right, you'll see him die right here on the floor in front of you."

He turned back to Tucker.

"You deserve to die!" he repeated, more loudly.

Tucker shrugged his shoulders.

"I warned you," said Malley. "I warned you that if you tried to make the break, or tried to hop onto one of the hosses, you'd be a goner, if I could make you gone."

"Yeah, you warned me," said Tucker.

"I told you a coupla lies about the chestnut, because I seen a sort of far-away look in your eyes that meant a good deal to me. So I warned you. I wanted to see what you'd do. And pretty soon I had my chance."

He leaned back in his chair and laughed heartily.

Then straightening, he went on: "Maybe I should 'a' finished you off, right then and there. But I didn't. I remembered that I'd knowed you for quite a long spell. I didn't hold it agin you, the way you let that Enderby manhandle you down there in Indian Gulch. I forgot even that. I decided that I'd give you another break for your life."

Tucker shrugged his shoulders again.

"Now," said Malley, "you tell the girl what I wanted you to do. See if she don't think that it's a good idea."

"He wanted me," said Tucker, "to write a letter to Tag, telling him that I'd spotted Malley, and that I had had a bad fall, and that I was laid up, in a certain place. And if he'd come out and give me a hand, I'd then pass on all the information about where to find Malley. That's the sort of a letter he wanted me to write. If I write it, he says that I'll be free to ride out of camp—as soon as their trap has chewed up Tag."

The girl nodded.

"He has a lot of pretty ideas—Malley has," she remarked. "He's what a lot of people would call a big help in a pinch, I guess."

"Yeah, a lot of people would call him a big help in a pinch," said Tucker. "But that's the letter that he wanted me to write."

He turned back to Malley.

"I won't write it," he said quietly.

"D'you mean it, man?" asked Malley pleasantly, with a sort of cheerful amazement in his voice.

"I mean it," said Tucker.

"The girl braces you up a good deal, don't she?" asked Malley curiously. "I know that you ain't any hero. You hate dying about as bad as most of us do. Maybe a little more than most. But I suppose to have a girl stand by and see you take your medicine—that bucks you up a good deal, don't it?"

"She's nothing to me," answered Tucker, as steadily as

before. "I don't even know she's in the room, hardly."

"That ain't very polite," Malley sneered.

"I ain't aiming at being polite," said Tucker gravely. "I'm aiming at dying as well as I can; that's all."

"And what holds you up?" asked Malley. "What puts the starch in you, you worthless, yaller cur?"

He roared out the words.

"Tag Enderby," said Tucker.

Malley bounded to his feet. In a stride he was around the table. One could see that years and increased weight had not robbed him of his old, catlike speed of action, when a crisis came. It was little wonder, watching him now, that his gang held him in a mighty awe.

"Tag Enderby" shouted Malley. "And what has he got to do with it? What's he got to do, bucking you up here? Enderby ain't here. He's nowhere near!"

"It's not his nearness," said the other, undisturbed. "But I've had my life back from him twice. And now I'm ready to die once for him."

Malley leaned, and struck the prisoner heavily across the face with the cup of his hand. Then he went back to his chair and sat down. The girl brought him a cup of coffee.

"Take a sip of this, Dan," she said. "It'll brace you up a lot. It'll give you a chance to be almost a human being again, instead of such a beast."

He raised his head and looked up at her with strange mixture of admiration and hate.

"There you are again," said he, "sinking your claws into me. But you're going to learn, before the night's over, what manner of man you deal with, when you deal with me."

"Why, Dan," said she, "I never doubted that you were

capable of a murder—even a murder before a woman."

She filled another cup with coffee and brought it to Tucker.

"Stand away from him!" shouted Malley.

"Oh, I won't touch the ropes that are holding him," said the girl. "But this will help him through—until the bullet smashes his brains out. I suppose you'll shoot for the brain, Dan?"

She held the cup at the lips of Tucker. He drank deep, and in drinking, his eyes were up to hers, tortured eyes, in a desperate seeking.

She went back to the stove again, suddenly blinded with tears. Malley, reaching out, caught her by the arm and jerked her close to the lantern. He peered up under her eyelids.

"Crying!" he sneered. "I knew that I'd fetch you, sooner or later. Crying for him, are you? You'll cry more when you see him flop out of his chair!"

"You can hold me without breaking my arm, Dan," said she. "D'you mind?"

He freed her, and drew a breath.

"If I was ten years younger," he said, "if I was ten years younger, I'd follow you around the world on my hands and knees. I'd let you kick me in the face. I wouldn't mind because, by thunder, you're wonderful!"

She made no answer. She drew back to the shadow beside the stove, and once more she was watching.

"Well, Tucker," said Malley, his cheerful tone returning, "I'm giving you your last chance. Write that letter to Tag Enderby, and you're a free man. Will you do it? Yes or no—and this is final."

"It's no, then," said Tucker.

"You fool!" murmured Malley.

Tucker once more shrugged his wide shoulders.

"Tell me," said Malley. "You got any messages that you want to leave behind you?"

"No messages," said Tucker.

"No friends, eh?"

"No," said Tucker. "I never was worthy of being a friend to Tag."

"The devil with Tag!" exclaimed the bandit.

"You'll leave a friend behind you, Tuck," said the girl from the shadow by the stove.

"Thanks, Molly," said Tucker. "That's right kind of you."

"By thunder," said Malley, "I kind of think that you'll die without any regret."

"No, I've got one regret," said Tucker.

"What's that? Tell me that?"

"I'm sorry that I won't be on hand when Tag Enderby finds you."

Malley stirred in his chair, but he restrained his wrath and simply answered:

"When I meet Tag Enderby, I meet him man to man, and face to face—and he's a dead man that day. Now, Tucker, your last hour's come on you. If you're a praying man, now's your time to pray."

"I don't mind if I do," said Tucker, retaining his wonderful calm. "But praying is kind of out of my habit, for twenty, thirty years. Molly, it might be that you could think up a prayer for me. I'd say it after you."

"You don't need a prayer, Tuck," said the girl in her quiet voice. "Surely God is close to heroes when they die."

"A hero, is he?" snarled Malley.

Suddenly Skeet Raleigh broke into a high-pitched, screeching laughter.

It seemed to grate upon the nerves of Malley.

"Shut up that noise!" he shouted.

And Skeet was still.

"Now let's have your prayer, if you want to say one," said Malley. "I don't mind. It kind of amuses me, though, to see a growed-up man turn soft and maudlin. I got five men standing and walking guard around this house, and I reckon that there ain't one of 'em that would believe how you're turning soft, Tuck."

But Tucker paid no heed. He raised his head. He closed his eyes.

"I'll try a prayer," he remarked. "It seems to me like I kind of need one."

And he said: "God Almighty, the things I have done have been mighty bad. I've had a hope of doing something better before the finish. You believe me if you can. Amen!"

"Well," said Malley, "it's a short prayer, anyway. Now, Tuck, are you ready!"

He laid a long-barreled Colt upon the edge of the table. Tucker turned deathly white.

"I'm ready," he whispered.

"You're turning yaller," said Malley triumphantly, "like I knew that you would turn."

"I'm scared," said Tucker faintly. "But I'm ready. Pull the trigger, Malley. I've done with living!"

Malley said slowly, gathering heat:

"You been a coward, a sneak, a traitor, and a failure. I'm going to wipe you out. Molly, this here is for you to see. I'm going to bust your nerves to smithereens. I'm going to make you screech. I'm tired of the smooth way that you've got of looking everything in the eye. Here's for you!"

He raised the gun and sighted along it at the forehead of Tucker.

At that moment a gun roared. It was not in the hand of Malley, however, and a sudden outbreaking of shouts shook the cabin. Malley started up and turned savagely toward the door.

~41~
The Captive

T HE yells of alarm ended almost as soon as they began, however, and in the place of them followed jubilations, almost as noisy, and a hand beat on the door.

"What's up?" called Malley. "What fool's trick is this?"

"Open the door!" called the voice of young Bender. "We got him, by thunder! We got him helpless, here!"

Malley turned toward the girl sharply, before he answered.

"It's Tag Enderby!" he said with a savage joy in his voice.

"It's not he," replied Molly.

"Throw the door open!" Malley said to Skeet Raleigh.

The door was flung wide, and into the room poured half a dozen of Malley's men, bringing with them the heavy shoulders, the stalwart body, the courageous face of Ray Champion.

"Champion!" called out Malley, half in delight and half

in disappointment.

Then he added: "It might 'a' been a bigger and a better bird, boys, but you got something worth while in the net. Who's the man to catch the birds, then? Is Dan Malley the boy? Is he the one? You tell me that, will you? Who set the trap, and who's catching the wild hawks in it?"

He laughed, and struck his thigh triumphantly. His joyous eye ran over the faces in the room.

Molly was already standing before Ray Champion, but Skeet Raleigh roughly thrust her away.

"You can whine over the body of him, later on," said he, brutally.

"Get out and watch," said Malley. "If this one is here, then Enderby's close by. Get up the rest of the boys. Call 'em in. By thunder, this is going to be a night for me that I'll remember. It'll be a night for you, Molly, my girl. I'm going to show you three shows instead of one. That's what I'm going to do. I'm going to do better than my promises to you, because big-hearted is what I am, me girl!" His head wagged from side to side.

"You'll not catch Tag Enderby," said Ray Champion. "He's not near here. He was hurt in a fall—and I came on alone—like a fool."

"Tryin' to stalk the house," said the rejoicing voice of Bender. "About as soft and quiet he moved as an elephant in a zoo. I had to laugh, pretty near, when I seen him comin'. We just dived in and got him. There was nothin' to it!"

He laughed long and loud. For he knew that this work of the capture would make him an important man in the band, in spite of his youth.

"Enderby's hurt, you say?" exclaimed Malley. "Hurt in a

fall, d'you say? I don't believe it. He never tumbled from a horse, and I've seen him ride the worst of 'em!"

"Any man can have a fall, when a horse breaks a leg," said Champion.

"What horse was he riding?"

"Bay, with black points—"

"Ah," said Malley, in real agony of heart. "That one is gone, eh?"

"Yes," said Champion. "Enderby shot it, after his fall."

"He had luck," said the other. "If he hadn't had the fall, he'd 'a' been here, caught in the same net."

"If he hadn't had the fall," answered Ray Champion, "he'd be here watching the heels of the Malley gang as they dived for cover."

"Shut up, you!" began Skeet Raleigh furiously. "I'm one that never would run from Tag Enderby."

"Keep out of it, Skeet," interrupted the leader. "Keep well out of it. When it comes to a show-down with Enderby, I've promised myself the finishing of him!"

"Do you boys listen to Malley when he brags like that?" asked the girl suddenly. "Don't you smile? Or do you do that behind his back?"

"You—" began Malley, whirling on her.

"Oh, come, Dan," said she; "you know how it is. You have to uphold your dignity. But don't make yourself ridiculous. All of the boys know that you're frightened of the very name of Tag Enderby."

She had worked so long, during her stay in the camp, upon that same theme, that the very brain of Malley seemed to have weakened in this respect. His sense of humor left him. As he had struck Tucker, he suddenly whipped the flat of his hand across the face of the girl.

She neither cried out nor moved. Her head was jerked suddenly backward by the force of the blow, but otherwise she did not wince.

There was a sudden, dangerous muttering from the members of the gang in the room. And the shrill voice of Skeet Raleigh cried out, as the spokesman:

"That's enough of that, Dan! We're with you everywhere else, but—keep—your—hands—off—that—woman!"

He spaced the last words of his warning, and shouted them out so that Malley, infuriated, turned upon him to make a savage rejoinder. But the hardened faces of his followers gave Malley pause, and suddenly he realized that he had stepped over the proper bounds.

Instantly he retreated from his false position.

"Molly," he said, "I'm mighty sorry that I did that. All at once you just seemed to me a mean kid, not a growed-up woman. I couldn't hold in, I tell you. Hearing the way that you've been badgering me about Tag Enderby—it sort of makes me hot. You know—and the boys all know—that I'll meet him night or day, with a gun or knife, on foot or on horseback. Everybody knows that Dan Malley never shrunk from meeting any man, face to face, in a fair fight!"

"Yeah," said Skeet Raleigh, "we know that chief. We never seen you back down, none of us."

"And if Tag Enderby was here right now—" exclaimed the other.

"He is," said a voice just outside the door of the shack.

That voice was sufficiently well known so that every member of the gang in the room dived suddenly for corners and the floor. Only Malley remained where he was. For he was directly in front of the entrance, and he knew that a gun from the dark would cover him perfectly.

So he stood where he was, his right hand still raised in the gesture with which he had emphasized his last speech.

Molly, as though a power had been removed from her, slumped suddenly back against the wall, with the faintest of moans. Tucker raised his head as though he had heard a voice from heaven. But Ray Champion, pale, stern of face, stared constantly at the girl, as though striving to drink up the last trace of meaning that appeared in her face.

"It's all right, Dan," said Tag Enderby, still lost in the darkness near the door. "You ought to teach the boys that they stand guard a lot better in the night outside a house than all crowded into one lighted room. But it's all right. I'm not going to shoot you down, Dan, from the dark. I never liked murder. It never was fashionable with me, as you might say."

Malley answered nothing, but his hoarse breathing could be heard distinctly through the entire room.

"We'll come to a little understanding—before I step inside, Dan," Tag went on.

"Yeah," said Malley huskily. "We'll talk—Tag."

He could not help adding: "Seems like you've got the drop on me."

"Yes," said Tag Enderby. "I have the drop. I have the drop right on the wrinkle between your eyes. It's a good place to plant a slug, wouldn't you say?"

"Yeah, I'd say that," said Malley.

"Very well," Tag went on. "The thing that I suggest is that I come in there and shoot it out with you, Dan, in front of the witnesses. The fight that you and I have, I think it's between ourselves. Have any of you other boys in there a single thing against me?"

"No," said the sudden voice of Skeet Raleigh. "If you come in here to shoot it out with Dan—right in the middle of the crowd of us—no, I've got nothin' agin any man with that much nerve, old-timer!"

"Nor me!" called another.

"I won't believe it till I see it," said the youthful voice of Bender. "By thunder, Tag, nobody's got nerve enough for that, though."

"Mind you, boys," said Tag, "if I come inside there, I come because I've heard from every one of you, and I know that I can trust you."

A sudden chorus answered him. Every voice was in it, except the voice of Dan Malley.

Molly Benton slipped suddenly down onto a stool. She buried her face in her hands, and trembled. And Ray Champion, white, tense, watched her. He hardly seemed to breathe. As for what else was around him, he was aware of nothing.

Then Tag stepped into the cabin.

~42~
Gun Duel

HE paused in the doorway, his glance steady upon the form of Malley. Then he drew the door to behind him. Malley said nothing. But into his eyes came a red fire, like that which appears in the eyes of an infuriated steer when it sees battle offered. Plainly there was no fear in him, even of such an antagonist as this. And neither was his cunning gone, but, hawklike, he watched every move of his antagonist.

"Boys," said Tag Enderby, "I'm glad to be with you all. I'd like to shake hands with you, all around, but you know that I have to keep my eyes and my right hand for the chief."

"You watch him," said Skeet Raleigh. "By Jiminy, I can't say that I want you to win, but I can't say that I want you to lose, either. I can't find it in me to want you to lose. We're goin' to give you a fair break here, Tag."

"We are!" said several hearty voices together.

Only now did some of them rise from their secure places of shelter in the room.

"Skeet," said Tag cheerfully, "what do you think? Do Tucker and Champion, here, have a chance to get guns and free hands? There's only two of 'em to five of you."

"Not by a long sight!" bellowed Malley.

"Oh, better be reasonable, chief," said Tag. "If I'd stood outside there and shot that wrinkle off your forehead, you wouldn't have anything to worry about now."

"That's true," declared young Bender.

And suddenly, taking himself at his own word, his knife slashed the cords that bound the arms of Tucker.

A very odd thing happened then, which few of them understood. For Tucker, raising his face, looked up, and then closed his eyes. Molly understood. No one else in the place could.

Tucker stood up. Ray Champion was already free. Guns were given them generously—the first impulse of generosity which more than one of the band probably regretted the moment that the thing had been done.

But perhaps all of them were now impelled by the instincts of the wolf pack, which rejoices to see the old leader pulled down, even though it has grown fat under his leadership.

Now Tag Enderby stood at the end of the table, and Malley opposite him.

"Are you ready, Dan?" Tag asked.

"I'm ready," said the outlaw chief.

"Tag!" gasped the voice of Molly. She was too unnerved to rise.

"I hear you, Molly. I can't look at you," said Tag.

"Tag," said the girl, "whatever happens, I want you to know—"

That sentence was never completed, for the cunning eye of Malley saw the glance of Tag, despite his will power, drift suddenly toward the girl, and in that instant Malley drew and fired. He fired low, the instant that the gun was free from his clothes.

The impact whirled Tag half around as, with instinctive speed, he whipped out his own gun. The blow of the first bullet was, in fact, the cause that made the second whir harmlessly past his body.

Then he fired, when the other already had discharged two bullets. As his gun spoke, Malley dropped his own weapon and brushed at his forehead, peevishly, it seemed, as a man will strike at an annoying fly which has persisted in its attack. Then he sank noiselessly to the floor.

Tag Enderby had already fallen, face down.

They got him onto the bunk—Tucker and Ray Champion and the girl. They cut or tore away his clothes and made the long, strong bandage that wrapped him round and round.

As for the body of Malley, it had been taken out by his own men, and by the morning there was a mound of raw ground upturned in the middle of the clearing. And every man of the band had disappeared, and every horse was gone with them.

That was the dissolution of the Malley gang. They passed into tradition, but as a force, as a unit of power, they were gone forever.

But the three in the cabin paid little heed to that. Tiptoe they moved, dreading lest the shock of even a heavy footfall upon the floor might snap the thin-spun thread of the life of the wounded man.

For the three remaining hours of darkness they watched. The girl, in whispers, gave orders to the men.

Then Ray Champion said to her: "I'm going down to Indian Gulch. I'll send up the only two decent doctors that they have there."

She nodded.

"I'll send your father, too," said he. "But I'm not coming back, Molly."

She looked him full in the face, and both of them understood.

"I'm sorry for that," said she.

"But you think I'm wise not to?"

"I suppose it's better," said she.

She went to the door and there shook hands with him. Then she heard him go down the steps, and the soft sound of his feet, with the grass whispering around them, as if a breeze were stirring.

But Tucker remained.

Two doctors and the deputy sheriff and several other men came up from Indian Gulch in the early morning.

They found that the life was still pulsing feebly through the body of Tag Enderby.

Tucker, exhausted, went outside for a moment, and sat in the sun. He smoked a cigarette, which he held in a trembling hand. And the deputy sheriff sat on the rock beside him.

"I suppose, Tuck," said he, "that I ought to say that you're under arrest again."

"Hush a minute," answered Tucker.

For one of the doctors was just then coming from the shack towards them.

Tucker started up.

"What's the word?" he demanded feverishly.

"He ought to be dead, but he won't die," said the doctor. "The fool doesn't seem to know that he's worse than dead, almost. And the result is, for all I can say, that he's likely to get well entirely. He's used to death, I suppose. There's nothing shocking or unnerving about it, for him."

"Has he opened his eyes?" asked Tucker.

"He opened them just now."

"Did he know you?"

"No, he didn't. He didn't want to. He knows the girl though. And, if he lives, I've an idea that she'll be the greater part of his knowledge for the rest of his life."

He added: "Molly told me to come out and tell you about it, Tucker. About his chance of getting well, I mean."

"Oh, I knew the other thing a long time ago," said Tucker.

He stood up.

"I'm going to go and say good-by to Molly," he declared to Locksley.

Tucker went to the door of the cabin.

"Hey, Molly!" he whispered.

She came to him like a shadow across the floor.

"Look, Molly," he said. "I never thought that I'd see you with tears in your eyes."

"It's happiness, Tuck," she told him. "God never made any girl so happy as I am this moment."

"Why?" asked Tucker.

"Tag just opened his eyes and smiled at me, like a baby."

"God has a lot to do with things," said Tucker seriously. "Molly, I wish you everything the best. I'm saying good-by."

She kissed him, her arms strongly around him.

"God bless you, Tuck," said she. "You were the truest blue of all!"

"Aw, no," said Tucker. "You know how it is. I just took my chances, as 'he' would say! And now I'm going to take my chances with the law."

Then he went off across the clearing, to the deputy sheriff.

But when Tucker's trial came, he was not convicted, for the people of Indian Gulch had come to believe in his version of the affray with the red-headed Swede, in which Tucker was forced to shoot in self-defense.

After that, living honestly, he remained in the county for years. And every Christmastide he rode down out of the mountains into Grove City and sat at the same Christmas table with Mr. and Mrs. Taggert Enderby, as a well-respected bachelor friend of the young couple.

Center Point Publishing
600 Brooks Road 1 PO Box 1
Thorndike ME 04986-0001 USA

(207) 568-3717

US & Canada:
1 800 929-9108